Winston Hewlett's Impotence

P.J. Blumenthal

Sagging
Meniscus

Set in Sabon with LaTeX.

ISBN: 978-1-952386-91-6 (paperback)
ISBN: 978-1-952386-92-3 (ebook)
Library of Congress Control Number: 2023952262

Sagging Meniscus Press
Montclair, New Jersey
saggingmeniscus.com

For Michael Hofmann—
Thank you for this book

All discord, harmony not understood.
All partial evil, universal good.
—Alexander Pope

WINSTON HEWETT'S IMPOTENCE

Prologue

THE LIGHTS go on. What seems to be a stage becomes visible. A Voice is heard in off: "Lily!" Silence, and then again: "Lily?"

An eagle draped in a golden robe enters from some corner: "Yes, my love?!"

"Another moon," the Voice says. "Call in the cast. Soon it will be time to celebrate."

The eagle nods, "The days will pass quickly in dreams and pain."

"Love is won doing injury. We celebrate in another key." What first sounds like words now fills the space with light and color, a swirling of patterns and echoes of consonants and vowels.

"Shadows, assemble!" It is impossible to determine who says this, because the words seem to be emanating from everywhere.

And suddenly they are there: figures, human figures, trudging in drowsily as if just awaking from a deep sleep. Counting these figures would be an impossible task. The more of them you see, the more they seem to increase in number. They are tall and short, some even dwarfed, and many in-between, they are plain, beautiful and ugly, obese and thin, aged and fresh. Their costumes are so varied, it would require encyclopedias to describe them. Some exhibit emotion, some don't. Some gaze about with curiosity, some not.

"My part is too long," says one.

"It has to be," says the eagle.

"Why is my role so small!? I hardly get to say anything!" a voice quakes from a darkened nook.

"There are no small roles, only small actors," says the eagle.

And the Voice? It has gone silent. It only listens now.

"What are we playing today?" one actor is asking another.

"A most lamentable comedy," says the other. "A very good piece, and merry!"

"Will there be tears?"

"Oh yes, many, and storm winds and music too . . ."

"And . . . intimacies . . .?"

"Some will blush. Some will not."

"How do you know?"

"I read the script. Something you might want to do."

"No. I prefer surprises . . ."

"Places! Places!" the eagle calls out. She is tense with excitement and concentration. "Cut your bow strings! It's time to begin!"

A moment of silence. A curtain, till now unnoticed in the play of light, opens, and we the audience see the cast for the first time. A blur of humanity. A young woman, twentyish in earth years, for the moment she has no name, steps forward, better said, she is pushed to center stage. Her hair is blond and cropped. She is wearing a white T-shirt and short shorts. A spotlight falls on her, and out of the silence, she recites:

> Over the hill and underage,
> full of mush and full of fire,
> lots of spark and scent of sage
> I wander through the mire.
> Your not so humble servant me,
> wondering what I please,
> meeting queens and fairies too, you see,

and everywhere I feel at ease.
But this time I shall feel a pain
sometimes greater than my years.
The moon will rise, the moon will wane,
like any music of the spheres.

The young woman steps back into the mass of actors.
Some are patting her shoulders, an expression of solidarity.

"Let the play begin!" the eagle says, and now she takes
wing, followed by other eagles, they too draped in golden
robes. They soar high above the proscenium, sometimes in
view, sometimes not. Meanwhile we perceive for the first time
a glowing symbol emanating from the back wall of the stage:

ONE

and it came to pass . . .

ONE LATE MORNING Winston Hewlett awoke and couldn't do it. His wife Virginia tried her best to coax him back to capacity, but to no avail.

It was approaching noon. Virginia watched him rise out of bed, a looming figure, clearly grim. *I wish I understood more about the male psyche.* "Open the curtains, Winston," she said wistfully, "and stop gnawing at yourself. It can happen to anyone. Maybe you're tired or worried about something."

"Ow!" He stepped barefoot on a drawing pencil, and his tall frame hopped over to the window. "Lead poisoning! Just what I needed!" He drew back the curtain with a single jerk, and a shock of daylight filled the muted room. Virginia winced at his silhouette in the window frame and pondered his silent, slumped-shouldered form surveying the blue Pacific. His curly brown hair had lost its luster and was beginning to recede at the temples. A little too much padding under the paunch. But, yes, he was as likable as ever and had the same winning smile (when he smiled) that had once won her heart, fresh from Los Angeles, a new girl in town.

Spring had come and the rains had dispersed the haze turning the air invisible. In the distance, he could make out the crisp contours of the Channel Islands and the bright profiles of sailboats carrying cargos of pleasure seekers under the picture book blue Southern California sky.

If there were any single place on this mysterious planet where the Garden of Eden might have been located, Santa Barbara surely had a major claim. There was nothing like it anywhere: a near-perfect temperate climate, lazy, lush vegetation, bourgeois comfort—a sleepy settlement of red-tiled white stucco haciendas and dark brown California wood frames, surrounded by a protective ring of mountains and situated along a broad southern reef that calmed the otherwise untamed Ocean that lapped at its shores.

Winston peered down the vertical of his body. I'm getting fat and old . . . and how tiny it looks. It never seemed so small before! Do they shrink with age?

Virginia had propped herself up in bed on a fluff of pillows, switched on her reading lamp and turned her attention to a novel, her reading glasses balanced at the end of her nose. No telling how many novels she had ingested during the twelve years of their marriage.

Like Winston, she was pushing past her mid-thirties, ultimate border of human timelessness. She was attractive in that way others describe as "unconventional," a thick head of straight black hair, which, when younger, she wore to her hips, a touch that made friends and admirers think of Victorian beauties from the nineteenth century. Currently, she kept it at shoulder length, and it was beginning to pepper with a few lonely strands of grey. Moreover, she was growing matronly, rounding out at places that had formerly revealed shape and grace.

If Santa Barbara was the Garden of Eden, then Winston and Virginia might be fitting candidates for its resident Adam and Eve, careless birds of paradise. Thanks to the POP-IT, they had no need to toil by the sweat of their brows—and didn't. Winston's late father had invented the POP-IT, a multipurpose gadget: corkscrew, can opener and bottle opener contrived on the principle of ionic displacement, a merger of laser and ultrasonic technology which ran on a single 1.5 volt penlight battery, was inexpensive and fit comfortably into any pocket.

Virginia glanced up from her "trashie" (that's how she described her favorite genre of literature). Her knees were raised, and her nightgown was stretched tightly over her heavy ankles, the bane of her existence (at least if you had asked for her opinion on that touchy subject), right down to her feet. She eyed Winston as he moped around the room. "Forget it." The words came out lackadaisically, and then she returned to her book. Winston could not.

He showered hurriedly and while getting dressed muttered that he would skip breakfast. Now, Virginia's expression grew sad and sadder still when she asked where he was going, and he answered curtly: "Out."

❈ ❈ ❈

He drove down the Mesa across the downtown basin and up to the Riviera, the city's charm whooshing by scarcely noticed, his destination a hillside street, generously green, palm trees, jacarandas and acacias hanging lazily over the sidewalk. He parked his car (O joy! A parking spot!) in front of a wood-framed structure with a red shingled roof and scurried up the steps to the porch, ducking instinctively to dodge a spider plant suspended high enough for all heads but his to collide with. He rang the doorbell.

Moments later, the door opened, and they stood face to face, or better said, face to shoulders, because he was easily a head taller than her, a young woman, pretty in a conventional way, oval face, fair complexion, large, brown eyes, a bright but sad expression that at first glance one might mistake for innocence, her blond hair cut to a longish pageboy.

She was twentyish, but one could discern fine gossamer lines furrowing from her eyes to her cheeks, visible especially when she flashed one of those shy smiles Winston liked so much. A white T-shirt and short shorts decked the roundings of her slender but womanly form, her legs bare from her thighs down to her lovely tapered ankles.

"Winston!?" Her voice tentative as he leaned over to kiss her perfunctorily on the mouth.

This was Gladiola Freytag, Winston's girlfriend.

"You're not busy now, are you?" The urgency was unmistakable.

"Well, actually, I was expecting a student, but she canceled at the last minute."

"Can I come up?"

Something about the way he was asking . . . "Well, sure . . ."

Up the steps to her flat, Winston hastily, Gladiola with deliberation. In the front room, large and bright with a southern exposure, every object had its place, clearly selected with loving forethought. The centerpiece was a daybed, flush to the wall and flanked by two easy chairs. A low bookcase stood opposite and next to it a drafting table topped with a neat pile of sketchpads and a box of charcoals. A music stand, an open score spread across it, was positioned near the window. An untarnished silver flute crossed the drafting table at a safe and aesthetically pleasing angle. The Roman poet Horace would have described this interior as *simplex munditia*, right down to the white walls and the few pictures hanging on them.

Winston stepped over to the window and gazed across the city, visible beyond a potted cactus rising high above the windowsill, his eyes homing in on the Mesa, his own house nearly discernable. Gladiola, hunched at the edge of the daybed, followed his movements.

Probably he was thinking, in all likelihood without words, that that short drive from one hill to the other in this small Southern California city was to him what navigating oceans are to other men or fighting wars or building empires. His quest for adventure bore the name Gladiola. Once he had actually confessed this private piece of braggadocio to her.

"Grrr," he growled, eyeing her impishly.

"Woof," her response, sitting straight-backed on the daybed.

"Grrr."

"Woof, woof."

It was the vocabulary of a ritual that had originated in silly, tail-wagging, toothy and panting spontaneity of which now (as is the nature of things, alas) more bark than bite remained. And then the dog in the man sprung across the room and pounced on Gladiola with unexpected ferocity, snorting, foaming and growling, his pants dropping below his knees with astonishing alacrity as he bit firmly and wetly into her neck. Surprised by the suddenness of this *élan*, she reacted at first defensively, muttering a not very convincing and giggly, "Winston, stop it!" as he managed deftly to raise her T-shirt and yank down her short shorts in what seemed a single movement, exposing her body to his feasting eyes, her breasts and hips bathing suit white. How divine thine ankles, Gladiola! Winston was grazing at her belly contentedly, she knotting her fingers into his hair, casting a glance down the length of her body and noting his eagerness. Her smile was motherly. And soon they were entrenched in delightful lovemaking, the sun bathing them in warm stripes of light that fell across the daybed.

Afterwards, Winston slumped over her limply, lazily breathing in the meaty sexual scents they had generated, and comfortably spent. When he finally rolled onto his back, freeing her from his length and weight, they passed silent minutes touching, sweat to sweat, intimacy to intimacy, motionless except for an occasional caress.

Winston was of course relieved. The irksome doubts were gone, but that he did not reveal. He just smiled wryly and said, "Thanks, I needed that."

Gladiola was eyeing him vulnerably, her pupils darting, looking for some meaning in his face. "When don't you?"

"Let's make a baby!" He was grinning.

"One big one's enough for me."

"Really, I'm serious."

"I know, and that's what worries me."

Their eyes remained locked, each reading the other according to a private theory. Finally, Gladiola rose and suggested they do some drawing—which was the *de facto* pretext for these trysts.

This affair had been going on for a year. Two lost souls had stumbled onto each other—and happiness—at a Santa Barbara Adult Education figure drawing class.

The primary impulse had been innocent. Moreover, it had been Gladiola's idea—he would not have dared—to collaborate in some extra-curricular sketching. But faultless as the situation was, he had told Virginia nothing about his sketching partner nor mentioned *what* they were sketching. For several weeks, the innocence did prevail. Only gradually did another level of intimacy begin stirring. When *it* finally did happen, Virginia was in Los Angeles visiting her parents. On those occasions, Winston rarely accompanied her, content to see his in-laws, two zealous Bible-beaters from the San Fernando Valley, as little as possible. For his part, it had been Gladiola's quiet intensity that had aroused his interest. Somehow she seemed older than her years and radiated an air of mystery. For her, it had been his good-natured ease. She saw him as a danger-free zone, a source of comfort, a balm against her loneliness, a squeezable pal. Yes, the same qualities that had once attracted Virginia to him.

Winston was stretched across the daybed, his eyes following her graceful nakedness as she stepped lightly across the room to fetch her art supplies; he admired her prettiness with quiet satisfaction.

She paused at her desk and reflected on his supine length, sunlight striping his skin, his body some peninsula surrounded by a mountainous reef. "Don't move," she commanded, pretending authority.

And so, he held the long pose, as she requested, ribs jutting out, abdomen sunken, arms extended behind his head and pectorals flexed.

"Woof."

"Shut up."

But he couldn't. He was feeling good, better said, relieved, and that was making him talkative. No, he did not bring up the subject of his ... *failure* ... that morning. Rather, art was on his mind and how happy it made him, which is probably why he mentioned his father's workshop, an annex to his house that had been sealed since his father's death. He described how he was intending to turn it into a studio. He also mentioned the thick layers of dust that blanketed that space and how when he had opened the door for the first time he immediately began coughing. "I want to replace the south wall with large glass panels. Perfect light! Then you can come over, and we can do some sketchin' at my place." His smile was mischievous. "What do you think?"

Gladiola wasn't thinking. She was lost in the hills and valleys of his surfaces, the light and darkness that divided his zones. She too was serious about drawing and not easily distracted. Thick charcoals were her preferred medium, which rendered her figures soft, larger than life. Gladiola saw bodies foremost as rhythm units. Once she recognized an intrinsic form, she filled out the details. Gradually, an image of Winston was taking shape on her sketch pad, an image anyone might have recognized as characteristically him, though idealized. For she was drawing Winston as she might have wished him to be: affable, generous and, well, fatherly, her impression when they first met. Of late, he had become so moody.

When she finished, she scrutinized her drawing critically. Winston rose, stretching his long body like a large boned cat, and approached her to examine her work. He leaned over, resting his hands gently on her petite shoulders.

"Is that my penis?"

She nodded.

"It's so big! You always draw it so nicely."

"Often it's the nicest part of you."

Winston's smirk demonstrated contentment.

Now it was his turn to draw her. "But no beaver shots today."

"Why not?"

"You've been abusing the privilege. I don't like to think of myself as an open-faced sandwich."

"Whassa matter? Think I'm going to blackmail you?"

"Worse than that."

Gladiola was seated at the desk and shifted into position while Winston, sketch pad in hand, retreated to the daybed. A classic pose: one foot to the floor, knee raised and clasped in her arms, hips turned slightly, head upright—a pose full of important exercise points.

Winston had a preference for thin charcoals. In contrast to Gladiola, he did not perceive a body as a formal totality. He focused on zones and unified them into a whole, like islands connected by bridges. Piece by piece the form took shape, the resemblance to Gladiola ever more recognizable, though more angular than his model perhaps and more severe. He was imagining her as queen of a magic kingdom. The wooden chair she was seated on transmogrified into a throne, and as a last gesture, he set a crown atop her head. Something was still missing though, an authoritative symbol of her royal pedigree. That's when it occurred to him to place the following icon at the apex of the crown:

He finished with an emphatic nod of the head and sweep of his hand. Gladiola rose, she too stretching after the strain of posing. She grew long and sleek, a fair skinned animal. Her knee was sore.

"Do you have anything to drink?" Winston asked while adding a few final touches to his drawing.

"Sure, how about some pop? Ow, my knee."

"Sounds fine."

She hobbled off to the kitchen and returned with two cans and a POP-IT; then sitting next to Winston, she looked at his picture and gasped.

"What's the matter? Don't you like it?"

"Why did you draw THAT?" She was pointing to the symbol at the apex of the crown.

And then he mentioned running into the postman a few days earlier when he'd gone out for the mail and how the postman had handed him a letter. It was just after he had come out of his father's workshop, and dust was still sticking to him. "Wait! I still have it in my pocket." He reached into his jacket and handed Gladiola a small envelope. She slipped out a card about the size of an invitation to a child's birthday party and saw the following:

DROPIT

Her face paled and her eyes grew wide. He had never seen that look before. "What's the problem?"

"The *MAENADS!!*" She was clasping the note tightly.

"Who?"

"Oh, this is TERRIBLE!"

"What are you talking about? What are mee-nads?" His gaze shifted repeatedly from his drawing to the note and then to her.

Her expression was serious, but she had regained her composure. "You've got to swear you won't repeat what I'm going to tell you."

Winston heard himself saying yes.

TWO

Meet Doctor Larez Pentius enjoying a final moment of idleness, alone at the summit of the San Marcos Pass, sucking the sweet sage into his lungs. He gazed southwards at the silent Pacific, then one last look at the thirsty Santa Ynez valley before skittering down the bluff to his car raising dust. A breeze was ruffling his white hair and lashing at his small, stubborn frame. The casual observer might not have recognized this rumpled figure with long face gnarled like root wood, large nose, floppy ears, porous drooping jowls, teeth irregular and in varied shades of yellow, as one of Santa Barbara's most respected psychiatrists. His glasses sat firmly on the bridge of his nose. His eyes twinkled with obstinacy.

He had been spending some days in a cabin at Lake Cachuma. Alone as usual and willingly dispensing with speech. His favorite holiday was a vacation from the spoken word. He'd awake early, eat or not eat as it suited him, angle himself into a rowboat, paddle over the green waters of the ripple-free lake across patches of shadow and light, eagles soaring above him. He thought they were buzzards. He'd light his pipe, a crusty piece of briar, as gnarled as his own countenance and patched three or four times, a gift from his late friend Leland Hewlett, and pass the day ruminating and reminiscing—in images without words.

His vacations had been solitary for years, which is to say, ever since Leland Hewlett's death.

In the old days, he and Leland, young Winston in tow, used to spend fishing holidays at Lake Casitas. Those were the days! And then there was that time Winston hooked a whopper, a thirteen inch black bass, the largest on record in the lake. Larez Pentius could still envision Winston, grinning the victor's grin: "A big one, dad! A big one, Doctor Pentius!" They celebrated that evening at the Fly and Reel in Casitas Springs, and Leland ordered Winston, then seventeen, his first drink ever, a screwdriver. Sure, Winston was under-aged and looked it, although he was a big fellow, towering over the Doctor and his father like a lamppost, but his dad winked at the bartender, who raised a knowing eye. When he brought the boy his drink, all were still partaking in that victory grin. And lord, what a face Winston made when he drank it. "Hey, why the grimace? It's not worm juice." That's what Leland said.

Sentimentality was not high on the Doctor's list of priorities; after all he was a psychiatrist. Only when the door to his thoughts swung open to that space Leland Hewlett inhabited did he float in the swell of sweet memories. But isn't that what a holiday is all about?

Here we should introduce the memory that was most cogent for the Doctor and will likewise take on a central meaning in the story that is unfurling: it begins with Leland Hewlett's death. Winston had found his father's lifeless body in the workshop. Before notifying the police, he called Doctor Pentius. "I was expecting this." That was all he would say. The autopsy report speculated that Leland Hewlett had been the victim of an experiment gone awry. Nevertheless, the pathologist was unable to reconstruct the exact circumstances. Larez Pentius had his own suspicions about why his friend's brain had turned to mush and could be seen leaking from both ears onto the high-polished floor of the workshop, but he did not share his theories with anyone. There *was* no one. Moreover, claiming that Leland Hewlett had been murdered by a secret society would have sounded like science fiction . . . or worse . . . especially as he lacked conclusive evidence. For this reason, solving the mystery of his friend's death had been the Doctor's major preoccupation the past fifteen years. What's more, he considered it his sacred duty for all to know that Leland Hewlett, whose POP-IT could be found in every kitchen utility drawer in America, had been at the brink of finalizing research on an invention as revolutionary as the wheel, and for which reason he had been eliminated by the most secretive cabal on this planet: the Empire of Chaos.

All his attempts to infiltrate that arcane society had failed so far, but the Doctor had amassed reams of corroborating information confirming possible concatenations that might be traced back to the Empire of Chaos and based on his intimacy with their secretive footprint, their circuitous means of exercising influence. These, he systematized under the following headings: *Trends*, *Tendencies*, *Crimes* and *Natural Disasters*. He had collected hundreds of entries for California alone. Nevertheless, he was missing that one crucial link that would unite all the threads. Frustrating as that was, Larez Pentius was confident he would recognize it when it came into sight. It was all he lived for. We will have more to say on this subject. Much more.

He filled this pipe, tamped down the tobacco, a blend of black cavendish and golden Virginias with hints of dark chocolate and vanilla, his favorite and Leland's too, started the engine and rippled down the serpentine access road leading to the San Marcos Pass, his pipe clenched in his teeth and still unlit. He turned left onto the steep pass towards Santa Barbara, passed a hitchhiker and accelerated, all the while sucking at his unlit pipe.

When he realized his brakes had failed, his face stiffened. He clamped his jaw onto the stem of his pipe firmly and pumped with a superstitious fervor at the limp pedal while the car continued racing downhill. He did not panic, people rarely do at such moments; he merely considered his options. Then it occurred to him to yank at the handbrake. It worked! He decelerated rapidly but the car would still not come to a stop. With great concentration he negotiated this narrow strip of highway which soon opened into a straightaway. To the right, a precipice, to the left, a road-bank. He held tightly to his lane, still straining at the handbrake, smoke rising from the floor of the car, eyes fixed ahead. Then he saw his opportunity, his only opportunity, a stretch where the road-bank widened to a turn-about. He threw the transmission into reverse, the engine screeching the whine of slaughtered steel. The stench of burning metal and rubber wafted through the interior. The car spun abruptly and thudded to a stop against the sandstone embankment, hurling the Doctor against the windshield, which miraculously didn't break. He lost consciousness.

When he opened his eyes, the ambulance had already arrived—a tip from an anonymous caller, he was informed. His pipe, his gift from Leland Hewlett, had cracked again. As for himself, nothing more than a minor concussion. Seatbelted in the ambulance and still dazed, he noticed a paper slip in the hand with which he was gripping his pipe. He understood the message immediately and grinned toothily:

The Deltagon! Why would they get in contact now . . . unless . . . my efforts have been bearing fruit at last? It's endgame!

THREE

GLADIOLA HAD OSSIFIED to a naked profile at Winston's side, her eyes fixed on a plank of parquet. Maybe she had somehow been waiting for this opportunity, because the words flowed urgently. Winston's hands were folded on his lap. He was on his best behavior.

She had not been the warm, wet issue of a mother's womb swaddled and coddled in loving arms, she recited in a monotone voice. Unknown hands had tucked her into a brown wicker basket and left her on the steps of the First Presbyterian Church of Woodland Hills in the San Fernando Valley, a pink, lamb's wool blanket covering her, and clothed in a cheap cotton pyjama with a bunny rabbit pattern, a handwritten note, in neat, focused letters, pinned to the blanket:

GIVE THIS BABY A GOOD HOME

She still had that basket, her "womb" she called it, pointing to the foot of the daybed, Winston's eyes following, and seeing it as if for the first time, tarnished and mute, now filled with skeins of wool, half-finished projects and knitting needles jutting at odd angles.

The following day, the story appeared on the front page of the *San Fernando Times* with photographs, and soon she was adopted by a childless couple from Tarzana, both musicians in the San Fernando Symphony Orchestra: Mr. Warren Freytag, first violinist, and his wife Florida, cellist, a fact which made Gladiola's later partiality for the flute advantageous for a variety of trios.

She had no complaints about her childhood; her adoptive parents had been attentive to her needs and loving, and although she had had playmates, she savored being alone (perhaps some trait inherited from her real mother—or father, she later reflected). Her parents broached the subject of her origins as soon as she was old enough to understand, and that knowledge furrowed deeply into her so that she was increasingly haunted by the mystery of the circumstances of her birth. Who could begrudge her that curiosity? Before her tenth birthday she swore a sacred oath to herself to solve that mystery whatever the cost.

She left home soon after completing high school, propelled by an inner voice, a call to adventure, advising her that if she searched assiduously, she would find what she had been seeking. Her parents were saddened by her resolve to set off on her own but promised their support.

She had no plan. She simply moved into an apartment in Hollywood and soon had a job as a flute instructor at a small private music school on Crenshaw Blvd. She was only seventeen but possessed a poise beyond her years that made it easy for her to lie about her age.

There she was, alone in the world, motherless and friendless too (a result of her infatuation with loneliness, she surmised), but she remained ever eager for answers to questions she had hardly formulated into words, determined to dig beneath the surface of things.

Maybe that was what attracted her to QUID PRO QUO, a self-help group she stumbled on in a newspaper article during the long bus ride home from work. QUID PRO QUO offered a practical training course, a seminar over two weekends, for those (she imagined like herself) seeking practical guidelines for developing the techniques necessary for self-discovery. The objective of the instruction was, to use the language of the QUID PRO QUO founder, Wyatt Amadeus Rosenbloom, to "get it."

One evening, Gladiola attended an introductory QUID PRO QUO seminar at the Century Hotel in Century City. She was probably one of the few participants who arrived there by bus as she was still too young for a driver's license.

The auditorium was packed, a gaggle of nervously chattering people, all wearing name tags on breast pockets, green or blue, depending on whether they were graduates of the course or newcomers like herself. The crowd froze to attentive stillness at the call to order. At the conclusion of the formal part of the program, including a rousing and rather entertaining speech by the founder, Wyatt Amadeus Rosenbloom, she signed up for the course.

On the following two weekends, from eight A.M. to eight P.M. with a single break at around two for a quick meal, she hunched together with sixty other seekers in a windowless lecture hall. An energetic young man who might have stepped out of an ad for Italian summer-wear, shirt open to the hair-line of his chest, battered them with insults, jokes, monologues, pep-talks. His energy was remarkable, and he had the power to sway them to laughter and tears. Participants were encouraged to respond to questions he asked, but when they did, they were clobbered with merciless criticism and often reduced to deflated, sobbing sacks of humanity. That at least is how she recalled the general procedure in this torture chamber of self-discovery. Another element that stood out in her memory was the awful pressure she experienced in bladder and bowels—with no relief possible, because the participants had agreed at the beginning not to leave the room, except for that one short late afternoon break, unless given permission. Her insides cramped with nerve impulses she could barely palliate through generous avenues of distraction. "Are you a tube?" their well-tanned, self-assured group leader queried again and again? "Food in, food out? Who's in control? You or your digestive tract? Does it tell you when to eat and sleep, or do you tell it?" Complainers were humiliated. Whoever left the room without permission was excoriated as a loser.

Towards the conclusion of the second day of the second weekend, the participants (which is to say, those who had survived the ordeal) had indeed developed new muscles to deal with the challenge. That applied to Gladiola as well. And yet, despite the desensitization process, she was still too shy to ask the seminar leader a question that increasingly demanded vocalization: What had they really learned here? There was no need to ask though, because as the ordeal concluded, the secret was revealed: It didn't matter what you did, everything was right; ultimately life could be described as a grand circus of possibilities and no one, yes, no one, had the right to tell you anything! Their handsome seminar leader verbalized this message as "getting it," and in no time everyone had really "gotten it," which precipitated a raucous round of laughing, laughing at him, at their neighbors and at themselves, a hilarious, free-for-all yuck-it-up. Even Gladiola was laughing. But surprisingly that laughter quickly transformed into anger because all at once she understood that she had learned nothing new. She rose, a lone figure standing there. While the others continued laughing, she stopped. And soon the others went silent too. Even their well-groomed seminar leader turned somber. "I'm sorry," she said, "but no, I don't get it." She stepped through the crowd like Moses through the Sea of Reeds and exited the room decisively, leaving an uncomfortable silence behind her.

A couple of weeks later, Stephen Lenz knocked at her door in Hollywood. He was wearing a three-piece suit more akin to middle-management than to the painstakingly casual garb of the QUID PRO QUO crew. Something about him appeared familiar, which might explain why she resisted her urge to slam the door on him. He handed her his card. INTERNATIONAL GROWTH RESEARCH FOUNDATION was printed on it along with a symbol, already familiar to her:

"You have been looking for us and we have been looking for you," he proclaimed in a voice that was both solemn and celebratory.

Without further questions, and perhaps against her better judgement, she invited him into her apartment. *Was that not the symbol pinned to her swaddling blanket?*

Initially, she was not certain what Stephen Lenz wanted or how he had found her. Moreover, his responses to those questions were politely evasive. And yet she was curious to learn more. Soon, he was coming to her Hollywood apartment two or three evenings a week. He was always neatly dressed and most definitely well mannered, and their discussions were, for lack of a better word, metaphysical and always interesting. Still, she remained on guard, though increasingly fascinated by what he had to say because their conversations were opening worlds within worlds in her mind, insight into personality structure and arcane laws of nature, information that reverberated through her body in waves of excitement. Finally, she sensed that in contrast to her experiences at QUID PRO QUO she was truly learning something. And yet, as much as she looked forward to these evenings with her private instructor, his intentions were not clear, even when she inquired directly.

What she did not know at the time, was that in patient steps Stephen Lenz was slowly metamorphosing Gladiola Freytag into *Agent* Gladiola Freytag, a *Maenad*, a member of the *Empire of Chaos*.

When Stephen Lenz initiated her into the mystery of the DELTAGON (no, that she dared not reveal to Winston), she no longer doubted that she had discovered her destiny on earth. Moreover, she was now confident that one day soon she would solve the mystery of her birth.

And yet, when she'd query Stephen Lenz about that pressing question, he'd smile vacantly and plead ignorance.

Fear disguised as a chill rippled through Winston's interior as Gladiola pointed to the symbol he had sketched and called it a DELTAGON, the symbol of the Empire of Chaos.

"But why have they sent *me* a letter?" He was swimming in words, and an undertow seemed to be sweeping his floundering limbs into a great, unknown sea.

Gladiola shrugged blankly and continued.

Stephen Lenz was never impolite, never fresh. Never once did she doubt his seriousness. Sometimes, however, she'd muse whether she and Stephen were perhaps the only *Maenads* in an Empire of Chaos that existed solely in his imagination. Increasingly, she'd insist on meeting other members of this . . . "organization" (what else to call it?) and expressed an interest in playing a more active role.

For a while, Stephen Lenz consoled her with vague promises to fulfill her request, but she remained adamant. That was her nature. Eventually, he did acquiesce, issuing what he described as her first "assignment." This consisted of contemplating a simple sentence until, to use his words, she "became one with it." Now she was hearing the echo of QUID PRO QUO jargon and was certain he was merely humoring her. Before long, it became clear that the Empire of Chaos meant business. No, they did not demand a tithe or preposterous amounts of money for courses meant to further enlighten her. There were no documents or contracts to sign nor any agreement that required her to relinquish her soul to dark forces. The "mantra" Gladiola was consigned was not to be muttered incessantly in the privacy of her own four walls. She was to be placed in a new social context where this contemplative exercise would serve as a key.

Within days, Stephen Lenz returned, informing her that she was to pack a bag and prepare for a long journey. She would be moving to San Jose where she would join up with the DEADLY DRUIDS, a motorcycle gang. Likewise, he handed her a small envelope in which she would find on a slip of paper the sentence she was to internalize. She opened it and read:

SOW THE SEEDS OF DESTRUCTION

By this time, she understood that she was involved in something more serious than anything she'd experienced— and potentially very dangerous. She knew instinctively that she would take on the challenge, spurred not only by an innate stubborn curiosity but likewise by the belief that this adventure would bring her one step closer to solving her personal mystery. A few days later, she quit her job, gave notice on her apartment and put her belongings into storage. With one small suitcase she boarded a bus to San Jose.

They were four *agents*, herself included, among the bikers, but she knew nothing about the nature of their assignments. They were all under oath not to share that information.

"Winston, it frightens me to tell you this. I have broken my oath of silence."

Soon, she had become the "old lady" of a biker named Scar Pete, a violent alcoholic with a scar like an earthquake fault cutting into his face from temple to chin, the souvenir of a bar fight, inflicted by a glass sliver from a broken bottle. Scar Pete was kind to her—and to cats. He called her his "tea pot," by which he meant that she was as delicate as china. She washed his clothes, fed him and slept in his bed or sometimes under a single blanket with him on hard ground in some remote field.

They rode up and down the coast from San Diego to Eureka, a pack of thirty bikers and their "old ladies," camping out or rooming with "brothers" along the way. Their home base was San Jose where the group spent their time at biker bars or camp sites. Gladiola found biker life on the whole boring, though sometimes, it got downright terrifying. Apart from their suicidal way of driving, the bikers were just ruffians and cowards. Still, despite her inherent boldness, she was careful not to criticize them. Nor did she express her opinions to her fellow *Maenads*, one a former schoolteacher whom the bikers called "Professor," another a dowdy ex-secretary and another, an airy-fairy teenage boy they'd nicknamed "Porky." The lot of them, herself included, were eminently unfit for membership in a motorcycle gang, but they were tolerated. But why were they there? Were the DEADLY DRUIDS somehow associated with the Empire of Chaos? And if so, what was this Empire of Chaos *really*? These questions stirred in her mind frequently along with another that particularly piqued her: What role had her unknown mother played in this *cult?*—if that were the proper word for describing this Empire of Chaos.

That pretty much summarizes her ruminations at the time. Then "Fingers" came along, an adipose biker with six fingers on each hand. From time to time, he'd rumble into the DEADLY DRUID camp on his chopper—no matter where they happened to be. On these occasions, he'd slip messages to Gladiola and the other *Maenads* on the sly, always in sealed envelopes. (Naturally, she had no information about the contents of her comrades' messages.) Hers was always the same, for which reason she assumed it came from Stephen Lenz:

I HOPE YOU ARE SOWING THE SEEDS OF DESTRUCTION

Over time, Gladiola was certain she had made a terrible mistake taking up this challenge. Her disappointment grew progressively. But she had no one to confide in and under the circumstances was afraid to run away. Even Scar Pete noticed her gloom, but his clumsy attempts at tenderness only served to make her feel more desperate.

One evening, the bikers got unusually rowdy in a bar. A fight broke out, and one of them, "Preacher" by name, was knocked unconscious. Those "brothers" who came to his defense, swiftly received the same treatment. Their challenger— as it seemed, a professional boxer—had managed to deck six DEADLY DRUIDS. The bikers were furious. It was a question of honor, and they planned to take revenge.

A few nights later, they abducted the boxer's girlfriend, a chubby waitress with long straggly hair, as she was leaving the restaurant where she worked. Helpless and frightened, she was whisked off to a field far from the nearest secondary road where she was to "stand trial"—as a proxy for her boyfriend. A ring of motorcycles illuminated the sobbing figure under a starry heaven, and a crew of drunken, mocking bikers, along with sundry "old ladies" and *Maenads* encircled the distressed figure. Cigarette smoke swirled through the beams of light along with zigzagging moths. Cases of beer crushed patches of dry, high grass.

A kind of cracked parody of parliamentary procedure ensued, whose major purpose was to determine what punishment to inflict on the victim. Some opted for lynching, others a quick bullet to the nape. The most just among them argued that if anyone should be shot, it should be her boyfriend. Once that motion had been unanimously accepted amidst nonstop harassment and mockery, they agreed to deal with her boyfriend appropriately and that as a preliminary measure they would "turn her out," that is, gang-rape her. The verdict had hardly been spoken when one biker stomped over to where she was standing and tore off her clothes executioner-like. She began wailing, begging and protesting weakly as they threw her to the ground. Gladiola experienced the scene in slow motion and in muted tones. Fat, ugly bikers, beer cans in hand, stooping over her like mad surgeons, pouring beer into her mouth and onto her body, extinguishing cigarettes on her breasts and belly, large undulating mounds of unhealthy hairy flesh humping her, panting and slobbering as she lay there mutely. Her good fortune was to pass out quickly. In the eerie glimmer of the smoky light of the motorcycle headlights Gladiola saw this pitiful ravished creature floating on a pool of beer, vomit, blood, semen and saliva.

Finally, Gladiola couldn't bear anymore. Unobserved, she retreated into the darkness behind the ring of headlights. Most of all she wanted to scream, which of course was not possible.

She hated the bikers with an impotent hatred. She hated the *Maenads* for placing her in this insane situation and encouraging her to sow the seeds of destruction and she hated herself for her naivety and even more so for her passivity. That's when it occurred to her to slip over to Sugar Jack's bike. The nickname was a reference to his addiction to grain sugar which he'd scoop from a linen sack into his mouth by the handful. She untethered the sugar bag from the saddle of his bike and dumped the contents into the gas-tanks of the churning motorcycles—a tried and true method for ruining any gasoline engine. She acted so silently and swiftly that no one took notice of her. The chugging of the idling motors and the carnival atmosphere of the gang-bang offered her cover.

When she'd completed the task, she slipped off across the field, walking first, then running until she reached the nearest road. She waved down a car that chanced along. As she climbed in to make her escape, she gazed back towards the field. The glow of the headlights had already begun extinguishing. She rode into town, made an anonymous phone-call to the police and took the next Greyhound bus to Los Angeles. After spending a few days with her parents in Tarzana, she collected her belongings and moved to Santa Barbara.

As for Winston, after hearing Gladiola's story, he couldn't do it anymore at all.

FOUR

"EYES CLOSED, deep breath. This won't hurt a bit." Dr. Becker's effort at soothing his patient while introducing the pencil-thick lubricated electrode into Winston's unwelcoming anal orifice. "Just relax."

Winston could not, would not, naked from the waist down, in the maws of something like an obstetrics chair, his long legs straddled, his feet braced in stirrups. Briefly he forgot how the man had persuaded him to take this position. The price of desperation of course. His *glans penis* was secured under a metal cap like a housewife at the hairdresser's. Other wire sensors, attached to something like a tongue depressor had been fastened to the shaft, and now this third one. He was quickly losing confidence in the Doctor.

But he was desperate. From the moment he had lost what he described to the Doctor as his "access" to his wife (conveniently omitting anything about "access" to his girl-friend), failure precipitated failure. He had entered that all too common danger zone best described as self-defeating self-prophecy. Which is to say: the more he strived to regain what he had lost, the more he lost what he strived to regain.

To overcome what he was now circumscribing as his "problem," he had tried various remedies (these were the days before Viagra): a yohimbine preparation, for example, but it made his blood pressure skyrocket, and the resulting tachycardia triggered a panic attack. Then there was the hypnotist, a

lanky, boney man, about his own height and age, with a prominent Adam's apple that made him think of a turkey. Moreover,
a stutterer with a nervous tick, characteristics that did not en-
courage confidence. Still, Winston attempted to cooperate as
the man intoned softly: "You'll b-b-b-be able to fu-fu-fu-fu-
fu-fu-fu-fu- function agai-agai-again." When the session was
over, Winston dared ask the hypnotist if he had ever considered hypnosis for his stutter and his tick. "I d-d-d-d-d-d- did,"
he answered, "You sh-sh-sh-sh-sh-sh-should have see-see see-
seeeeeen me be-be-be-f-f-f-f-f-f-f-fore." The hypnosis had no
effect and Winston grew more n-n-n-nervous.

Finally, almost desperate enough to send off for a mail-
order sexual accessories catalogue, he stumbled on the following classified ad in the Santa Barbara News Press: SEXUAL
PROBLEMS? TRY ELECTRIC-PSYCHIC TECHNOLOGY!
PAINLESS AND FAST! SUCCESS RATE ASTOUNDING!
EROTO-STIMULASTIC INSTITUTE. DR. ANTHONY
BECKER M.D. What inspired confidence was the "M.D."
title. Virginia agreed. Not Gladiola, however; she remained
skeptical. Now he wished he had taken her advice.

"Fine! Everything in place." The voice friendly and concentrated. Now the Doctor pressed on a button and engaged a ser-
vomotor. Winston's back arched and his legs rose so that from
head to foot he was like two hills descending into a basin—not
very different from the geography of Santa Barbara from the
Mesa to the Riviera.

Winston peered at the smiling man as unobtrusively as
possible. He was bald-pated and wore thick black-rimmed
glasses, a myopic egg in a white coat. Winston wished he could
say *stop!* But he couldn't. The Doctor sat down on a swivel
stool and focused his attention on a control panel, plugging
the wires affixed to Winston's nakedness into the appropriate
jacks of his feedback monitor so that from Winston's perspec-

tive they resembled tenement clotheslines. Subsequently he began adjusting various dials.

Of course the Doctor sensed Winston's unease. "Really, there's nothing to be nervous about, Mr. Hewlett. Please, just breathe deeply."

Winston was not looking cooperative.

"As I have explained, the factor or factors responsible for your . . . disturbance . . . may be traced to any number of segmental phases in the arousal process." Repeated smiles punctuated his sentence. "This examination will enable me to locate the phase where the interference is occurring." Again a smile. "Please don't feel intimidated by this high-tech. The test is really quite elementary. The machine will monitor the specific phasal bio-feedback responsible for the disturbance. More precisely, it measures the charge, which is to say, the erotogenic irritation generated by the probable etiological factor. Do you follow me?"

No, Winston was not following him, nor did he ask for a translation. It might also have helped had he been listening. But he was thinking: Why don't I insist he remove these wires?

It should be stated here that the Doctor usually sensed when a patient was not suited for eroto-stimulastic therapy, a therapeutic form that demands cooperation. Winston Hewlett's body language was unambiguously uncooperative. Normally, the doctor was not shy about confronting a patient with his frank assessment. Something was going wrong today. But what?

"Before we begin the actual monitoring, Mr. Hewlett," the Doctor was clearly straining to maintain a friendly, better said, businesslike tone, "I'll need to ask a few routine questions, if I may."

Winston nodded.

"Were you a frequent masturbator during adolescence?"

The Doctor was already assessing Winston's reaction to this question on his feedback monitor. Arcs of light were bouncing and blinking while the Doctor took notes. Judging from the patterns, it should have been clear that Winston's reaction was not related to the question posed. And that was true. Winston was just irritated that this man, a stranger, should be asking this question. He was feeling utterly at this person's mercy. Maybe I should ask if *he* masturbated as an adolescent. To be fair: until his recent "access problem" Winston had never been obsessed with sex. He was just a normal guy. But the question had been asked and he could not act as if it hadn't. He was mad, very mad, but he knew that he had only himself to blame. After all, *he* had asked the Doctor for help. If answering this question was what was required, well . . .

His eyes were focused on the Doctor. He noted the expectant look and analyzed the face with a figure drawer's sobriety: the thin lips, the narrow old maid's chin, the black rimmed insect eyes and globous pate. That is when he decided he didn't like him, not one bit.

Against his better judgement, Doctor Becker remained optimistic that his balky patient might still cooperate. Moreover, he was confident that his procedure was more advanced than conventional treatments for impotence by lightyears. Unlike deep psychology, gestalt, behavioral theory, psychoanalysis and even bio-energetics, his treatment was based on clearcut mathematical objectivity. Facts alone counted. Infallible diagnostics were followed by a made-to-measure treatment. His premise, expressed as simply as possible, was that a neurotic stasis could be reduced to its lowest common denominator in the form of *measurable* sexual impulse congestion, a concept which he conceded had been inspired by Wilhelm Reich. In a well-known, albeit controversial paper on this subject, published in the Journal of Cybernetic Medicine, Becker had defended Reich's long debunked orgone theory and courageously redefined it. Granted, he did criticize Reich's later tendential mysticism that ultimately led to the scientist's tragic megalomania and resulted in a false objectification of OR-energy into something like a world formula. Likewise, he regretted his mentor's commitment to the effectivity of orgone accumulators. In Becker's opinion, an objective quantification of individual sexual information depended on—and this was the catch—patient cooperation. That being the case, it was highly suitable for rendering the necessary information—yes, objective correlations—that governed inclination and disinclination in human sexuality, a fact which was of immense value for the treatment of a variety of sexual disturbances. In accordance with this premise, he developed what was no doubt a flawless methodology. As a primary analytical tool, he subjected his patients to a visible display of sexual fetishism via a holographic slide show accompanied by olefactory ancillary stimuli. The Doctor had confirmed the efficacy of odors as a tandem for activating memory on the most primary prerationalistic level. Once this diagnosis had been objectified, the precisely measured reactions that resulted could be utilized as a reliable basis for prescribing an appropriate treatment involving a highly individual frequency modulation capable of reliably reprogramming the body's sexual signals microelectrically. In truth, Becker's degree of success had been relatively high. Nevertheless, he managed to excite little or no interest in his research or its practical application in the medical profession, and, sadly, he frequently encountered outright mockery from fellow specialists, for which reason he had set up his practice in a place like Santa Barbara, away from the fray.

Winston could not have known any of this. He was feeling hostile because this person was, in his opinion, embarrassing him. Oh, and there was another thing Winston did not nor could not have known. Doctor Becker was also *Agent* Becker, an agent, that is, of the Empire of Chaos, i.e. a *Maenad*, and although this fact was of little relevance at the moment, it would soon be affecting Winston's life in unexpected ways. But more about that later.

More importantly for now: Winston was drifting into escape mode. You might say it was the most convenient means possible for a timid man to say "no." Then suddenly he fell into a "what-if" fantasy. In a single bound he vaulted out of the mad Doctor's obstetric chair to make his escape. But being shackled to the bio-feedback equipment, he imagined hauling the whole clanging mess of gadgetry into the street by his penis. And now, the "what-if" fantasy grew even more cartoonish. In addition to dragging the doctor's machinery in tow, he had yanked out the entire electrical system of the building as well. Anything plugged into that system was now attached to him as he fled: including assorted TVs, stereos, irons, hair dryers, clocks, washers, driers and even a flurry of housewives flapping about like flags, fat men on exercise bicycles, dancing teenagers, grandmothers in vibrator chairs clasping their earplugs for dear life as the walls of the building crumbled around them. Moreover, in his urgency, he managed to unearth miles of subterranean cables as well as uprooting a dynamo at a distant power station and even causing violent eruptions in the Colorado River, source of all electricity in these parts, all of this, we should add, attached to his omnipotent elastic organ locked firmly under an electrode cap and stretched as thin as the most infrangible steel wire.

Meanwhile, the Doctor was still waiting for a response to his question, and the uncomfortable silence had gone into overtime. Winston was beginning to wish he could be cooperative, but something in him was resisting.

"Ahem, Mr. Hewlett, were you a frequent masturbator during adolescence?" The Doctor was losing his patience.

"Look, I don't understand why you are asking about . . ."

The Doctor was following Winston's volatility, visible as jags of light on his monitor. It was evident that his patient was upset. But why? "Mr. Hewlett," again a routine smile, "there's no necessity for you to get defensive . . ."

"I'M NOT GETTING DEFENSIVE!"

"Perhaps if I explained. I'm asking a few . . . preliminary questions in order to better calibrate your highly individual treatment." Again a smile.

Did I just yell? Did I lose my temper? It felt good to let out a little anger. Maybe the doctor *isn't* a quack if he managed to get me to yell. Hmm, what can I lose? "OKAY, OKAY." He raised his hands as if surrendering to the Law. "The answer to your question is yes."

"Fine," said the Doctor, smiling, "I see we're going to be good friends" (words that made both cringe).

Winston's resistance had at any rate developed cracks, and he agreed now to answer the follow-up questions without a fuss. Doctor Becker was beginning to believe that he might be able to help this patient after all. He'd always taken pride in his ability to judge human character.

I mean, he's a doctor. *He must know what he's doing. He went to medical school. He studied. He's got a diploma on the wall. He has OTHER patients, doesn't he? He must do something for them, otherwise he wouldn't be in business or they might take his license away. What can I lose? If he cures me, I've gained something. If he doesn't, things can't get any worse . . . can they?*

"That was fine, Mr. Hewlett. Let's move on now to the next procedure." As he spoke, the examination chair began flattening. The whir was audible. "Relax, relax," the Doctor cooed, rising and approaching his patient. "May I ask you to raise your head a moment? There!" He placed a pillow beneath it. "Comfortable?" Was that pillow . . . scented?

The Doctor returned to his stool. There was a moment of silence and anticipation. The room dimmed and then grew dark. "Hey!?" It was like being on a gallows when the trapdoor drops open. Suddenly, he was snapping into the unknown. He held his breath briefly, and then came the syrupy muzak. He thrashed his head from side to side. A fragrance like jasmine and lilacs and sweat filled his nose. He imagined he was suffocating. "What's going on?"

"Relax, Mr. Hewlett," Doctor Becker was speaking in the hushed tone of a sweet persuader, the one who urges you to spill the beans before the torturer is called in; or maybe the friendly voice of a pilot describing the details of the flight over the public address system. "Just keep your attention on the ceiling. Free your mind. You are about to embark on a gentle sen-SYU-al journey. Have a nice trip!"

CLICK. FLASH

HOLOGRAM ONE: Two boys, early teens, androgynous, girlish long hair. One is hunched forward. The other, behind him, expression ingenuous, is crouching and scrutinizing his playmate's anal region with interest. He is ithyphallic but clearly unfazed. The other boy is gazing skywards, as if communicating with the angels. He is smiling. He too is ithyphallic.

WINSTON'S REACTION (AS MEASURED ON THE DOCTOR'S MONITOR): none.

DOCTOR BECKER'S REACTION: none.

WINSTON'S THOUGHTS: Is this how he plans to cure me!? Showing me 3-D pictures (how does he make them anyway?) of little boys doing dirty things? Does he show pictures like this to all his patients? How does he stay in business? Is this legal? What smells so funny? Like . . . ugh, yuck! etc.

CLICK. FLASH

HOLOGRAM TWO: A boy and a girl, teens, lying in the grass. A sunny day, and they are naked. Behind them, a swimming hole. The girl is on her back, arms propped under her shoulders. Her knees are raised, legs spread, and her bright, pretty face radiates nonchalance. Her breasts are small and firm, the nipples sprite, upturned. The boy, a lanky fellow, is stretched out on his belly beside her, his head nesting in his elbows. Mischief in his eyes. She is reaching out towards him.

WINSTON'S REACTION: none.

DOCTOR BECKER'S REACTION AND COMMENT: Hmmm, very curious.

WINSTON'S THOUGHTS: (suppressing a giggle) Where does he get these pictures from? And in 3-D, I never saw anything like that before. Do the parents know? etc.

CLICK. FLASH

HOLOGRAM THREE: A full-breasted girl, maybe eighteen, tapered waist, hips and thighs like Praxiteles' Aphrodite and her face a paragon of schoolgirl innocence; around her neck a black collar. She is crouching, hands on the ground, body tipped forward, buttocks raised. Behind her, a hirsute young man, mid-twenties, ithyphallus prominent, seems to be on the verge of *intromissio a tergo*. In the foreground, a male thigh in profile is visible along with its state of arousal. The girl is eyeing that region with unambiguous attention.

WINSTON'S REACTION: none.

DR. BECKER'S REACTION AND COMMENT: This is highly unusual.

WINSTON'S THOUGHTS: Is this what he calls therapy? Am I expected to get aroused and then, boom! I'm cured??!! etc.

CLICK. FLASH

HOLOGRAM FOUR: Two sailors. One, very masculine and cruelly handsome, is sitting on a barrel, his pants rolled down to his ankles. The other is younger, slender and girlish in appearance. His legs are straddled over his partner's lap, his breeches dangling from one leg below the knee. *Coitus per anum* can be assumed and is nearly discernible. The younger participant is arching his back and chest, his hands cupped over his own (unseen) *genitalia*, mouth open.

WINSTON'S REACTION: none.

DOCTOR BECKER'S REACTION: He is checking his equipment, his grunting almost audible.

WINSTON'S THOUGHTS: Ow. Are they really doing what I think they are? etc.

CLICK. FLASH

HOLOGRAM FIVE: A woman, mid-twenties, attractive features, supine on a bed spacious as a sea, her legs raised at the knees and asunder. Circling her a wolf-pack of male adolescents. One, with an expression of cruel braggadocio is grasping her ankles and poised for intromission. Another, equally aroused, is prying her mouth open, his intentions unambiguous. Two others are visible only from the waist down. They are standing on the bed, ithyphallic.

WINSTON'S REACTION: none.

DOCTOR BECKER'S REACTION AND COMMENT: Could there be a loose connection in the electrodes? A short circuit? Hmmm. There must be *some* explanation!

WINSTON'S THOUGHTS: What's the point of all this? Really, I don't want to see other people *doing it*—if that's a reasonable way to describe what they are doing! I want to be able to *do it* myself again . . . Does he take these pictures himself? This man is not normal! And those awful smells! I think I'm going to retch! etc.

CLICK. FLASH

HOLOGRAM SIX: A bird's-eye perspective. Two women lying on a blue carpet, one voluptuous, large-breasted, smooth fleshy hips, red hair, the other boyish, blond, small shapely breasts, thighs long and muscular. They are caressing and kissing. Flanking them, two men, fortyish, masculine in appearance and each clearly in a coital embrace with the women, *phalloi*, half obscured, half visible, reflecting light.

WINSTON'S REACTION: none.

DOCTOR BECKER'S REACTION AND COMMENT: No reaction! What's wrong with him? He's not normal!

WINSTON'S THOUGHTS: I wonder if he looks at these pictures when he's alone. This is sick. Filth! Yes. That's what it is. Filth! etc.

CLICK. FLASH

HOLOGRAM SEVEN: A post-menopausal woman, sagging skin from neck to legs, stooped shoulders, burdened breasts, and yet attractive, a face with character. She is sitting naked on a sofa, feet planted firmly on the floor and looking into the camera as if watching television. Her long salt-and-pepper hair is in a single braid and hanging over one shoulder. A wispy youth, clearly an aesthete, shiny brown longish hair, supine, his head cushioned in her lap. She is stroking his forehead maternally. Neither is paying attention to his ithyphallus.

WINSTON'S REACTION: none.

DOCTOR BECKER'S REACTION AND COMMENT: Come on, Hewlett! There must be something that turns you on!

WINSTON'S THOUGHTS: I know what his problem is. He has an Oedipus complex! They're always saying that psychiatrists are sicker than their patients, just know how to cover it up better . . . etc.

CLICK. FLASH

HOLOGRAM EIGHT: She is sitting at the edge of a bed. Maybe she is seventeen, coy expression, her blouse unbuttoned to her belly, her skirt tucked around her legs to the knees, an image of untried innocence. Her legs are open at an angle of forty-five degrees. A boy, probably her age, still dressed, though the top buttons of his shirt are undone, revealing his pale chest, is leaning over her, one arm across her shoulder, his face, half submerged in her breast. He is wearing light khaki pants and the swell of his ithyphallus is discernable beneath his pantleg. The girl's expression is one of embarrassment and curiosity, her eyes fixed on his trousers.

WINSTON'S REACTION: none.

DOCTOR BECKER'S REACTION AND COMMENT: "Hardly a delta vibration!" The words are spoken in a silent whisper.

WINSTON'S THOUGHTS: What if he *isn't* a doctor?? What if he's a pervert *posing* as a doctor?! Well, I wasn't born yesterday buddy . . . etc.

CLICK. FLASH

HOLOGRAM NINE: She is the parody of a schoolgirl, like in a pornographic film; voluptuous, panties down to her ankles, legs spread, her plaid skirt turned back over her waist, her white blouse unbuttoned, her large, womanly breasts looming above her chest. She is lying on a gym mat, a muscular, hirsute man naked beside her and leaning towards her. She is clasping his ithyphallus, tongue extending over her lip as an expression of interest. His hand is buried in her *mons Venus*. Her eyes are shut tightly. You might expect her to cry out in delight at any moment. The man is mustachioed, his expression merciless.

WINSTON'S REACTION: none.

DOCTOR BECKER'S REACTION AND COMMENT: Impossible! Not even a negative reaction!

WINSTON'S THOUGHTS: This can't be real. Does he buy these 3-D pictures at adult bookstores? Or does the AMA sell them to psychiatrists? Phew! Smells like someone hasn't showered in weeks. The Doctor maybe? etc.

CLICK. FLASH

HOLOGRAM TEN: A domina, fullfaced leather mask, breasts bound under a black-studded leather harness, the nipples peeking through. Her legs are girthed in leather, and she is wearing shiny black high-heeled boots that rise above her knees. A whip in hand, she is standing, one high-heeled foot planted on the ithyphallus of a naked, well-proportioned man with a friendly face. He is supine at her feet. She is urinating on his groin.

WINSTON'S REACTION: none.

DOCTOR BECKER'S REACTION AND COMMENT: He has something against me, is doing this out of pure aggression. etc.

WINSTON'S THOUGHTS: I sure hope Blue Cross will cover this . . . etc.

CLICK. FLASH

HOLOGRAM ELEVEN: Young love, pretty like flowers and conjoined in the coital act, her arms and legs straddled around his back. They are under a thin sheet, but the contours are visible enough for the details to be left to the imagination. We are invisible guests, *succubi*, witnessing a moment of intimacy that seems to be approaching its climax.

WINSTON'S REACTION: none.

DOCTOR BECKER'S REACTION AND COMMENT: I admit it. I was wrong. He's not suitable for the therapy. I was too ambitious, too eager. No, I shall not . . . I refuse . . . to take him on as a patient.

WINSTON'S THOUGHTS: How much longer is this going to go on? etc.

CLICK. FLASH

HOLOGRAM TWELVE: A window in artificial light. Orange glow. A body builder in profile at the foot of a bed. Light falls on his nudity. The shadowy profile of a woman's head and shoulders can be seen kneeling over the edge of the bed and fellating him, muscular arms and hands clasping her head. He seems to be gazing out the window . . . absently.

WINSTON'S REACTION: none.

DOCTOR BECKER'S REACTION: Silence.

DARKNESS

Suddenly light. Winston blinked. The syrupy muzak went mute and the diverse scents, both the floral and the unruly, dissipated swiftly. "Impossible!" Doctor Becker was muttering, shaking his head, obviously irritated, and waving his hands. "Not the slightest reaction, not the most miniscule syncope! Dead. A corpse. Not a single vibration above the delta level! Not even a theta disturbance! Really. Life is not possible at two vibrations a second!"

Winston was propped up on his elbows, somehow resembling one of those hologram figures he had just viewed, apart from the tangle of wires connecting him to the Doctor's feedback monitors, of course. His eyes were fixed on the Doctor who must have forgotten he was not alone. A brief look of mortification.

"Oh dear, how embarrassing. Please excuse the outburst. It's just that . . . frankly, Mr. Hewlett, I have never seen a case like . . . yours . . . before." Sweat beads had collected on his bald forehead like lost opportunities.

Now it was Winston's turn for mortification. Maybe there *was* something terribly wrong. "Please, what is it, Doctor?"

"Mr. Hewlett . . . there's just . . . *nothing* happening there . . . not a single reaction above," he was struggling to find a friendly tone, "what is technically described as 'delta sexuality.'"

"Delta sexuality?" Now he was worried.

"You see, Mr. Hewlett," he slipped off his glasses, a prop to conceal his irritation, "Sexual impulses can be measured in waves, like brain waves. To identify these wave values, I have developed a descriptive apparatus similar to that used for measuring electro-encephalographic impulses, which is to say according to per-second frequency. We distinguish between delta, theta, alpha and beta levels. Your response ratio never once rose above the delta level, which is about the equivalent of, well, living in a coma, in the current context, a sexual coma."

What the Doctor did not say: Winston's reaction to this preliminary eroto-stimulastic examination had managed to raise crucial questions about the system's cybernetic viability. To wit: Not being able to identify Winston's condition within the framework of his system could be explained by one of two factors: either something still uncharted was at the root of Winston's problem or something was wrong with the Doctor's cybernetic model.

"But I know that already. That's why I came to you!"

"I'm sorry to disappoint you, Mr. Hewlett, but facts are FACTS!"

"You don't have to get defensive."

"I'M NOT GETTING DEFENSIVE!" A full stop. Time for a slow, deep breath. The Doctor slipped his glasses back on, his face pruned up. "Mr. Hewlett," he was hunting for the semblance of a smile, "I am an electro-psychic technician. Finding the individual *emotional* etiology for your . . . umm . . . problem is not relevant to my approach. Or maybe you were uninformed about the nature of my method. You never explained why you chose eroto-stimulastics as a form of treatment for your . . . umm . . . condition. Perhaps I should have enquired. Unless you're here to DISCREDIT me!"

"Discredit you??!"

"Oh dear. Forgive me, Mr. Hewlett. That's not what I meant to say. I'm not myself today." He wet his lips and smiled thinly.

"Then who are you?" Winston was satisfied with his cheeky repartee.

The Doctor perused Winston's long body, his naive expression and absurd nakedness and knew that he just didn't like him. There was something about Winston.

"Mr. Hewlett," his voice grown calm, his face steadily smaller, "I am a researcher. I have developed a system of personality taxonomy as individual as fingerprinting. If, and I say IF you were to continue treatment with me, I would in the course of therapy, that is, after carefully determining your galvanic identity, subject you to faradic inducements of the appropriate frequency, which is to say, suited to your unique constitution in order to, well, to re-modulate the nil-frequency of your sexual individuality. But I sense, Mr. Hewlett, that you would probably be better off with a more conventional form of treatment, which is something quite alien to what I could offer you . . . with *guaranteed* success, I might add."

"Re-modulate my nil-frequency! What am I? A radio?"

"In a manner of speaking," the Doctor smiled, a hint of indignance, "yes."

"And what *are* faradic inducements?"

"Something resembling what you may know as electro-shock therapy."

"On my . . ."

"Yes, Mr. Hewlett, on the *glans penis*."

"You can't be serious!"

"Serious? You don't think I'm serious?" His cheeks reddened. His eyes turned to glowing points. "You *insult* me, Mr. Hewlett. You keep INSULTING me. Ha! I'll show you . . ." and he lunged for his feedback monitors.

Winston was sitting upright on the obstetrics chair. "You keep away from those dials! And unhook me from this clothesline! Immediately!"

The Doctor froze, then sighed. Tears, yes tears, were swelling behind his eyes . . . He raised his hands in a helpless gesture. Then he began cleaning his glasses. "What's happening?!" He slipped his glasses back on. "Please Mr. Hewlett," his face bloodless, "there's no need to get excited."

"You just untangle me first from this contraption!" In the back of his mind the thought: what if he won't?

"Yes of course, of course." The Doctor was fumbling with the electrodes, feeling the heat of Winston's glare.

"Ow!"

"Sorry, Mr. Hewlett, I don't know what's getting into me."

"Just as long as you get it OUT of me. OW! You're trying to kill me!"

"Please, you're making me nervous."

"Smut peddler!"

"SMUT PEDDLER! SMUT PEDDLER!" He shook a finger at Winston. "How dare you insult me! Haha! I'll show you!" He dashed back to his monitors, leaving Winston with the expectation of a worst case scenario.

"Don't do it! Don't do it!" Images of splattered sexuality flashed in his mind. "Stop! STOP!!!"

"Oh my God! What am I doing?" The Doctor braced his arms against the rim of the table. "What is going on??!"

Yes, what *was* going on? To be fair, Doctor Becker's stimulastics test had always worked reasonably well—sometimes masterfully—as a preliminary to a custom-fit psycho-electro treatment. Winston was most certainly not the Doctor's only patient. In fact, the doctor had scored quite high in treating dysfunction. But suddenly . . . and inexplicably, his system had dysfunctioned, had itself become . . . impotent! What was wrong? Something about Winston was anathema to the Doctor; he just could not put his finger on it. And something about the Doctor was anathema to Winston. He too could not put his finger on it. Twin blindspots in another's frame of perception, a collision of *antipodes*. We mention this phenomenon here because it is more common than one might imagine. Everyone has an antipode. To what extent this will influence this story remains to be seen.

❊ ❊ ❊

Once the electrodes had been detached, Winston and the Doctor exchanged glances, puzzled, exhausted looks, scrutinizing each other shyly with a mixture of embarrassment and suspicion. There was a long silence during which both readjusted their frequencies to a civil band.

"I think we should end our doctor-patient relationship," Doctor Becker said weakly.

Winston nodded meekly.

"Perhaps I might be able to recommend a colleague with a more conventional approach," the Doctor added with bashful circumspection.

"Thank you, that's very kind," Winston low key and polite, "but I may just consult an old family friend who happens to be a psychiatrist . . ."

"May I ask the name?" The question was meant as polite small talk, a way of concluding this encounter on a superficially friendly note.

"Doctor Pentius." Winston responded, equally blasé, "Do you know him?"

"Larez Pentius?" A note of interest sounded in Doctor Becker's voice.

"I see you do. Most people think he's pretty eccentric, but I hear that he's got a good reputation in the profession."

"Indeed." But now Doctor Anthony Becker's expression metamorphosed, as if another force was in control of the muscles, nerves and sensory receptors that constituted that face. Unknown to Winston, Doctor Becker had vanished momentarily, leaving him to confront a new interlocutor, *Agent* Becker, an informant, a very minor functionary of the Empire of Chaos.

"Mr. Hewlett," *Agent* Becker asked, "It didn't occur to me before . . . are you by chance a relation of . . . Leland Hewlett, the inventor?"

"Why yes, he was my father. Did you know him?"

"No, I never had the pleasure, I was much too young, but I've heard quite a lot about him. He and Doctor Pentius were close associates as I recall." He was raising an eyebrow, his look probing. *Agent* Becker seemed to know something.

"Yes, why do you ask?"

"Simple curiosity, Mr. Hewlett, nothing more." He smiled briefly. "Well, I hope you'll extend my best regards to the Doctor."

"Of course, and I'll be sure to tell him about my, how did you call it, Deltagon sex impulses?"

"*Deltagon* sex impulses?" Now *Agent* Becker could barely restrain himself, "What do you mean?!"

"No, not Deltagon, that's something else. I mean delta waves. Isn't that what you said?"

Agent Becker's brain waves were modulating in quick peaks. *The Deltagon, what does he know about the Deltagon? I must report this.* "That's right, Mr. Hewlett, delta waves. Um . . . you may get dressed now."

FIVE

H E GROWS OLD Mr. Morris, he grows old, his bushy eye-
brows greying on his tired, thin-lipped merchant's face.
Virginia could have slipped the lead crystal paperweight she
was cupping right into her bag. He would never have noticed
or suspected her. He'd grown weary of following sleight-of-
hand movements though he knew: any customer was potentially a thief, even Virginia Hewlett. Hardly likely though.
"Thou shalt not steal" was deeply engraved in her program-
ming.

Virginia was caressing the contours of the cold, smooth
object. "How darling," she exclaimed.

"It's authentic Bohemian crystal, must be at least seventy-
five years old. They stopped making em that way after the
First War."

"Just look at the details!"

He adjusted his thick-rimmed reading glasses and partook
in a moment of admiration and salesmanship. "Natural dyes,"
he said. "Chemical ones were pretty uncommon back then.
The blue of her cape probably comes from forest berries."

"Imagine that." A hungry eye fixed on the delicate Virgin
with child. She was nestling the paperweight to her breast, similar to the way the Virgin was nestling her baby. "How much
did you say?"

"Well, for a good customer like yourself, I'm willing to go
down to seventy, and take my word, that's a good price."

She pursed her lips pensively, while stroking the object with blind fingers, her eyes surveying the corners of the darkly lit store, shades of brown and grey. Victorian tables, dresser drawers, secretaries, spinning wheels, Singer sewing machines, proto-dictaphones, zinc baby bathtubs, washboards, glass vitrines full with varnished silverware, tarnished oil paintings in chipped frames, everything dingy and musty, and all of it weighing heavily on the sagging, wood-planked floor. "What about sixty?" She raised her eyes, vaguely interrogative, a hint, just a hint of a coquettish smile at the corners of her mouth.

"Well, hmmm," feigning a troubled expression as he folded his glasses into the sheath that jutted from his shirt-pocket, "You know, you don't find them around so often anymore, especially not so finely crafted as this one. Seventy is a fair price—coulda sold it for that this morning to a young lady who came in here and was interested in it, said she might come by again later."

But Virginia was clearly holding her ground, her eyes fixed on his. There was a short silence.

"Well, all right. I'll give it to you for sixty-five, but that's my final offer. No sense quibbling over a few dollars."

Larcenous satisfaction, a release of tension in Virginia's extremities. She was proud that she'd kept her nerve. Felt good. She smiled back broadly, "A deal."

We don't know much about Virginia yet beyond what appears to be a certain domestic passivity mixed with some evidence of business acuity. Now perhaps might be a good opportunity to fill in a few details. She was what later might have been called a "Valley girl" (not in the popular use of that label), born and bred in the San Fernando Valley, specifically in Canoga Park, once the homeland of Tongva-Fernandeño and Chumash-Venturaño tribes, though since the 1930s a comfortable bedroom community north of Los Angeles. She was an only child, and family life centered around church activities, her parents being members of a certain Protestant denomination (or sect) whose name we will not reveal and somewhat older at the time of her birth. In fact, her father had been a "doughboy" in the First World War, and like her mother, scion of old Anglo-Saxon stock, perhaps "Mayflower" people. Family life was dour, and early on, Virginia found her only solace in reading. Some books she had to smuggle home from the public library, her parents' own library limited to sundry pamphlets and prayer books and of course the King James Bible, their favorite chapter being Leviticus XVIII. Already as an adolescent she began yearning for something different in life. And so, like her rival Gladiola Freytag, also a "Valley girl," at a young age she too migrated—albeit for different reasons—to Santa Barbara to seek her fortune. She was no musician however but had managed to secure a job at a Santa Barbara bookstore. And likewise similar to her rival Gladiola, she too met Winston, the scion of an old Barbareño family, soon after arriving in town. Back then he was a sweet, lanky and goofy young man who quickly won her heart. It was love at first sight. Yes, that does happen. But so much for now.

Mr. Morris was wrapping the piece in a sheet of newspaper and then settling it gently into a paper sack. Virginia reached into her deep handbag, a perfect receptacle for plunder, and fished out her wallet. Would she tell Winston she had bought yet another *objet*? She'd been spending so much money on antiquities these days. She was sure he would ask if she was unhappy. Then he would start looking for reasons and end up blaming himself . . . for the usual reasons. No, no, she wouldn't mention it, at least not for a while.

Focused on their business deal, Virginia and Mr. Morris took little notice of another customer slinking around the shop, picking up objects here and there with little discrimination, fingering them briefly, putting them down and picking up the next one, all the while casting nervous glances at Virginia.

It was *Agent* Becker. This being a Wednesday afternoon, all doctors—probably worldwide—were off duty, and most of them, at least in California, were shooting a few rounds of golf. Not *Agent* Becker. He was on duty—officially. He had been shadowing Virginia all morning and had followed her into three antique stores. She still hadn't noticed him. Now she was leaving this one, her long muumuu swaying tent-like, her new *objet d'art* firmly in hand, her bag hanging from a shoulder, heading for her car.

"Anything I can do for you?" Mr. Morris queried, his bushy brows forking into a half-skeptical frown.

"Thank you," *Agent* Becker stammered, nervously polite, jerking his head for a quick glance out the window. He was wearing a freshly pressed half-sleeve white shirt, khaki trousers and burgundy shoes. "I've seen everything I care to." He exited hastily, his eye still on Virginia who had climbed into her bright red compact. She loved its visibility. He jumped into his car, started up the engine and continued the pursuit, ever the shadow.

There was something about that man, Mr. Morris was thinking, but he couldn't put his finger on it. He jotted down *Agent* Becker's license number, just in case. Then in a sudden fit of consternation, he started pacing through the store, wondering whether *Agent* Becker might have shoplifted something. You just never know, no matter how respectable they may look.

SIX

"C'MON, HONEY, stop crying. Please. What did I do now? Why is it always my fault?" Winston had been trailing Virginia from room to room, Apollo pursuing Daphne, and Daphne futilely trying to shake him. Now they reached the kitchen. Last stop. Dead end. "Tell me, what did I say this time?" His bewilderment was framed in the doorway.

Virginia's lips were sealed, though an occasional whimper did rupture through. Her face was red, cheeks swollen and uncomely, eyes focused inward. Standing there in her muumuu, she was like some exotic tent without a door. Which did not stop him from searching for a secret opening in that closed system. She looked so helpless and—he could not help thinking this—so unattractive when she made a scene. "Tell me what I said? Will ya?"

She sunk into a chair, her elbow on the kitchen table, a hand wedged under her chin. With the other hand she was playing with the paperweight she had bought that morning. Dammit! She'd left it on the table! Well, he wouldn't notice it anyway.

Unrest in the Hewlett household. But why? Something was happening to disrupt the status quo, and one step seemed to precipitate the next. "Are you mad because I said I wanted to call Dr. Pentius? Huh? Is that it? Huh?"

No response. She was fondling that heavy piece of crystal, a lifeline, her eyes concentrating on the serene mother with child sealed safely in glass. How peaceful it must be in there.

"What am I supposed to do? Huh? Go back to that pornographer?! I've never been so scared in my life! He tried to kill me or castrate me! What was I supposed to do? Say thank you? Make another appointment? If you had seen the guy, you'd know what I'm talking about! Or would you like me to do nothing? Just accept my fate? Should I become a Buddhist monk? Is that what you want?"

"You're an idiot," she muttered that without looking up.

"Aha! I'm an idiot! And may I ask why? Because I'm trying to help myself? You should be proud of me! I'm tired of being a . . . a . . . *lug*. Look," he slapped the heavy steel door next to the refrigerator, "*I'm* the one who decided to open this door and go into Dad's workshop."

"I told you to do that ten years ago," her eyes still fixed on the paperweight.

"Okay, do you want a Nobel Prize? I wasn't ready ten years ago. Now I am. Besides, I've got ideas. I want to do something constructive in there. You just wanted to get me in there for . . . for . . . therapeutic reasons. What can I say? I wasn't ready. So sue me!"

"I don't like Dr. Pentius." The words were spoken unemotionally. Why couldn't she say what was on her mind? *Why do I have to be so chicken?!* What she feared was that the Doctor would blame Winston's impotence on *her*. Breaking up marriages: wasn't that what psychiatrists did best? How to explain that to Winston? She was biting her lips.

"That's it! I knew it was something like that! Aha! You don't like Dr. Pentius! Wonderful!" He sat across from her at the kitchen table, grabbed at a cylindrical saltshaker and began tapping it. "And what would you suggest I do, if I may ask?"

"Drop it, Winston."

"Drop what?"

"Just forget it."

"I don't understand."

"I don't like Larez Pentius."

"Do you think I do?" He was fondling the round metal cap of the saltshaker. "But I've got to do *something*."

"No, Winston. You don't. It'll go away just like that. Just stop dwelling on it."

"That's easy for you to say. You're a woman. If it hadn't been for women's liberation, you'd never have figured out you were supposed to have orgasms. Men are different. You know what they used to do to tribal chiefs in Africa when they couldn't do it anymore? You wanna know? They'd chase em into the forest, hunt em down and fry em for dinner. It's true. I read that in a book. That's what it's like to be a man. Always vulnerable! And lemme tell ya, I'm not ready to get my goose cooked yet. Besides, who knows, maybe someday I'll be able to convince you that we should have a baby . . ."

"Don't start up again. You promised . . ."

"I know I promised. I'm sorry. But I'm only flesh and blood. Maybe I should talk to Dr. Pentius about that *too*. Or maybe you should. I mean, if you want my honest opinion, it's just not normal . . ."

"WINSTON HEWLETT, I HATE YOU!" She stood up, throwing her chair over, and stamped out of the room.

Winston was about to yell something out, but then he noticed the paperweight. "More junk," he grumbled. "How much did this one cost?" he called out, but not loud enough for her to hear. He scrutinized the smooth object in his fingers and was soon charmed by it (yes, Virginia did have good taste). Still, he was angry at it in a surrogate sort of way. Something in him was tempted to smash it on the floor, but no, he would never do that. He wasn't that kind of guy. He turned it and turned it in his fingers, viewing it from all sides. But what was this? On the Virgin's breast, where normally the blood red sacred heart is, he eyed something that had become all too familiar and yet all too unknown:

It was a Deltagon! What was it doing there?! Just chance or was something else at play? Now he was really getting worried. That evening he called the Doctor.

Winston was roused out of sleep by an elusive erection. It towered above him like a cop with a warrant for his arrest, looking down at him with policelike dispassion, as if to say, "All right, Hewlett, get dressed, you're coming downtown with me to answer a few questions." On closer analysis, it became clear that this erection was also capable of feelings, and as Winston watched it poking up from under his blanket, all at once, it opened up, baring what till then it had kept concealed. Winston, it said, I didn't always want to be a cop. Honest. It's just that I didn't know what else to do. I was scared, defenseless, and what with all those people, insensitive to my needs. I was afraid that unless I found some way of protecting myself from *them*, I'd be a goner. Laughed out. Rejected. Beaten. Abused. Used. And to be honest, I always believed I was doing it for you. I mean it. Can you believe me? I didn't know it would turn out this way. Oh Winston, I love you. I really do. It's just because I'm a little drunk that I can say that now, but I mean it. If only things could be the way they used to be, I would know better. Yes, it's true; doesn't everyone talk that way? Oh, what's the use? Can you ever find it in your heart to forgive me? I know how you must hate me. But please forgive me. Please. And then it began to cry, bawling pitifully. Poor guy, Winston thought. Oh, it felt warm, so sensitive, so giving and friendly. Winston reached out to caress it, an expression of his forgiveness, to let it know that bygones were bygones. The strong-limbed friend twitched gratefully, spurred by the generosity of the affection. There, there, Winston soothed, his chest warming and flushed. Everyone makes mistakes. And he stroked his erection with brotherly affection to wash away its tears.

As Winston and his erection were reconciling, neither was aware that a third party had been observing them. This third party was wearing a mask in the form of a smiling face to secrete its identity. Now it approached the reconciling friends and addressed them in an exaggerated stage whisper. I know you two are in the process of resolving your differences, it said, but hey, how about you guys sharing the wealth? He nudged them and pointed to Virginia's sleeping form beside them. I bet she'd be real happy if you, well, surprised her. Don't you think?

This sudden appearance of the masked figure startled Winston and his erection at first, and they asked who he was. The smile of his mask merely smiled, and he said, "Just a Friend." Well, how about it? he prodded. Don't you guys want to do the lady a favor?

The reconciled friends exchanged comradely glances. Why not, they shrugged, grinning broadly and feeling ever so free. They turned towards Virginia to poke her awake. Virginia. Virgi-i-i-nia, they called out. But she was sleeping fast. Vir-gi-i-i-niaaaa. Wake u-u-up. And finally, she did.

Winston and his erection took her by the hand so she would understand what had happened, and after an initial disorientation, she was happy indeed and began caressing both lovingly. It seemed like it was going to be quite a party. It's so nice when we get along, they all agreed. Why don't we toast to our friendship? Each raised a glass and drank a little punch. How odd to imagine that only recently we were still enemies, but what's past is past. A little honesty is all it takes. Yes, honesty, trust and friendship. What good is pride? It only makes for unhappiness. This and other things they said while continuing to make merry.

But then, the masked figure, who called itself "Just a Friend" approached Winston and whispered to him out of earshot of his erection: Winston, your erection just told Virginia that you're not to be trusted, which is why he became a cop in the first place. He said WHAT? Are you sure? Absolutely, the masked figure with the happy face responded and slinked away. The party continued, but if you listened carefully, you could hear a sour note in Winston's frolic. Both Virginia and his erection were puzzled.

Now, the masked figure sidled up to Winston's erection, murmuring so only the erection could hear. Pssst, I heard Winston say that you're a prude. Are you sure? asked the erection in a tone revealing righteous probity. The masked figure nodded affirmatively. Why that ungrateful fucker. He'll pay for this. And then, the masked figure seemed to vanish.

In a nonce Winston and his erection resumed their conflict. It was horrible, each accusing the other of terrible wrongs. The struggle grew quickly in intensity. Stop! Virginia cried. She was horrified. Stop! I hate seeing you this way! But she could not influence them. They were wrestling, slapping and choking each other—it's horrible to tell—till finally both dropped into limp exhaustion. Oh dear! Virginia exclaimed bewildered, why must you treat each other like that? Can't you just be friends?

But that was not possible, and the losers strove to salvage what was left in sleep.

❀ ❀ ❀

Winston could not sleep. He was scared. My God. What if I can never do it again? What if I become a sexual cripple? An image of his penis imprinted itself in his imagination. It continued shrinking rapidly, a skinny worm, flapping limply at every step. Maybe I have an incurable disease? Maybe this is just a symptom? Maybe . . . I'm . . . DYING! My strength sapping from me. A rush of the willies hurtled through him. A sour taste rose to his throat, and he began to belch, to feel nauseous. He inhaled deeply. I don't want to be sick. I want to be *normal* and *healthy*. His palms were damp, and he clenched them as if praying. In fact, he did begin to pray, like an atheist on the battlefield. Please God help me to . . . to . . . he could find no other word . . . to *fuck* again. Please God help me to *fuck*. I don't want to be . . . he couldn't say it . . . don't let me be . . . he fought against the word, afraid to voice it . . . don't make me . . . oh hell . . . shit fuck . . . I don't want to be IMPO-TENT! It was as if he were plunging into an abyss. So dizzy. If only Virginia would wake up. But maybe she wouldn't take me seriously or think I was being self-indulgent? Maybe she would reject me. Maybe she would take on a lover! Maybe she *already* has one! THAT'S why she's been insisting it doesn't matter to her. Who is he? I'll kill him! How can I compete? What's wrong with me? Hopelessly diseased! He had the urge to throw up on himself, relax all excretory sphincters at once. Just give up. EEK! I'm a eunuch! No. I don't want to be a eunuch. What's wrong with me? Why am I falling apart? He was tossing from side to side, unable to find a comfortable position, hoping to wake Virginia with his little ruckus. But no. She continued sleeping, safe in her dreams. He curled into a fetal position, but that didn't help either. He felt a vertigo as if the bed were tilting. His body began to shake. This is the end, he was thinking. He could concentrate on nothing except that maybe he was ill, that thought strobing through his mind. He was breathing rapidly in the wake of his nausea. Finally, he climbed out of bed. The air felt chilly on his sweating body. He staggered into the bathroom and urinated. His own urine frightened him, as if he were losing something irrevocably important, some segment of his mortality. Compulsively he began arranging the jars in the medicine chest. Then he reached for a vial and tapped a blue valium tablet into his palm. He placed the tablet onto his tongue fastidiously and cupped his hands under the water faucet, then sloshed the pill down. He inhaled deeply, already slightly relieved. In a few minutes, he was thinking, yes, in a few minutes the valium will take effect. A soothing thought. He shuddered. At least I'll sleep. He wet his face with cold water then looked into the bathroom mirror. He did not think he looked attractive. He stuck out his tongue at his own reflection and smiled. Gradually, he was feeling calmer. He sighed and rubbed his face. It was cold out there. He trundled back to bed. Virginia did not awake. He lay down next to her and stared blankly. The musty smell of sleeping humans filled the air. The valium began blanketing his thoughts. Yes, he was feeling good. A wave of well-being swept through him. He breathed deeply. Ahhhh. He rolled over towards Virginia and threw an arm across her shoulder affectionately. You're so good to me. If I were really sick, I know you'd take care of me. Would I do the same for you? I would I would I would.

SEVEN

M EANWHILE out in the desert. Mid-afternoon. Cloudless, bloodless blue sky. Brown yellow stretches of landscape. Pale dry tufts of yucca and pampas grass. Twisted Joshua trees. Low rock hills. Desiccated, craggy. Eagles circling overhead. The grey freeway, a zipper stretching to the horizon, transmogrifying in the distance into slick black mirages. The tires rumble, constant whirr. The engine's running hot. The gas tank's reading empty.

Nathan Weiss switched off the radio. The Las Vegas frequencies had begun disintegrating into a scatter of electrovibratory components, hardly more than static, and Los Angeles was still out of range. Except for the engine whine and the steady roar of the tires, silence. A car raced up from behind out of nowhere, whooshed by and disappeared in a huff. A road sign up ahead came into focus.

BAKER 12 MILES

"Damn. Looks like that's where we make our last stand, Custer," Nathan Weiss said to *Agent* Porky of the Empire of Chaos. "Baker, California. What a great name for the place we're going to get cooked in, huh?"

"Don't you worry," *Agent* Porky calmly. His face boyish, a few scraggles of blond beard hanging from his chin. He was smiling. "We'll make it through."

"Easy for you to say. You're still a hippie. You can afford to arrive in places when you want. If I don't get back to Santa Barbara in time, I'm S.O.L., not to mention rehearsal. I've got a show opening next week, for your information."

"You'll get there."

"If you had to be at work in five hours, you might wipe that self-satisfied smirk off your face," Nathan Weiss was referring to his part-time job as a waiter at the Lobster House. "I mean, Jesus, what the hell were you doing out in the middle of the Nevada desert anyway?"

"Waiting for you. What else?"

"Yeah, well that's just great. You sure saw me coming! Huh? From miles away. You don't find a sucker like me every day. I bet you must be into astrology too. Well in case you're interested, I'm an asshole with penis rising and moon in Miami."

"You don't have to get so upset just because you're running out of gas. Last night you were much more fun." He brushed his long blond hair out of his face.

"I sure was, and I sure wish I hadn't been. Then at least I would have had enough money to get back home today without all this hassle."

"You just don't have any faith."

"Now you talk to me about faith. What are you, a Jesus freak? I mean whose idea was it to stop in Las Vegas. And whose money do you think we got drunk on and played blackjack with? Yours? You're a hippie. You don't have money and don't need any either because you've got faith. I'm the slob who scrapes shrimp shells off dirty plates just so I can eat and pay the rent. If I had faith, I would have driven right by you out in the middle of nowhere, and I would have been home by now, because, alone, it would never have crossed my mind to pitstop in Las Vegas and piss away the few dollars I had. But no. Why do I always have to be such a nice guy?"

"I think I liked you better yesterday."

"Well, I think I liked me better yesterday too, so that makes two of us; but that still doesn't get us to Santa Barbara any sooner. God knows how I got so personal with you anyway. I mean, you aren't even a girl and I'm not queer, even if you are a little cute."

"It's because I tell you the truth."

"Fantastic. Well, tell me when I'm going to get home then."

"In five hours."

"Well, I only hope you can stay so sure of yourself when you get to be my age."

"You're not that much older than me. Maybe ten years."

"You'd be surprised what can happen in ten years. I mean, I used to be a hippie too."

"Probably part time, like everything else you do."

Nathan turned to *Agent* Porky, "You're a little weasel, Porky, a real little weasel."

The town of Baker appeared up ahead. Nathan signaled right and exited the freeway. The area came into focus in slow motion, very slow motion. Town is not quite the word to describe it. It was a junction of two broad streets: one lined with motels and the other with gas stations, these interspersed between the usual fast-food havens. For all appearances, it looked like there was no part of this sandy flat where locals might live—unless they owned motels or slept in some back room at their businesses. No grocery, barbershop, post-office in view as they cruised slowly along the main drag—let alone a school or even children. Nathan counted seventeen gas stations, some of them duplicate or triplicate, three Exxons, two Texacos, two Gulfs etc. The buildings were flat, pale pastel, and the afternoon shadows accented their boxiness. Everything looked extremely thirsty.

"Oh damn. Baker. Now I remember why I know the name," he lowered his head to the steering wheel. "We've picked a swell place to hope for charity. Just look at all those cheerful faces. Of course. Baker. The first stop out of Las Vegas. Most everyone who passes through is broke. Yeah, that's it. People will trade their shoes, their guns, TV's, cassette recorders, rings, jewelry, or whatever else they've got left, for a fill-up. I read somewhere that a guy who's really desperate can sell his wife here for gas. What've we got to sell? My old Timex? A pair of worn-down Florsheims? Hey Porky baby, how's about you bending over for the Flying A man, if he's interested, huh?"

Agent Porky was busy gazing at the pale, plastic town. "Try that one," he motioned, pointing to a Gulf station off to the right. "Why don't you pull over to the curb. I'll wait in the car while you ask the attendant."

"Another hunch, huh?"

Agent Porky smiled boyishly.

"Okay, Billy Graham. Can't lose nothin'."

Nathan pulled over and climbed out of the car, first stretching his cramped limbs. He was thin, medium height and was wearing sandals, blue jeans and a T-shirt with the imprint "I left my heart in Santa Barbara." His hair was black and curly, but the curls were hanging limply in the dry air. His face was narrow, his expression vexed, and he needed a shave. A hot dry wind slapped at him, and he was forced to squint in the bright sunlight. He groaned, his body still vibrating from the buzz of the freeway. He stepped over to the pumps where an attendant, his skin old and parched, was wiping dead bugs off a windshield. The sight of the water he was squirting on the glass reminded Nathan how thirsty he was.

Nathan did not interrupt. He waited, acting as unobtrusive as possible, reading the labels on oil cans and engine additives, even growing interested in a paper towel dispenser and figuring out for the first time how one of those things was constructed. Then he studied the prices and gallon indicators on the pumps, all the while eyeing the spigot longingly. Finally, he began turning his head left and right as if reading the oil stains on the hot shadowless ground, seemingly fascinated by something anyone who cared to watch him for more than a few seconds would have recognized as not there.

When the car he had been servicing drove off, the attendant walked past Nathan without the simplest acknowledgement.

"Excuse me," Nathan warbled, pursuing the man and mustering up his most polite tone, "Wonder if you might be able to help me."

"Heaven helps them who help themselves." the attendant twanged, spat and continued on his way.

Nathan knew immediately that he could expect nothing, but it was too late; he was already caught in the momentum. "No, I mean, can I ask you a question."

The man stopped and stared blankly at him."Askin' costs nothin'." There was no mercy in those deeply crow-footed eyes and gaunt, sunbaked cheeks.

"Uhm," Nathan cleared his throat, "I wanted to know if there is anything I can offer you for a, uh, fill-up."

"Yep. Money."

"No, I mean, well, maybe my shoes, or my spare, or my jack or my watch or something." There was no reaction. "Look," well, here goes everything, he thought, my theatrical reputation to boot. Putting on his most pitiful expression: "I've got to get back to Santa Barbara or . . . or I'll lose my job . . ." The attendant didn't twitch or blink. "Don't you understand?" Nathan's voice turned recognizably teary, "It's a matter of life or death. My wife's sitting in the car. She's pregnant, very pregnant in fact, and she's started having contractions. I'm afraid her water's gonna break any minute; and my mother-in-law's dying of cancer and wants to see us one last time to give us her blessing . . ." The attendant did not appear moved. "How can you be so callous?" Nathan demanded indignantly. "I'm sure in my situation YOU would be as desperate as I am!" His voice tremoloed.

"Maybe so," the old man smiled, "but I sure as hell wouldn't waste my time asking someone like me for somethin' I knew I wasn't gonna get. Anythin' else I can do yer outta?"

Nathan harrumphed away, outdone and insulted, and stomped back towards the car. Wise guys! he was muttering. All I run into are wise guys! I thought I was supposed to be the funny guy. They should go on stage not me. He reached for the door handle. Ow! It was sizzling under the beating sun, and he bounced into the stuffy front seat, raising dust as he plopped himself down.

"Great idea, O prince of the sublime. I think your magic powers are flaking out, or your radar's on the fritz."

Agent Porky shrugged indifferently.

"Any other hunches?" Nathan was tapping his fingers against the steering wheel.

And then they heard the loud rumble of a motorcycle.

"Oh hell, now we're really in for it. The damned Highway Patrol. We must be in a no parking zone or something. Just what I need. Add insult to injury. Pour salt on the wound. When it rains it pours. Huh, Porky baby?"

Nathan turned to his left expecting to see the shiny leather leggings, the gold wire-framed mirrored sun-glasses, the bulbous white helmet, black strap slung under the chin, ticket book flapping in the dry, hot wind, and to hear the familiar request for "license and registration please"; but no. Instead, the blazing splendor of a fully customized raised-forked-front

Harley-Davidson, almost entirely chromed except for its jet-black gas tank, sparkling like the light of some heavenly body, a sissy-bar like Jacob's ladder, rising into space at least four feet and topped by the fluffiest racoon tail he had ever seen, dazzled his eyes, blinding him in reflected sunrays. He could barely make out the image of the person riding that chopper, and he had to strain to hear the raspy booming voice over the roar of the engine.

"Goin' to Santa Barbara?" The voice was bellowing over those awesome four cylinders.

"Sure hope so," Nathan quipped back loudly, then . . ."Say, how did you know . . .?"

"Wonder if you could do me a favor . . ."

"Oh, I'm very reliable," he was straining his voice but feared the irony was lost in the volume.

"I've got a letter here that's got to be delivered in Santa Barbara, and I wonder if you could do that for me."

Very strange. Very strange, Nathan thought, and cried back, "Why don't you just drop it into a mailbox? It might get there faster."

"Can't. Don't trust the mail," the voice roared. "You'd save me an awful lot of trouble if you would."

"Well, I'd like to," Nathan was squinting in the direction of the imposing voice and was about to explain his financial troubles when a leather-gloved hand reached into the window of his car clasping a small envelope and likewise a fresh fifty-dollar bill. Nathan's eyes bugged. But for another reason. He counted on that gloved hand one, two, three, four, five, six, yes six fingers! Hard to believe, but it was a six-fingered hand. He jabbed *Agent* Porky in the ribs to catch his attention, but *Agent* Porky was showing no interest in what was going on.

"For your troubles," the voice roared.

Nathan's fingers snatched the envelope and the fifty-dollar bill before his brain could register what his hand had just done.

He was about to say thank you when he heard the clank of the clutch engaging. A loud roar and the dark speck of a rider disappearing into the distance on what seemed like a gleaming sunbeam was all he saw.

"Jesus H. Christ! Did you see that! I can't believe it. Out of nowhere. I never heard of anything like that before. He just rode up. He KNEW I was going to Santa Barbara. And six fingers! I NEVER saw anyone with six fingers! NEVER! Once a guy with webbed toes, but SIX FINGERS and then WHOOSH and he's off. How creepy. Wassamatta? Don't things like that impress you? You above all that or something?"

Agent Porky smiled. "I knew you'd make it home in time."

"Keerist. You're too much." He raised the fifty-dollar bill to his lips and kissed it. "Ulysses S. Grant, am I ever glad to see you. Porky baby, you're right. The show will go on!"

"What's on the envelope?" *Agent* Porky prodded.

"What envelope? Oh that." He read the printed address:

WINSTON HEWLETT

1234 EDGEWATER

SANTA BARBARA, CALIFORNIA

Nathan scrutinized the sealed envelope carefully, held it up to the light, shook it, even smelled it. "Strange, huh, not even a return address. Hey Porky, why don't you just stick it into the glove compartment. Let's you and me get some gas and hotfoot it outta this fryin' pan, okay?"

"You won't forget to deliver the letter, will you?"

"A real boy scout you are, Porky. That's what you are. Say, while you're at it, there's a script in there too. Why dontcha take it out. You can cue me on my lines while we're driving. Be useful. You little devil." Nathan winked at *Agent* Porky, started up the engine and drove to the next gas station.

EIGHT

L AREZ PENTIUS lived (and worked) in a vintage ranch house nestled in a quiet neighborhood not far from the Santa Barbara Mission. Its rustic brown exterior (which could have done with a paint job) was obscured behind a thicket of scrub oak and eucalyptus trees. His yard was unkempt, a playground for weeds and high grass, a good place for ghosts to find cover. The screened-in patio at the side of the house served as a waiting-room for patients, a soothing ambience albeit a couple of notches beyond the norms of informality. Winston was sitting there on a weather-beaten, metal-framed, cushioned garden chair waiting for the Doctor to finish a consultation. He was nervous.

A scent of mustard wafted through the screened-in window, origin unknown, and it wakened Winston's animal spirits so that briefly he was able to forget where he was and why. For some reason the sour yellow smell of mustard always triggered his appetite. Mmm, mustard. His mouth was watering, and he was imagining a thick cold-cut sandwich on coarse rye bread.

As a boy, he had spent many hours here in the company of his father. While Leland Hewlett and Larez Pentius engaged in the usual intense verbal exchange about things Winston neither understood nor cared about, sometimes in this very patio, Winston would amble off from room to room to take in the Doctor's exotic trophies: a stuffed kiwi for example, or a massive cannon cartridge which Larez Pentius used as a waste-paper basket. In one corner of the Doctor's office a bundle of arrows with menacing tips was propped against the wall. The wood was dark and dry, and the Doctor would inculcate young Winston with warnings for him to avoid contact with those tips because they had once been dipped in poison. African masks glared blankly at visitors from various walls; ivory figures from China or Japan, vase-like containers, figurines carved from diverse woods or cast in metal adorned sundry table-tops. In some rooms kelims not unlike Navajo blankets hung on the walls, maybe some vestige of the Doctor's place of birth. All these images were still fixed in the incandescent light of Winston's memory.

He knew little about the Doctor's past. There was a faint whisper of a foreign accent in the music of his speech, some exotic verbal detail. Maybe his father once mentioned something about the Balkans (Bosnia? Macedonia? Albania?). But Winston had never been one to ask probing questions, nor were answers forthcoming. What he did know: Larez Pentius and his father had been bosom friends before he was born.

He heard the door to the consultation room open, and soon a man around Winston's age and tall like himself stepped into the patio to exit at the side of the house. He nodded grimly, exchanging an *ave Caesar nos morituri* glance with Winston. The screened door swung open with a creak, and the man disappeared down the garden path, the crunch of footsteps fading on the unswept walkway.

Soon after, Larez Pentius scuttled into the patio. A toothy "Winston!", a vigorous handshake. Next to him Winston looked like Saul among the Israelites.

How thin and white his hair is. He's aged. The Doctor's forehead was still discolored and scabbed as a result of his recent accident, but Winston, if he noticed, didn't inquire about it.

And then they entered the office, executioner and condemned man, or was it priest and condemned man? Winston's role was clear (at least to himself). The Doctor's was yet to be defined. No, nothing had changed. The same dark leather upholstered couch, sagging now from the weight of so many problems. And look, the kiwi was still perched on the Doctor's desk along with other smaller objects, some recalled, some not. Was the Doctor a collector? Interesting thought. And there were the poison arrows, dustier and smaller than in memory. On the wood-paneled wall behind them, he spotted a thin-rimmed brass frame with a photo of himself as a boy, the Doctor, hair black and bushy, an arm slung over Winston's shoulder, both smiling somberly.

It was always the same: a warm greeting and little opportunity for Winston to interrupt the swell of words, usually in the past tense. And then the refrain: "All we have left are memories!"

Soon they were sitting face to face in comfortable doctor-patient armchairs, but without professional distance. And then more reminiscing on the part of the Doctor, hard to know about what—maybe among other things that screwdriver long ago at Lake Casitas—but Winston was not listening anyway. He was gazing around the room. A low table near at hand caught his attention because he noticed a few figurines including a paperweight similar to the one Virginia had recently bought. He reached for it. Phew, no Deltagon. Then a few perfunctory questions about hearth and home and when there'd be a cake in the oven, but Winston only waved a hand disparagingly. He was beginning to regret his visit.

"Such a nice girl, but she isn't getting any younger and soon, all she'll be able to say is I didn't but maybe I should have! Her upbringing maybe."

Then silence and blank stares. And now Larez Pentius shifted to the subject that especially interests us: "Sometimes

I think there are no coincidences," he said with a hint of seriousness in his still cheerful voice. "I'm glad you came. It's as if you were reading my mind. Winston . . . I need your help."

"My help?!"

Larez Pentius sprung up and began shuffling through the mess of papers on his desk, fishing out a small card he extended to Winston:

"A Deltagon!" Hard to describe the tone of that exclamation.

"You KNOW about . . ." They had finally found their subject, and the room was filling with question marks.

Now it was Winston's turn. He reached into his jacket pocket and handed the Doctor the envelope he had recently received . . . was it just a few days ago?

DROPIT

Soon Winston was recounting everything Gladiola had divulged to him about the Deltagon, the Empire of Chaos, the Deadly Druids, and yes, all pertinent information about his impotence which in this context was taking on a new relevance. Gladiola's admonition not to repeat what she was about to tell him flashed briefly into mind, but now he was tangled in the grip of necessity, which, as everyone knows, is more powerful than all the gods.

The Doctor, plucking pensively at the loose skin of his neck, listened attentively, as one might expect of a psycho-analyst, but on this occasion he was not mapping out a dia-gram of a neurotic disorder. He was thinking: why has the Empire of Chaos chosen to reveal itself to Winston? and why exactly now? They must want something, but what? He was hardly more than a boy back then when ... Larez Pentius leaned back, eyes alert and far away. He reached for a pipe—not the one from Leland Hewlett; it was beyond repair. Aha, the pieces of the puzzle were falling into place. The battle lines were being drawn, clear as the points of the Deltagon. THEY had sent Winston to him. What they wanted was clear: DROP IT the message and Winston the unwitting agent. The Doctor was filling his pipe, satisfaction spreading across his face invis-ible as wind. This is the sign I've been waiting for. Now it's *our* turn to sow the seeds of destruction.

And then the decisive question: "Have you brought up your ... father ... to anyone recently?"

"My father? What does he have to do with my impo-tence?"

"No, my boy, forget your impotence ..."

Forget his impotence! Doctor Pentius was lighting his pipe, his eyes fixed on Winston with the penetrating glare of the psychiatrist. First Winston mentioned Doctor Becker's "delta wave sexuality," but Larez Pentius dismissed this diagnosis of his colleague whom he described as a "wiener roaster" with a wave of his hand. And then Winston mentioned his plans for his father's workshop, that venue long buried in the dust of neglect.

"The workshop! Yes! That must be it! Tell me more!"

From Winston's perspective, there was not much more to tell, except to explain his plans to transform it into a studio and to describe the ubiquitous dust. But now he was about to become privy to yet another story about events past. This time not his girlfriend but his father was to play the major role, though somehow both stories seemed connected. He was feeling like a small animal in the maws of a serpent and being sucked into darkness. "My boy," the doctor intoned, "your father did not die a natural death—as the coroner claimed. He was murdered . . . by that very Empire of Chaos." The room in which they were sitting had all but vanished. Winston's attention was concentrated on the Doctor who was sucking deeply on his pipe, and the words he spoke were enveloped in a cloud of smoke: "Your father was a great inventor . . ."

"That's for sure. I've been living off POP-IT royalties for years!"

"No, there's more, much more." The Doctor scurried to the window and shut the curtains with a single sweep of his hand. He switched on a floor lamp, which threw an orange glow, campfire atmosphere, on them. Puffs of smoke streaked the musty air and twisted into lazy, floating knots in the incandescent light . . . as if he were about to tell a ghost story. "Just a little precaution," the Doctor's uneven teeth peeking out from behind his lips in a sullen smile. "You never know when THEY might be listening." His eyes grew intense, and he spoke with a gravity that resembled calm. And now we take another trip into the past, a place as we've mentioned where Larez Pentius was especially at home . . .

Winston's father, he began, had secretly been working on a project that may have been as revolutionary as the wheel in its effect on human life. He had stumbled on an energy source so simple and so inexpensive to produce that it would have rendered the petroleum industry obsolete overnight and secured unlimited energy for all. Somehow, THEY had managed to get wind of it and had attempted to sabotage it for twenty years! Those were the facts. And no, the Doctor reassured, the Empire of Chaos were not agents of the petroleum industry, which—clandestinely—had been subsidizing the elder Hewlett's research.

In a nutshell: Leland Hewlett had devised an inexpensive process for converting carbon dioxide into a stable, solid form—not like dry ice, but rather something like a tablet or a powder. Dissolved in plain water, his PHOTOSYNTHESIZER—that was his name for it—could unharness vast amounts of energy. Specifically, he had designed the prototype of an engine that could channel that energy, producing exhaust fumes consisting of *pure oxygen!*

"Sounds like my father invented Alka Seltzer." Winston allowed himself a smirk.

"The comparison is not as far-fetched or as glib as you may think," said the Doctor.

The research was fraught with danger. At any time, THEY might attempt to sabotage the project, for which reason Leland Hewlett decided to work from home. It was an environment he could most securely keep under surveillance. As an added precaution to protect his family, he constructed a heavy steel door between his reinforced workshop and the kitchen and was careful never to reveal anything about the nature of his work except to Larez Pentius and of course to his business associates. But it seemed *no* precautions could ever truly keep THEM out. On the day of Leland Hewlett's death, reams of notes, vials and beakers full of tablets and powders and even a prototype of his PHOSYNTHESIZER engine in miniature— vanished and no one could imagine how that was possible.

That was the sad conclusion of a story whose beginnings could be traced back to a time shortly before the Second World War when Leland Hewlett and Larez Pentius were working as young colleagues on a top-secret project at the War Department. For those familiar with Santa Barbara, Headquarters was located in a subterranean aggregate where currently the El

Paseo stands. The site was an outer post for an operation code-named MAGIC which anyone can read about in history books. Leland Hewlett and Larez Pentius shared an office, which is how they met and became friends. Both had attended the same university back east at the same time but must have passed each other like ships in the night. At MAGIC, they were part of the corps intercepting messages from the Japanese High Command in Tokyo to its diplomatic attachés in Washington. Their job was to decipher the codes. It was a task the elder Hewlett was well suited for. Not only was he an accomplished cryptologist; thanks to the years he spent in Hawaii as a boy, he also spoke perfect Japanese. In the case of Larez Pentius, his skills as a psychologist were also considered valuable. Moreover, he had spent much of his early life in Japan, his father having been a liaison between the Imperial Austrian-Hungarian government and Japanese industrial interests. Thus, he had an intimacy with the Japanese mentality. As early as 1940, the staff at MAGIC had cracked a code confirming that the enemy was contemplating a surprise attack. They even suspected that Pearl Harbor would be the target. In fact, they were aware of the actual code words that would signal the onslaught: "East Wind Rain." A couple of days before the attack, those words were heard in a Japanese news broadcast. In other words: Washington was aware of the imminent threat. Nevertheless, the destruction took place. This anomaly remained inexplicable. Moreover, strange things had been happening at the War Department in those days. Files were disappearing, some even tampered with; couriers were not managing to relay communiqués properly, and phones weren't working. It was as if all *chaos* had broken loose.

This was happening not only in Washington but likewise at the West Coast MAGIC Headquarters in Santa Barbara. There, a message was heard again and again crackling across a variety of radio frequencies, but no one could make sense of its content. It was unlike any code that had been successfully cracked till then. Sometimes, Leland Hewlett and Larez Pentius would find scraps of paper in their in-basket . . . and no one could explain where they came from! It was always the same pattern of dots and dashes. It seemed indecipherable. It was not even possible to venture a guess regarding what language it was in—like trying to decipher a fragment from an unknown, ancient script. And because it was always the same code, decrypting it was even more difficult as cryptographers depend on quantity, variety and repetition to crack a code. Here, the code in question:

_ •••• •• ••• •• ••• ••• ••• •• _ • •• ••• ••••

In this case, the task at hand turned out to be less complicated than expected, because Leland Hewlett soon ventured a guess that the message was not written in some complex cipher but in garden variety Morse code! Moreover, in plain English! It read: `thisisshiteish`. The meaning of the first part, apart from its semiotic context, was evident. It was the `eish` the colleagues puzzled over. Was it a Japanese word? If so, a number of translations might have fit the bill: words, for example, meaning "doctor," "leg," "teach," "salt," "one," "eight," "chair," "late," "tasty." Nevertheless, they remained nonplussed. Nor could they imagine who might have sent that seemingly absurd piece of scatology. It was then that Leland Hewlett had the idea of interpreting that final sequence of dots iconically rather than semantically. He arranged them in rows of ascendency rather than linearly. They yielded the following pattern:

•
• •
• • •
• • • •

That was their first encounter with the mysterious symbol. They still had no inkling about the Empire of Chaos, but even then, Leland Hewlett managed to intuit a hypothesis that might have hinted at such a likelihood. The fact is: that symbol was not unfamiliar to him. Being well-versed in ancient history, he recognized that pattern as a TETRAKTYS, which is to say, the trademark of the ancient Pythagoreans, a vegetarian cult from the Greek island of Samos, followers of the famous philosopher Pythagoras.

And yet, something still didn't jive: the Pythagoreans were a peace-loving sect. The message Leland Hewlett had decoded was anything but pacifistic. For which reason he now proposed a bold theory that impressed his friend Larez Pentius very much. Knowing that the Pythagorean movement had evolved from an earlier sect that worshiped the poet-divinity Orpheus and that this Orphic cult in turn had its origins in Dionysus worship, a wild, orgiastic religion, he surmised that they were dealing with some sort of modern day Dionysians. His exact words, which still resounded in Larez Pentius memory: "Whoever sent us that message, must fancy themselves worshipers of Dionysus. How else to explain that ridiculous chaos?" *Chaos.* That was the word he had used. As for this symbol he had deciphered, he saw it as an upper-case Greek "delta," which also happens to be the first letter in the name *Dionysus,* in this case embellished with a mystical point at the center. As chance would have it, the followers of Dionysus were called *Maenads,* a word, which means . . . *maniacs.*"

"Are you saying that an ANCIENT GREEK CULT killed my father?!"

"At least a group that uses symbols from such a cult. Yes, I know this all sounds preposterous—after all, I'm a psychoanalyst—but as you can see . . . the pieces all fall into place. Besides, everything about the Empire of Chaos confirms—and this I can vouch for personally—that they are very *un*-Japanese."

The question remained: why had they homed in on Leland Hewlett and Larez Pentius? And now the PHOTOSYNTHE-SIZER comes into play. Before the morse code messages began arriving, little was happening at MAGIC. Sometimes Leland Hewlett and Larez Pentius, both young men at the time, would clown around to pass the time. Somehow, Leland Hewlett knocked an elbow against a coke bottle. It tipped over, rolled across the desk and fell to the floor, but didn't break, the quality of glass still being good in those days. Later, when he pried open the bottlecap, foam shot out volcanically. "Can you imagine how much energy was locked in that bottle!" Leland Hewlett exclaimed. It was like Newton sitting under the apple tree when the apple dropped. Suddenly, he began spouting ideas about a new source of energy. Was there a mole at Headquarters who overheard everything? That is what they later surmised.

Winston had been a small child when all this had been happening and was living with his parents in the same house on the Mesa which he now shared with Virginia. He saw little of his father in those days, and when he did, the elder Hewlett showed only perfunctory interest in his small son. Maybe he was just too busy or burdened by the weight of his responsibilities. The opposite was true of his mother: she indulged him and bathed him in love and attention. Then she got sick, very sick. As her illness worsened, Leland Hewlett grew even more impatient with Winston, and the boy was increasingly compelled to fend for himself.

One day—it was shortly after the War had ended—she left the house with his father. She could hardly stand and was very thin. "You be a good boy," she said, "and don't forget to water the plants." He never saw her again and could only remember her red hair.

Soon after those sad events, Leland Hewlett, having too little time or interest himself, hired a governess named Lily to supervise his son. His projects occupied ever more time, and now that his wife was no longer there, he began ensconcing himself in his workshop from morning to evening. Perhaps his way of dealing with his grief. That at least was Larez Pentius' theory.

Winston recalled very little of that time with Lily except for frequent excursions with her for which she would prepare cold-cut sandwiches, always with lots of mustard. He knew that his father was somehow nearby, which is to say in a room right behind the kitchen, and yet he seemed far away as if he had gone off on a long journey. Winston rarely entered that space. Leland Hewlett was afraid the boy might upset things. Only Larez Pentius had unlimited access to that sacrosanct precinct and spent much of his free time there with his friend, sometimes helping or advising him. It was in the workshop that Leland Hewlett had—accidently—invented the POP-IT which had led to great prosperity. He was actually attempting to develop a remote-control device for opening and closing the door to the workshop. That workshop was a secret refuge, and the door leading to it was an interface between two worlds or maybe two centuries or two dimensions. Moreover, the bolt closing it off to the outside world was probably as thick as the one on the vault of the Bank of England. Leland Hewlett was especially fussy about security. Only two people, he himself and Larez Pentius, had keys to that door. Then one day they began noticing small breaches. Nothing much: a notebook mislaid, a tool on the floor (which was hardly likely because Leland Hewlett was terribly fastidious about things being in their place), a light left on. At first, he and Larez Pentius were prepared to attribute this carelessness to their own physical ex-haustion, both being very overworked. But as these anomalies continued, they surmised that someone *wanted* them to notice that security was being breached. Soon, the frequency began increasing. It became clear that someone had been rummaging in the wastepaper basket; sometimes they'd find cigarette butts crushed out on the floor—although neither of the two friends smoked cigarettes, only pipes. There were even indications that someone had been handling models and shuffling through notebooks.

They became increasingly nonplussed and finally began checking for fingerprints but could only find their own—and neither of them could seriously be suspected of being the miscreant.

Finally, they set up a trip-wire that would release the shutter of a camera focused on the door should someone enter the space of the workshop. And indeed, someone did. Unfortunately, the interloper on the photo was concealed behind a sheet of tin foil. A reflection of the camera flash is all they saw. It was like examining an abstract painting.

There was no recourse but to begin holding nightly vigils in the workshop, sleeping in shifts and waiting for something to happen. A grueling time for both. Leland Hewlett couldn't concentrate on his projects, and Larez Pentius couldn't focus on his patients' needs. No one appreciates a psychiatrist falling asleep while you confess your most intimate quirks.

They were at their wit's end, minds like empty cannisters. And still they had not trapped the intruder. Then one night, around three a.m., Larez Pentius heard the sound of a key slipping into the door. He nudged Leland Hewlett to wake him, and both snapped to attention. The door opened, and a figure as if on tiptoes and waving a bright flashlight entered the workroom. The two friends pounced on the invader like predators in action. There was a scream, some struggling during which Leland Hewlett managed to switch on a light. Their prisoner went limp. It was Lily, a surprise because she had excellent references.

They interrogated her, but she remained tight-lipped. Then Leland Hewlett sketched the Pythagorean symbol he had hypothesized as the logo of that mysterious organization that had been hounding him since the War. She was clearly impressed by his deductive skills. Perhaps it was then that she understood how formidable an enemy he was. She immediately initiated the two friends into a vocabulary that chilled their insides: words like *Deltagon*, *Empire of Chaos* and *Maenad*. There was no mistaking: she meant business.

And then she made it clear that the Empire of Chaos, for reasons she declined to elucidate, vehemently objected to Leland Hewlett's research on his PHOTOSYNTHESIZER and demanded he shelve the project unless advised to the contrary. That was her tone, like someone from middle management sending an intra-office directive. Leland Hewlett remained defiant. He was not one to buckle under to bullying. Moreover, he was under contract with an energy company—whose name we shall not reveal here—to continue developing his PHOTOSYNTHESIZER. For which reason he speculated that this Empire of Chaos might be connected with the competition. Stranger things happen in the business world! At any rate, he bluntly dismissed Lily's request. That very morning, she packed her things and left.

Leland Hewlett was now acutely aware that he had powerful enemies, for which reason he assumed that hiring another governess might always harbor some risk. Thus, he decided to take charge of Winston's upbringing personally. After all, working at home did offer certain advantages in this respect, and from then on, father and son managed to share meals regularly. Nevertheless, Winston was usually just left to his own devices, though his father did help him with his homework when necessary. Larez Pentius had encouraged his friend to marry again, but Leland Hewlett showed little interest. He liked to describe himself as a "one-horse carriage."

"From what you've told me about your dalliance with your friend Gladiola, I see you're a horse of another color!" The Doctor winked.

And now we return to the present. It was too late for Winston to imagine he hadn't heard all this. Moreover, the Doctor had already devised a plan of action, and Winston had been assigned a leading role, despite the fact that he was still not sure what any of this meant.

"I want you to interrogate your 'paramour' for more information." Again a wink.

"But I promised I would never repeat her story. She would never forgive me."

" Don't you worry about that. Remember, I'm a shrink. Women may say things like that, but it's not always what they mean. And most importantly, my boy, I suggest that you and I have a good look at your father's workshop. There may still be important clues there under all that dust, and it's essential that *we* find them before THEY do. We've got to play THEM into our hands. And then . . ." the Doctor swiped with his hand as if snatching some flying object out of the air. "And as for your impotence, there's no doubt that THEY are behind it. What crueler way to vex a young man!"

"But why me?"

"The Empire of Chaos defies logic, my boy. And never forget: You're a Hewlett! That means you *have* the stuff it takes! I'm so glad I've found an ally . . . at last!" The Doctor drew on his pipe, and his face disappeared behind a puff of smoke.

NINE

JUDGING FROM APPEARANCES, it was a pleasant day. Winston and Virginia were lazing in the backyard. Their chaise longues, bright orange and green plastic straps on an aluminum-frame, were at random angles to each other but deliberately positioned to the sun, each according to an individual need for light and warmth.

Winston's gaze was fixed on the silent Pacific, but his thoughts were landlocked. He was wearing boxer bathing trunks and scratching mindlessly at a scab on his thigh while hunting through the vault of his body for memories, in particular memories about Lily, a personage long vanished in the nebula of childhood. Slowly, the slender person with gaunt face and long, straight black hair took shape in his mind's eye, though he couldn't be certain whether he might just be transforming her into the sorceress she had now become. Did she really have long, straight black hair? After all, in that niche of time they were acquainted right after the War, women were still perming their hair. Her cold-cut sandwiches with mustard, mmm, remained his most prominent memory, apart from a trip to the zoo where he had seen a monkey urinating. And then there was her frequent exhortation: *Let's get this show on the road!* Yes, that's what she used to say.

So, let's get this show on the road. First question: Why would the *Maenads* want to make him impotent? Granted, he was the son of his father but hardly the executor of his scientific testament. When the irascible inventor of the POP-IT, the PHOTOSYNTHESIZER and God-knows-what-else died—or had been murdered—as Doctor Pentius claimed, Winston and his father were living like two boarders under the same roof. The Leland Hewlett he knew was a moody, uncommunicative stranger prone to unpredictable paroxysms of rage. Second question: What might motivate the Empire of Chaos to strike at him *now*? "Drop it" was the message, and dammit he did! All he had in mind was doing a little sketching in the workshop, not inundating the world in carbon dioxide tablets. Did that space still harbor secrets that might come to light if he renovated it? Is that what got this show on the road? Were they bent on preventing him from revealing something unknown to him? And what was this Empire of Chaos anyway? Some esoteric group out for power and money like everyone else, or . . . or were they *really* just . . . EVIL? Impotence. That's really hitting below the belt. And now he'd been enlisted by Doctor Pentius. There was no doubt. The Doctor had bamboozled him with all that fast talking. Why couldn't he just say no? Yes, why not?

Success! Winston finally managed to tear off the scab and open his wound. He was smearing the blood on the skin of his thigh in a forest of leg hair. The flesh smarted, a welcome distraction. He licked a finger, idly diluting the blood in saliva. Then the antiseptic sting. A breeze floated in from seaside, and the sun beat warm on his chest. Very soothing. A quick glance at Virginia who was leafing through the SANTA BARBARA NEWS-PRESS and nibbling potato chips, the bag wedged beside the armrest. Her black, one-piece bathing suit did not cover the rolls of fat that had been forming at her thighs. A towel lay across her ankles, her way of forgetting. On the grass, a thick novel waiting for her attention. Her reading glasses balanced at the edge of her nose. She was at peace, feeling warmly domestic. Everything she wanted or needed could be found within a radius of ten or twenty miles or maybe ten or twenty feet.

"Hey," Virginia said with muted excitement, eyes still fixed on her newspaper, "WEISSGUY REVIEW STARRING NATHAN WEISS AND HIS WEISSGUYS is opening this week. Maybe we should go?"

"Hmm?" Winston responded from very far away, *Maenads* on his mind.

"Do you want to see WEISSGUY REVIEW STARRING NATHAN WEISS AND HIS WEISSGUYS? It's opening at Baudelaire's."

"Hmm? Nah."

Silence again. The comfortable silence of intimacy. Feet tapping, toes curling. Scratching sounds, some snorting. An occasional ahem or cough or sneeze. Swiping or brushing movements, wind, hollow echoes of distant sirens, automobile horns, thin voices from the beach below the cliff. Bird sounds, crows cawing in the date palms, eagles slicing through the air above, a radio playing next door, a door shutting or opening somewhere. Nothing too loud, all sounds muffled by space and air and breeze.

"I meant to tell you," Winston broke the silence, "I went to see Doctor Pentius."

Virginia lowered her paper, emotion gears shifting immediately. "No, you didn't tell me."

"You won't believe what he said."

"What?" Why was she expecting to hear something horrible?

Winston drew up his knees and folded his arms around them. "It's completely crazy, I'm not sure I can explain it."

Her voice silenced at the edge of a word.

And then the sentences cascaded out of him. Meanwhile, a lonesome cloud puffed across the sky and managed to blot out the sun. It was a brief interlude, but long enough to cast a shadow over the Hewlett backyard.

"*Maenads*?" Virginia was voicing skepticism.

"That's what he called them." Naturally, Winston excised all details about Gladiola from his narration.

"They murdered your father?"

"I know it's hard to believe. I don't know what to make of it either."

"Winston, are you making jokes? You're just trying to frighten me, right?"

"Honey, I wish I was. I guess I'm not the strong and silent type. I didn't want to tell you any of this, but, well, *somehow* I just had to."

For a brief instant it was possible to observe the spreading of a disease: the actual moment when infection leaps from one victim to the next, infecting each according to his immune system.

"Wait. I want to show you something. I'll be back in a minute." He got up from the chaise longue, the pattern of the straps impressed on his back and legs, and immersed into the house.

Virginia raised a knee and began picking at a favorite toenail. What to make of this? The transition from newspaper fiction to this science fiction posing as reality had been just too abrupt. In a nonce, her safe corner of this vast universe had been invaded. Spies in the date palms. Microphones in the orange trees. Sailboats on a menacing ocean whose insidious crews were surveying them through high-powered binoculars. That stubborn little cloud was still canceling the light of the sun. She felt a chill. She folded her glasses and cupped them in her hands. Then she caught sight of what seemed to be eagles or vultures circling above her as if they'd spotted carrion below. Why were the neighbors so loud? Doors slamming all about. The ominous cawing of crows. Thank you Larez Pentius. At least the Doctor hadn't blamed Winston's impotence on *her*. Thank you, Empire of Chaos, whoever or whatever you are.

Winston returned, light of foot, and handed her his DROP IT note. "That's the Deltagon," he said, his voice cheerful.

Even before she ventured a closer look, the tears began raining down. Within moments, she was whimpering.

"Hey, you don't have to worry." He was squatting at her side and stroking her arm. But she was out of control and dropped limply against him, her body jerking in rhythm to her sobs.

"I know it sounds awful," his voice heroic, "but you'll see, everything will turn out all right. We'll get to the bottom of this. Okay?"

"You don't understand! You don't understand!"

"But honey, I do, really I do."

"No . . . oh . . . I'm so unhappy!"

"Oh Virginia," her tears warm and damp against his bare chest, "I'm so glad you care."

Ten

THE FIRST TIME she sighted him, she thought it was her imagination. But yes, *Agent* Porky was sitting on a bench in front of the museum, eyes closed in the sun. There could be no mistaking. She recognized him clearly from the patio of the restaurant across the street: that angel face, the long, unruly truss of hair and that blank, better said, inscrutable expression. There could be no doubt now: the nightmare had returned. First Winston's DROP IT note, now Porky. Gladiola lost her appetite, paid and slipped off onto State Street hoping he hadn't noticed her.

Then at the beach. She was ambling in the damp sand, her attention fixed on the Mozart sonata she was practicing, her audition for the Santa Barbara Symphony rapidly approaching. Mozart was a reliable cure for a sour mood. She was tripping along to the rhythm of the playful allegro. She loved the way it tongued its way out of silence at the beginning of the second movement, eighth notes, light as sandpipers flitting across wet sand. She was feeling good, wholesome, swathed in Mozart's timeless optimism, bathed in sunlight and sea breezes. Then she spotted him. He was crouched barefoot in the sand, maybe twenty feet from her, staring vacantly, his knees raised and tucked under his arms. She altered her steps to a more invisible pace, all the while pretending not to notice him and hoping his attention was elsewhere. It was like walking by an aggressive dog and trying to conceal the scent of your fear. He did not call out to her.

The third time was at the supermarket. She was pushing her shopping cart down an aisle, heading towards the Mexican food section. Only afterward did it occur to her that she had passed him. He had been standing, his expression idle, at the cookies and snacks shelves, a thin guy in a T-shirt and jeans, hair bushy, a long, unshaven face, next to him. Another *agent*? They seemed to be discussing something, though Porky was doing more listening than talking. She was sure he had briefly cast a glance at her from the corner of his eye.

By then it was clear to her that their paths would eventually converge. She saw herself as a person with an incurable illness in regression who had been living the illusion of health. And now, her disease had returned. She contemplated flight, but she knew there was no escaping. She would have to make her stand in Santa Barbara.

"Winston, you really have to go. I'm expecting a student in an hour and I have to prepare. Besides, I still need to practice for my audition."

"I know, I know," the whining in his voice unmistakable, "but I had to get away." They lay stretched out on the daybed, unclothed. His sketchbook, his pretext for being there, orphaned on the wooden floor.

"It's not going to work. You have the . . . well, wrong attitude. You can't force yourself."

"I know, but Virginia has been so morose. We look at each other, and we both get depressed."

"What about me?"

"Somebody here has to be strong, and I'm afraid it's you."

"Thanks, Winston. Good to know I can depend on you if ever I need help."

"Why should you need help? You're the freest person I know." He jerked his head up. "Don't tell me you have some problem?"

"Oh no, of course not."

"You had me worried for a moment."

And then it happened. At first just a few tears welling at the corners of her eyes, heralds of an approaching inclemency. They began trickling down her cheeks, and soon the trickle turned into a stream and the stream into a torrent. Dammit, Dammit, I don't want him to see me this way. But she was sobbing and there was no stopping it.

"Oh no!" Winston sat up. "Not you too now! What's the matter? Why are you crying? I love you, Gladiola, I really do."

But the crying only intensified, and soon she was hurrying out of the room, leaving a puzzled Winston behind. He stepped over to the window where sometimes he would gaze across town and gloat, but he had lost that ability. In fact, he made a point of avoiding eye contact with that distant hill he called home, focusing his eyes onto the street below for the moment where he observed a long-haired, blond boy passing Gladiola's house. He began counting that person's steps. Anything to distract himself, especially because he knew that he still had to fulfill that promise he'd made to Doctor Pentius to interview Gladiola about the *Maenads*. The entire business was making less sense to him daily; he knew he was slipping into a cognitive infarct that defied all logic.

Gladiola returned. She was dressed, her face puffy, but she had herself under control. "I'm sorry, Winston. I don't know why that happened. It was, well, like an attack of the blues. I don't want to burden you. You have enough problems."

She was regaining her poise and charm rapidly, and Winston was happy to believe her. "Oh, forget it," generosity in his tone. "I understand. And don't forget, I'm always there if you need me. You know that."

She nodded.

"Umm, Gladiola," he was leaning against the window frame. "There's something I've been meaning to tell you."

Uh oh, danger, said her mind's radar. He was definitely about to say something that would catapult her into greater misery. What's that expression? If things can get worse, they will? Through willpower alone, she feigned an inquisitive look . . .

"I know I promised I'd never repeat what you told me about THEM, but . . ." And then he related his encounter with Larez Pentius, making an effort not to omit a single detail . . .

ELEVEN

"YOU KNOW WHAT your problem is, Porky baby?" Nathan was framed in the doorway between bedroom and living room while unbuttoning his shirt. "You take yourself too seriously."

Porky was sunk in the sofa, his attention fixed on the television and eating cookies. He did not respond.

"Really." He stepped into the small, messy room and propped an arm on the back of a frayed upholstered armchair as makeshift as the rest of the furnishings in the apartment. "I know your kind. Teenagers from the Midwest escaping to California from some lousy home situation to find godknowswhat. In your case, probably nirvana or the Garden of Eden or something like that, because you're obviously one of those guru types. Don't get me wrong, Porky, I like you, but you're lazy. And God forbid you should ever reach samadhi, or whatever they call it. You're the kind of guy who'd probably force the rest of us to be as enlightened as you."

"Why are you leaning on me?" *Agent* Porky looked up with an expression of bland curiosity.

"I'm not leaning on you. It's just that I'm from New York, and when people like me go to California, it's only for the sun."

"You're unhappy today."

"Of course I'm unhappy. I'm unhappy every day. But don't try to change the subject. Whether I'm unhappy or not doesn't alter the fact that you're a lazy bum. Don't get me wrong. I enjoy you staying here. You don't get in the way. You're polite. You're clean, cleaner than this place maybe. I don't even mind you emptying my refrigerator. You're a growing boy. But you're just full of crap. Which is to say, your guru talk is getting to me."

"You're frustrated because your show got panned." He was referring to the WEISSGUY REVIEW STARRING NATHAN WEISS AND HIS WEISSGUYS which closed down because it was playing to an empty house.

"Whaddaya think? Of course, I'm frustrated! You think I don't have feelings? But you're still full of crap. I mean, what do you live from—besides suckers like me who are willing to put you up for a while. I've never seen you open a book. Can you read? Or are you one of those TV babies? I mean, if you're studying to be a guru, you gotta think about the do re mi—like that QUID PRO QUO guy, what's his name, Wyatt Amadeus Rosenbloom. I saw him on TV. That's one smart cookie, I tell you. He knows how to toast his buns. Or have you already entered samadhi? At least I work, even if I am a failure."

"I don't think you're a failure. In fact, I think you're a good actor. You can be pretty funny sometimes."

"You really think so? Now I've got two fans, you and my mother. But wait a second. Don't try to change the subject with flattery, though I love being flattered—even if it's from you. I'm trying to find out what makes you tick, and all I get is smart-ass answers."

Agent Porky propped himself up, his expression serious. "I think you need to find yourself a larger apartment and nicer furniture. Besides, these walls are the most hideous green I've ever seen. A new environment would do you good. It would make you work better too. And then you'd probably become more successful."

"Jesus Chrysanthemums! I should rent you out to parties. I just need to install a slot behind your ear so people could stick in a quarter and you could give advice. Look Porky, you may have a pretty face now, but in ten years it's going to start losing its youthful bloom and develop character like mine. And if all you got to offer people is good advice, let me give you some advice. Don't."

"You're trying to hurt my feelings."

"Thank God. At least you've got feelings. Now I know all this wasn't in vain."

"I'm sad now."

"And I'm happy."

Their eyes locked, beyond the comfort zone; neither spoke.

Nathan slid onto the chair he'd been propping himself on. "Tell me something about yourself."

"What do you want to know?"

"I don't know. Like where you come from or whether you've got any hobbies besides watching TV, eating cookies and meditating—which, if you ask me, all seem pretty much the same thing."

"Is all that important to you?"

"Is all that stuff important to me? Why do you always talk in circles? You're damn straight it's important. Why do you think I'm asking?!"

"Why are you yelling at me? I thought you want to get to know me. Now I'm not going to tell you anything."

"God, I talk to you like a Dutch uncle and wind up in a ju-jitsu match. Listen, Porky, I've had a long hard day scraping people's lobster shells from their plates. I'm starting to smell like a fish myself. As for my acting, I got the worst review I've ever received in my entire life. I was even accused of mugging! The horror! And no woman in a radius of a hundred miles wants to sleep with me. I've reached a new all-time low. I even put a red mark for today in my calendar, and I'm going to celebrate the anniversary every year by burning a black candle. All I want is a little solace when I get home. Instead, I find you sitting there with those wacko television eyes."

"How would you like me to be?"

"What kind of question is that? I don't know. Friendly."

"Okay, Nathan," Porky smiled, "I'll try to be more friendly."

"I'm glad you're going to try. Hearing that makes me feel better already. That's great. You're going to try. And I'm going to try something too. I'm going to try to go to sleep and make believe today didn't happen."

❀ ❀ ❀

Once, during his student days at Queens College, Nathan received an invitation to a garden party at Professor Damur's, whose "Cultures of the Ancient World" was a required course for undergraduates majoring in the Humanities. Unknown to him, the invitation had been sent by mistake, some confusion of names, which might explain why Nathan was surprised to receive it. After some initial hesitation, he decided to accept anyway.

Because he had been invited unintentionally, he was not aware that this annual event enjoyed an especial reputation among a select coterie of students and faculty members who referred to it as "The Competition."

It was no ordinary social gathering. For the past five years, the Professor had been handpicking men from the local academic community whom he considered most suitable to compete for the hand of his daughter, Melanie. It was winner take all. Celebrating Melanie's perfection—in body and soul—had become the stuff of legends in this elite circle.

The rules were well known. Competitors were challenged to solve a conundrum, a feat still not accomplished after five years. The only consolation for the losers was to enjoy a brief moment in Melanie's proximity, actually more a punishment than a reward because no one was given a second chance.

The defeated, unless endowed with great fortitude of character, were often haunted by the recollection of Melanie's sublimity. Some, after the experience, found it impossible to love another woman. A few failed suitors, students and faculty alike, had sadly taken their lives or drifted into madness or depravity. There was a rumor that there existed a secret society dedicated to the worship of her splendor, a pastime that clearly led to permanent dereliction.

Nathan knew none of this, and though he was flattered to receive an invitation to *something* . . . to *anything*, his social life at the time being quite impoverished, his instincts—and nature—normally led him to steer clear of student/faculty get-togethers. Not because he was shy; he was just too much of a non-conformist to find his niche at such events. In the end, he did accept, reasoning that under the circumstances he could not afford the luxury of being fussy.

The Professor's villa was in Bayside, the property surrounded by tall hedges, high as fortress walls and equally impenetrable. Nathan arrived late—not as a display of insolence or haughtiness. He had once read that arriving at parties punctually might be interpreted as overzealousness or bad manners. In this case however, his tardiness precipitated scornful looks from all present, including the Professor. Moreover, he was not dressed properly for the occasion. His corduroy suit, the most formal piece of attire in his wardrobe, might have been considered casual when compared with the dinner-jackets the other guests had donned. The condescending glances quickly made him feel unwelcome, and soon he regretted accepting the invitation. Soon too, he noted that the guests, some young like himself, others nearing dotage, were all male, no women far and wide. Now he was wondering whether he had chanced upon a sexually aberrant "do" or perhaps just a stag party. Above all, he sensed a tension in the air.

Shortly after his arrival, Professor Damur approached him and discreetly informed him that this was a private party, invitation only, and asked him politely but unequivocally to leave. Nathan barely recognized his teacher. Granted, Damur had always been somewhat of a stuffed shirt, but today, dressed to the nines in black tails and cummerbund, his silver-grey hair combed back austerely, he seemed like a figure from some dimension unknown to Nathan. Not in the least intimidated, he showed the Professor his invitation. His host scrutinized it, returned it, harrumphed and walked off brusquely.

After cocktails and a paltry though ambrosial brunch, the Professor mustered his guests to attention. They hurriedly gathered in a broad semi-circle around him; the nervous chatter hushed swiftly. As the Professor began presenting his introductory remarks, suddenly a gasp rose from among the assembled. Melanie had stepped into the garden, a figure of grace and purity who soon took her place at her father's side.

Describing her is not easy. Her complexion was dark, as was her hair, and yet her skin had a delicate pallor, while her hair seemed to glow translucently. She was slender and of medium height but seemed tall and full bodied. Her burgundy silk dress was sleeveless and hung loosely, emphasizing and concealing her contours at once. The hint of nakedness attested by her bare arms was enough to awaken yearning in the most anodyne imagination. A perfumed scent like the fragrance of roses and violets further tempered by a more severe note wafted over the assembly.

Meanwhile, she surveyed the circle of suitors, more out of curiosity than interest. This ritual had become all too familiar to her. Then her eyes fell on Nathan, who was looking blankly or perhaps interrogatively in her direction. When their eyes met, she blushed, a fact that did not go unnoticed, and a barely audible murmur arose from the crowd. The Professor eyed Nathan caustically.

And then the contest began. What contest? Nathan was thinking he ought to ask someone but was loath to reveal his ignorance. But the Professor had already begun telling what struck Nathan as an entertaining little story. The guests were listening tensely to the words spoken with deliberation and clarity:

On a Saturday, a judge condemned a delinquent to death by hanging. The execution, he advised the condemned man, would take place in the afternoon on one of the seven days of the coming week. You will not know which day in advance and will be informed on the morning of the execution. This judge was known as a man who kept his word. Returning to his cell, the condemned man, clearly despondent, was accompanied by his attorney who was smiling. Can't you see? the attorney said, the judge's sentence cannot be carried out. I don't understand, said the prisoner. Look, said the attorney, it's obvious that you can't be executed next Saturday. Why not? Because Saturday is the last day of the week. That means being alive on Friday, you would have advanced knowledge that you were to be executed on Saturday, which is to say, you would know a day before your execution and not on the morning of the actual day. That would be a contradiction of the terms set by the judge. If Saturday were out of the question, the same would hold true for Friday because, if it were not possible to execute you on Saturday, then Friday would become the last day of the week. Which is to say: if you were alive on Thursday, you would also know a day in advance that your execution was scheduled for Friday. That too would contradict the conditions the judge set, so that Thursday too would be out of the question as an execution date because you would already have advance notice on Wednesday . . . and so on. Now I understand, the prisoner said to his attorney and was clearly relieved. In other words, the judge has made it impossible for me to be executed on any day of the week.

Your task, gentlemen, said the Professor, his tone ceremonial, is to tell us whether or not the execution takes place, and please elucidate. We want details.

One by one the names of competitors were called out, each approaching the Professor and his daughter who were standing under a striped garden awning, just a few feet from them, each aware that this was the decisive moment. Some were so overwhelmed by the proximity to the object of their yearning that they managed to bring out little more than a couple of stammered words, struggling desperately to form sentences and failing that, lingering for a few final moments in the proximity of that prize that would never be theirs. Others expounded eloquently and longwindedly in the language of algebra and logic, clearly self-satisfied with their solution to the problem until abruptly cut off by the Professor with an icy thank you. A couple of wooers feigned attempts to take their own lives in full view of the others. A few broke down and had to be carried off by what seemed to be an ambulance service in attendance. The atmosphere was chilling, painful to experience. Meanwhile, Melanie was casting flushed glances at Nathan, who, to say the least, was still very puzzled by these goings on. In fact, he was contemplating asking that pretty girl to go out with him to the movies after this nonsense was over. After all, he definitely sensed that she was flirting with him.

When his name was called out, he did not react at first, his mind too distracted. The Professor addressed him a second and third time and finally, his neighbor to the right, who might have been his history professor, jabbed him in the ribs. Nathan snapped to attention, stepped forward, still puzzled about all this and swaggered over to host and daughter. Melanie's heart fluttered as he approached, and when he grinned at her, her cheeks turned deep red. The Professor and the remaining suitors glared with hostility. The Professor was still puzzling about Nathan's invitation; but it was too late now.

Murmuring, then a hush. All eyes were fixed on Nathan, especially Melanie's. Am I supposed to answer that question? Nathan asked calmly. The Professor was dumbstruck by Nathan's audacity and only managed to nod. Well, if you want my opinion, the whole story is gobbledygook. Hey, do you really think that prisoner has a leg to stand on? Look, his lawyer got everything, if you'll pardon my French, *ass backwards*. He should have started his counting from the first and not the last day of the week. I mean, that judge can hang him anytime he wants. Any day would be a surprise. Besides, you don't seriously think a judge who had to work on a Saturday— why on Saturday anyway?—would let himself get tricked that easily!

This . . . *gentleman* . . . has solved the problem! Professor Damur exclaimed and let his list of contestants drop into the grass, unable to conceal his disappointment. The defeated suitors roared aghast. Nathan was grinning. What's going on here? he asked Melanie. Hey, how about you and me going for a walk? I'm yours! she exclaimed, I'm all yours!

Eventually Nathan did find out what was going on and what he had won, and he didn't like the business one bit. He was inclined to say thank you but please find someone else. You don't win people in contests. But Melanie's sad, friendly expression touched him. Besides, he thought she was cute. And soon he grew genuinely fond of her. In fact, he fell in love with her.

Melanie was pleased by this reciprocity. Professor Damur, who should have been, was not, despite the fact that Nathan had fulfilled the conditions he himself had set or that his daughter actually loved the winning contestant. What more could he wish for? Quite simply: he wanted his future son-in-law to be an academic. Nathan, by contrast, was aiming for a theatrical career, which meant, from the Professor's point of view, he was a man without a future. And so, Professor Damur added a new condition as a prerequisite for matrimony: he insisted the winner enroll in a course of studies of his own choosing—as far as he was concerned it could even be Theater Studies—and earn a Ph.D. Only then, would the Professor consent to Nathan's marriage with Melanie.

Had this been another era or a different culture, Nathan might have had to defer to the will of his future father-in-law, like Jacob in the tents of Laban; but we are describing an incident that occurred in the second half of the twentieth century, and furthermore, in the United States, and everyone, including Nathan, knew that there were easier ways of getting things done. And so, Melanie and Nathan moved together into a small but charming apartment in Flushing.

There, they led a happy life *à deux*, well, almost. There is one circumstance we have not mentioned up to now. You see, for as long as Nathan had known his beloved Melanie, he had never been in her company after sundown. Not once. Strange but true. From the earliest days of their romance, they were inseparable: but only by the light of day. Nathan hadn't considered this at first, attributing the hours of their rendezvous to some machinations of the moody Professor. Eventually, he did begin to wonder . . .

All the more, once they moved in together early in the year. Because now Melanie set her own condition for life together, one that truly baffled Nathan: for a full year, he was not permitted to see her after sundown. If he did, she stipulated, she would be obliged to return to her father's house. Initially, he objected to something so preposterous, but there was no mistaking her seriousness. Moreover, he loved her, and so, finally, he did consent, despite his misgivings. Of course, he asked for an explanation, frequently, in fact, but none was forthcoming. And so, he and Melanie shared a daylight love. At the first signs of sunset, she'd withdraw behind the door to her room and not reappear until dawn.

Despite this unusual circumstance, they were happy together.

Half a year passed, and Nathan patiently accustomed himself to this peculiar situation. Nevertheless, the enigma of her nocturnal disappearance continued to unsettle him. What was behind it? Certainly, not prudery, for by day the sweet mysteries of her lovely body were his to explore and lavish in. What secret was she withholding in the dark? The question tormented him, but he always managed to fight off the urge to satisfy his curiosity. After all, he had promised her his trust. And yet, some nights, he'd stand before her door, hand on the door-knob, at war with temptation, until, exhausted, he withdrew in frustration to his own room and fell asleep, only to find her at his side in the first light of dawn.

As this year of disciplined waiting was reaching its culmination, he might have celebrated the rewards to come. Instead, his curiosity only intensified.

Night after night he'd ask himself why it had to be this way? But then came the day again, and there she was in his embrace assuaging those urges, filling him with warmth, with love. The nights grew longer, the days shorter, and he'd muse: to see her just once, just once before the conditions have been met. Maybe I'm missing something I will soon never have an opportunity to experience.

Finally, the cracks broadened, and his resistance broke. It was late December when he decided, candle in hand, to enter her room sometime after midnight. Yes, he did hesitate at the threshold, but he was no longer master over himself. Quietly he opened the door, which was unlocked, and entered the room, tiptoeing until he stood by the bed where she lay sleeping.

He held the candle over her and gasped. He had to stifle a cry. What he saw was not the Melanie he knew and loved, but a faint, translucent version of her, barely visible. She was so nearly without substance that through the transparency of her body, he could see the impression of her head on the pillow and the pattern of the pillowcase. Suddenly he felt faint; his hand shook, and a few beads of hot wax dripped onto her sleeping translucency. She awoke with a shriek. The sheets shuffled. He heard a gasp and then a weeping voice, but he could no longer locate that voice. Now you've done it, the voice was lamenting, now you've done it. If you had only been patient just a little longer, Nathan, I'd have been yours forever. YOU would have filled me with visibility, and I would have been yours day and night. Your love would have completed me. But your curiosity was more powerful; and now, though I love you with all my heart, though I shall long for you, I must leave you, and perhaps never see you again. It was too soon too soon too soon . . . and then even the faint voice of Melanie Damur had vanished.

Nathan cried out. He called her name. He begged her to come back, but it was too late. The invisibility had turned to vacancy. There was nothing more to see nor anything more to say. She was gone, and emptiness moved into his heart.

❀ ❀ ❀

Nathan was dreaming. He was changing a tire. Behind him, the house was on fire. The tire iron kept slipping off the lug nuts. After each try, Nathan would say: "no dice, no dice," intoning the words rhythmically. "A POP-IT!" his dream-self exclaimed, "That's what I need to change my tire. 'Anything goes. Just POP-IT.' Isn't that what they say in the commercials?" But his POP-IT was indoors, and the house was on fire; and the closer he got to the door the more intense the heat, and soon it became unbearable . . .

Then his dream went deaf, dumb and blind. The sleeping S of Nathan's body sighed. And then he felt an unaccustomed warmth at his back, a double S. Was he plural? "Huh? Wass-goin' on?"

"Shh. It's okay. It's only me, Porky." A hand was snaking over Nathan's hairy chest.

"Oh." Three, two, one . . ."PORKY!" His head shot up, his brain suddenly aware of that warm, smooth nakedness clinging to the curves of his own body, a new skin that was somehow making his own skin tingle, and then a hard insistent pressure in the neighborhood of his loins . . . "What!?"

"It's all right, Nathan. Just relax." Lips pressing against the musty sleep smells at Nathan's shoulders, stirring his skin awake . . . and wait . . . releasing the scent of sweet, pungent sexualized molecules from millions of stimulated cells, nuclei clearly going insane with interest and, yes, with pleasure.

Nathan's heart was beating faster. His facial muscles were growing tensile. A hand swept along the hairs of his body as if gathering flowers or whooshing through high grass in fragrant spring, fingers entwined in pubic hairs that shivered and sprung autonomously. A bicep, hairless, smooth, taut and smelling of evergreen, musk, sex and wisteria coursed near enough to his face to make him want to bite it. Bite it??? What's going on here??? Porky!!! What are YOU doing in bed with me??!! Wait a second. You're a GUY!!!

All too late. By now Nathan's hand was sweeping shyly and curiously along Porky's blond downy thighs. Oh my God. I think I'm going to faint. Nathan's neck throbbing with fear and O the heavenly pleasure of that sweet tongue savoring him. Oh horrors. It feels so good, his hand climbing will-lessly towards Porky's smooth round tight-skinned buttocks, delicate hairs protruding from the crease, like reeds on the shore of a river of honey, and the skin on the soft full cheeks turning to ripples of goosebumps when Nathan touched them so that Porky sighed and cohered more intently to Nathan's body so that without warning, Nathan's penis unfurled and throbbed. What's going on!? This is homosexuality!! I'm not queer!!! But his heart was racing, and he found himself bearing down on Porky, and then he breathed deeply. O so deeply. As if he were breathing for the first time. So nice, and Porky's finger-tips were exploring his nipples, and his skin began to sweat, as if each pore had exploded, and Nathan ran his own fingers into the hairy seam between front and rear, and it was as if the room filled with the perfume of excrement, sweat and excite-ment, and Nathan tried to reach for Porky's hard, persistent appendage, first from behind, where he lunged for the root of the swollen stem. He was overwhelmed by the need to touch it, to touch the whole thing he perceived pushing against his but-tocks, making an effort to force his fingers through the cleft between their bodies, but Porky would not yield and cleaved more tightly to Nathan.

Now Porky's hand swept down to Nathan's belly, leaving trails of gentle eruptions of nerve ends in the wake of his finger-nails. He gripped Nathan's twitching thing which had swollen to capacity, a balloon threatening to burst at the slightest in-crease in pressure. His body shuddered and throbbed in com-munion with Porky's finger movements, so that he thought he had reached the epitome and would explode momentarily, ex-plode momentarily, his heart missing a beat, no loss; and he believed he had died for a second so sweet. Had he climaxed? What did it matter? Then he sensed it was about to happen again and again and again. No part of him was not liquidiz-ing now.

Porky was licking sweat from his shoulders and neck and ear. Nathan's mouth was a cavern, his body, a hollow that wanted to be filled and emptied. O the ear. He was all ear now. And then Porky reached for his rough unshaven cheek, cheek to cheek, and Nathan sprung around and kissed him on the mouth, slurping the taste of his own skin from Porky's ohgod-howsweet tongue, and Nathan twisted round till he lay mouth to mouth, chest to chest, member to member with Porky.

The thought of Porky's gender crossed his mind again, but too late for reflection. Now he was focused on touching that hard thing that had been poking him from behind. An image flashed through his mind. A room, Victorian in style, furnished in burnt crimson. A child he was, cushioned in the plush of an armchair. A dark-haired woman with countrygirl eyes, full damp lips, a lacey chambermaid's uniform, was kissing his bare feet. "Bite, bite!" he said. He heard far off music, trumpets and violins, mixing mournfully. A singer crooning:

> I wonder who's kissing her now.
> I wonder who's showing her how.

Nathan's hand was gliding down Porky's smooth chest, stopping momentarily to twist his fingers in the few stringy hairs sprouting around his nipples and brushing over the soft, blond down at his belly. The gently sweeping curve of his male thing bumped against his wrist, warm, more than warm, and he accelerated his journey through the damp garden of plush that encircled the stalk. And then Nathan touched it. It was the first time he had ever touched one that wasn't his own. It curved differently than his, was thinner and longer, though at the root, perhaps a little chunkier. He glided his fingers up and down its length. It was hard yet soft and warm like a nest is warm. How to describe it? A hot oily bead dotted the tip, and he rubbed it into slick skin that seemed to have eyes. The thing was taut like a bow about to shoot, snapping tightly against Porky's belly when he released it. This he repeated a number of times, not sure whether to continue exploring or to kiss him. It was all so new. Like Disneyland maybe, (at least the first time). You've got a fist full of tickets, a heart full of eagerness and anticipation and a linear path of possibilities. What rides to go on? What will you wind up missing? What will you forget to do? Will there be a second time? Must it be now?

Now Porky raises Nathan's legs in a spread-eagle. He hovers above him for an instant. He is faceless with sex, Porky's penis twitching above him. Nathan feels very ridiculous in this position, though his own penis does not share Nathan's preconceptions and is standing in the thick of eagerness. Porky pushes Nathan's legs back as far as they will go, revealing the pink curled worm of Nathan's anus. He lowers his head to that goal and begins to feast noisily at the tight sphincter muscle. It tickles, and Nathan can't help but giggle, partially out of embarrassment, partially because it does tickle. And then, it begins to feel good, and Nathan finds himself reaching towards Porky's swollen center with a longing hand.

Porky has inserted a finger into Nathan's orifice. O my God. It feels good! Nathan recalls bending over for a medical exam. "Tell me if you feel anything," the Doctor asked, "that is, ahem, in addition to the expected discomfort." By now Porky has two fingers in there, distending the opening. A feeling like stretching in the morning when your muscles awaken and welcome the new blood, and willingly Nathan pulls Porky towards him. Porky introduces that swollen warmth, gently first, ow it feels so filling, then deeper, my God, I'm being buggered! and deeper and deeper until Nathan is full of Porky thrusting till they are as close as humanly possible. Oh, Nathan thinks he will faint. God, it's happening to him. It's as if his body has been perforated and any part of him suitable for penetration. Porky is heaving to and fro. He is breathing ever more heavily. He is arched like a sphinx or an eagle. Nathan thinks he's about to cry. His own organ rocking with the premonition of explosion. Oh God, how long is this lasting?

What time is it? Where are we? Who belongs to what? What belongs to whom? Are they crying? Both of them? Whimpering sounds sputter from their mouths. It's as if Porky's rigid tangent has fingers. Whatever he's doing in there, I just hope he keeps it up. And his downy smooth belly manages to meet Nathan's own protrusion halfway, and the pressure is simply wild. How fast they are moving is hard to say, only only, that they are riding, like on a motorcycle that is simultaneously the motorcyclist. Who begins and ends where is no longer a question. It is a theoretical concern. Only the thumping sloshy pumping now. The music is everywhere, and God, its rising to a crescendo. Like running up staircases in a dream, in an attempt to reach the top, only to find more stairs to climb, and here and there a window exploding in light. Oh my God. I'm so high. And then the staircase vanishes, and you are back on the earth. But what an earth. Not the one you know. Maybe one you've read about in a fairy tale. An earth full of unknown pleasures and pressures and music and the strange feeling of rising without rising until until . . . where are you going? What is happening? I'm oh oh oh Oh Oh OOOOOOh . . . a long silence during which manifest existence disappears no other way to describe it unless you've been there yourself. Oh blankness. O death. O love. Ohh. Ohh. Look at him? Where did he go? Where is he? Oh I'm falling. This is the end. The music of insanity, the bow going berserk against the strings. Do you hear it? Mother. Oh, hello Aunt Fanny, what are you doing here? Fainting. Oh I may cry. Oh I am crying. Ohh collapsing drenched in fluid in each other's arms. Hearts thudding, tears flooding, every cell empty and exhausted. Dreamless sleep absence of memory . . . did I say dreamless? Because then Porky says, "Is that friendly enough, Nathan?" and then they drifted off to sleep.

❀ ❀ ❀

The next day, Nathan was cleaning his car. A sudden need for self-discipline. He was feeling like a bride the morning after and singing dreamily. From time to time, he would press his thighs together to experience the pleasurable soreness. Each time he did so, he would think, yes, it really did happen, and then he'd smile. He was stretched across the front seat of his car fantasizing about setting up house with Porky, life together, chil . . . wait a minute, let's not take this too far. But what could he do? He was head over heels in love, or at least infatuated. I'm not even queer, he'd remind himself. Still, he'd catch himself anticipating the coming night, eagerly imagining the new terrain he might explore. It was the newness, the encounter with the unknown that excited him most. How often do you get to experience things that are truly new? Then came the fear. Hey, am I carrying this too far? Am I making a fool of myself? A failure, a bore, irresponsible. And now this. Another nail in the coffin of my self-esteem. He constricted his thighs again, seeking soothing solace in memory. Just one more night like that one. That's all I ask.

In the midst of this reverie, the glove compartment snapped open with a WHACK right above his head, missing his nose by a fraction of an inch and snapping him out of his daydream. Hey, how did that happen!? Then he remembered the envelope the six-fingered biker had given him. He had promised to deliver it. Why can't I keep promises?! God, what if Porky finds out? Melanie drifted dimly through his mind invisible. Good grief, irresponsible again.

TWELVE

"**W**HY DON'T you ever draw me?" Virginia looked up briefly from her book, reached over and scooped up some potato chips from a bowl on the table next to the armchair she was nestled in, her legs folded fawnlike beneath her.

Winston grunted from the sofa, his attention fixed on the house of cards he was building on the coffee table. The four A-frames of the foundation were already securely roofed over, as were the three on the next level and one on the third level next to which he was now gently positioning a second one, his fingers light and tense, his tongue peeking out from between his teeth.

"If you asked, I would pose for you." Virginia's look was probing, her lips were pursed as if more words were to follow.

"There!" triumph in Winston's voice. "One row to go. I've never made it this far. This is exciting." He turned towards her. "Why don't you turn on a light, honey. You're gonna kill your eyes."

"We never go anywhere. We don't even see our friends anymore."

"Oh come on, not now. I'm trying to concentrate. Anyway, after you reach a certain age, you start getting more domestic. That's just life." He was lowering the pinnacle of his card house into place. "Don't move, don't move," he was mumbling. Flop! "Damn!" The top two rows collapsed.

"Mr. Morris at the antique store said he saw a man follow-ing me. He was bald, had beady eyes and wore glasses. Do you think he might have been interested in me, or that maybe he was a *Maenad*?" She was clearly trying to bait him, but only she knew that.

Winston had repaired his house of cards and had reached the top again, once more lowering the last two cards ever so gently. "Let's not talk about them now, okay? Hooray! There! See! I did it! I did it!" He glanced over at Virginia. "What are you crying about?"

Her head was tucked into her chin, the sluice behind her eyes had opened, nose running, cheeks red like a mourning Buddha. "I have a headache."

Silence.

"You want me to get you an aspirin?"

Silence.

"You want an aspirin?"

She shook her head no.

"Oh God, what's the matter now? Isn't it enough that I'm going bananas? I don't see why you have to too."

Wheezing and squealing sounds.

"What did I say now?" Exasperation in his voice.

She shook her head again.

Winston stood up.

"Where are you going?"

"To get you some aspirin."

"I don't want any aspirin."

"How about a valium?"

"No!"

"Well, at least I'll get you some water. The way you're go-ing, you're going to be running on empty." He returned to the living room, glass in hand, stopped and stared. "Crap."

"What's the matter?" Concern in her voice.

"Don't you see what I just made?"

"Where?"

"On the coffee table. My house of cards. It's a Deltagon!"

❀   ❀   ❀

To sleep perchance to dream, Larez Pentius mused, but the wish was serious. The last gulp of hot milk always made him gag. He hated the taste but forced it down his throat anyway. A warm white film and a ghostly rim of foam was all that remained. "Ugh." He clanked the glass into the sink and trundled off to his bedroom.

He was propped on his pillow in the auburn glow of the bed lamp. Should he write in his diary tonight? Afterall, it had been a portentous day. This time, he was certain they would take the bait, and then bang! He would cripple their insidious plans! He still did not know how. Especially alone (unless Winston came on board, though he still wasn't sure he could rely on that). He reached for his diary and began turning thoughts into words:

"Logic and clarity have always been anathema to things chaotic; a correct answer and righteous action skewered the Sphinx and banished Typhon to the bowels of the earth. When the time is right, I too shall find the fitting instrument and disable these nefarious enemies. My most potent weapon shall always be the power of reason, the only tool capable of defeating them. In this holy war against disinformation and misappropriation, the voice of truth shall be victorious. Is that not the lesson hinted at by the ancient myths, a struggle as old as the birth of reason? When the dust settles, the forces of order and harmony shall always be victorious."

He intended to write more—imagining himself a mythological hero—but the promise of sleep grew increasingly persuasive, and he clung to it. Placing his diary on his night-table, he switched off the lamp. For a moment, he heard the crunching of grass underfoot. Foraging racoons, he figured. Then silence, restless silence. Why do old men forget how to sleep? O the bane of insomnia! No, don't call it that, no sense turning a situation into a condition merely by giving it a name. Names are the root of all conditions. That is what empowers *Chaos*. But what about those forces without a name? Are they any better? Interesting question . . . to be shelved for another time. Speaking of invisible forces. At that very moment one was taking control of the Doctor's hands, steering them under the covers till they came in contact with an old friend for a secret rendezvous. A few loveless strokes and a passionless sigh. Hot milk and THAT release of tension. Currently his most potent recipe when sleeplessness befell him.

The sound of grass was still crunching underfoot, but the Doctor was barely aware of it. In the dangerous world of nature movement is frequently cautious and tentative. Somewhere out there, a car whooshed by, faraway a foghorn hooted, but by this point, Larez Pentius had surrendered to the seduction of his mattress and was drifting off. But hark! That rustling would not desist, and somehow it was an unaccustomed rustling, like reeds lashed by a sharp breeze, a faint tingle co-mingling with it, sounds that were increasing in volume till finally he forced his sleep-drunk eyes open. Warily, he surveyed the parameters of his room. Whatever it was seemed to be approaching. Then he heard a clearly audible clanking. Fright billowed through his limbs. Unusual for him. Afterall, he was in the business of combating fear. Was it THEM? Wait. Deep breath. Never surrender to fear that great trickster. But somehow he knew that he was not alone in his room. What's worse: a stench filled the air, an odor like swamp gas or flatulence, so strong it was suffocating. Are they trying to POISON me—or frighten me, attempting to penetrate through the gateway of my imagination?

The Doctor was still hesitating to look in the direction of those auditory signals. Very unusual for him, because he prided himself on his intrepidness and sensibility, the only reliable weapons in the fierce battle against irrationality, as he frequently claimed. Instead, instinctively he pulled the covers over his head. All in vain, because then came a familiar voice.

"Larez, do you not recognize me?"

I know that voice, he was thinking and slowly lowered the blanket. He opened his eyes as courageously as possible and surveyed the darkness until the world came into focus. "Leland!" Yes, it was his old friend, spectral but easily recognizable, right down to the white lab coat. But wait. Somehow his deceased comrade resembled a Christmas tree draped haphazardly with clanging objects. And then the Doctor saw that Leland Hewlett was entangled in a mess of POP-ITs.

Larez Pentius sat up, a little embarrassed at the thought that his old friend might have passed through the walls in time to observe his bed-time ritual. "Leland," he uttered, "Why are you here?"

"Mark me," Leland Hewlett said.

"I will." Larez Pentius nodded obediently, unsettled and fascinated.

"My hour is almost come when I must render myself up to sulphurous and tormenting flames."

"Come on, Leland, what manner of talking is that?"

"How shall I put it, Larez, so that you will understand?" He gestured and numerous POP-ITs began rattling. "Dear friend, it is different than you think."

"I know," He didn't know why he said that. Politeness?

The specter's expression was serious. "That's the problem, Larez, you don't know. And I am not able to explain it in a way that will make it clear. The effort I have made to appear to you has been substantial, and now that I am here, it occurs to me that we speak different languages, and that the one I am using will make no sense to you."

"What is it like where you are?"

"I have not come to make conversation."

"Tell me anyway. You know I have always been terribly curious."

"How shall I put it. It is a little like the Montecito Country Club, the buildings, the lockers, the pool, the ocean, the people. Yes, it is similar. But also different. The air is sweet and even pleasant, but the spider is never far removed. No, I see. You will not understand, Larez. Now it is clear. They told me it would be that way. But I had to try. In that respect, I am a lot like you. Yes, of course we are similar."

"They?"

"Yes, *they*. But I cannot tell you who they are without harrowing your soul and freezing your blood. Each hair would stand on end like the quills of a porcupine."

"Leland, were you murdered?"

The ghost gazed at Larez Pentius but did not respond.

"Were you murdered?"

"Yes." He raised his arms, and POP-ITs began rattling menacingly, "But it is not what you think. None of it. And I am unable to explain myself. Larez, have you ever known me to act this way?"

"No, you were always very sure of yourself."

"Yes, that is the proper answer. Perhaps you will be able to find the words that elude me, because I ... I ... cannot remember why I've come to see you."

"I don't understand."

"And I cannot be any more explicit."

"Why have you come here?"

"To understand that I shall never return again."

"Do you have a message for me?"

The ghost was endlessly still, then said, "No." The voice trailed off, and there was a hint of resignation.

"Do you have a message for Winston?"

"Yes. Nothing."

Ghost and host were eyeing each other emptily.

"You know, old friend," Larez Pentius, broke the silence, "there's a lot I want to tell you and have long wanted to. It's lonely here without a friend. But now I see. I can't find the words either. Something about this interface, Leland, something about this interface."

"Larez," the ghost responded, "You have described the dilemma in a nutshell. Maybe you can tell me later." And then he was gone.

"Leland!" Larez Pentius called out, but except for a residual trace of swamp gas or flatulence, Leland Hewlett was nowhere to be seen. How long had they been talking? Their discussion seemed so brief, and yet it had been incredibly strenuous. Now the Doctor was really feeling tired, more tired than he had in months or maybe years, so tired . . . and it occurred to him in his last dim sparks of consciousness that he had forgotten to ask his friend why he smelled so awful.

Thirteen

ANTHONY BECKER did not notice the evanescent apparition as it whooshed by, nor did he hear the rattling of POP-ITs. Only the faint, noxious whiff of swamp gas or flatulence reached his senses, prompting him to raise his legs one at a time in the moonlight to check whether he had inadvertently stepped into animal excretion in the high grass around Larez Pentius's house. Moreover, he was irritated, convinced that what he was doing here was an insult to his dignity—just as shadowing the Hewlett woman was, and he was grumbling. Grass rustled and crunched underfoot as he made his way back to the sidewalk. Fortunately, this undignified vigil at Larez Pentius's window was finally over! Just in case, *they* had said. Just in case of what?! But *they* had offered no further instructions. Anyway, he had observed nothing out of the ordinary, and that was that. The air was cool, downright chilly in fact for a spring night in Santa Barbara. A mist had swallowed the streets, enveloping even the high ground, the moon playing peek-a-boo where the fog grew threadbare. In the distance, he heard foghorns, traffic, flushing toilets, coughing, sneezing, snoring, discussions and monologues from behind open windows, sounds that broke the nocturnal silence around him. He was feeling lonely. Sundry lights had gone on and off in Larez Pentius's house during his vigil. A code for fellow conspirators? He had tried to identify a pattern. Impossible. From time to time a silhouette of the man darted by behind the curtains.

Becker was dressed in a jogging outfit. It was meant to be a disguise, and now he wished it had had pockets or that he might have taken a short jog around the house to warm himself. He made his way off the trespassed property as unobtrusively as possible, all the while muttering.

Indeed, he had more important things on his mind than spying on Larez Pentius. *Agent* Becker, better said, *Doctor* Becker was still troubled by the episode with Winston. He had yet to find a reasonable explanation for Winston's failure to respond to the preliminary tests he had conducted on him and continued to ponder where the fault lay: in the subject or the system. Can a patient exist outside the system? Wilhelm Reich, he recalled, had once hypothesized the existence of DOR, *deadly orgone*, the antithesis of OR, an element I chose to ignore in my research because it sounded too much like some reflection of Reich's *personal* problems. Was I wrong? Is Hewlett a DOR carrier, whatever that might mean? Had eroto-stimulastics met its cruel antipode in the person of Winston Hewlett? If so, the Doctor's system would require an essential re-evaluation. Of course he regretted all that silly talk about shock therapy. It wasn't fair to scare Hewlett that way. Besides, the treatment was *not* cruel, at least *he* didn't think so. Maybe it was shortsighted to reject Winston Hewlett as a patient. Nothing but a knee-jerk reaction attributable to his injured pride. Hubris! Had he feared failure? Or was it an antipathy caused by a clash of characters? Did he feel . . . *threatened* by Winston Hewlett? Yes. Yes. All that and more. But what was the *more*? The Doctor still had no explanation. And now this figure named Winston Hewlett was clinging to him like an incubus. The problem was serious, and he was convinced that he needed that man's help if he were to progress in his research. There was something about Winston Hewlett he needed to know. He had to speak to him again. Yes, exactly. That's what he would do, contact him, apologize for his rudeness and, in the name of truth, suggest they meet again.

Anthony Becker was so enwrapped in this reverie as he ambled along the street, the distance between himself and Larez Pentius's garden increasing with each step, that he failed to notice the three sheriff's cars converging on him. Suddenly he was blinded by blazing lights. Shock, paralysis. "Hands up!" a voice snapped, and then he heard a clicking sound like guns cocking. He raised his arms. His jaw tensed and his eyes were squinting behind his dark framed glasses. Three sheriffs, two with shotguns and one brandishing a pistol stepped into visibility. From his vantage, they were three silhouettes. "I.D.," one barked.

"Is there anything the matter, officer?" he was using a tone all honest citizens switched on when intimidated by the police. Then it occurred to him that he had no I.D. with him. Of course not! His jogging suit had no pockets! "Oh my God!" he exclaimed, "I don't have any I.D. with me. You see, I only live about ten blocks from here and was out jogging . . ." He was feigning a smile.

"Yeah, yeah. You can tell us all about it down in the cooler, pal," a sheriff with a fat, red, acne-scarred boyish face, sneered, directing a ferocious rifle at him. "Seems like you've been doing your jogging in other people's backyards, buddy. We've been on to you for a half hour."

That was a surprise, and Doctor Becker had no fit response. "But what's the charge?" he asked, hunting for his most innocent voice.

"Suspicion of rape."

"Rape! But . . . but I'm a doctor!"

"That's just grand, Doc. Then you'll be smart enough to tell us everything. 'Cause someone in a monkey suit like yours just did something real dirty about five blocks from here not more'n an hour ago."

"But . . ."

"You just get your butt into the black and white and pronto."

After *Agent* Becker had been handcuffed and shoved into the back seat of the sheriff's car, he pressed his cheek against the window and did what any normal person might in this situation: he began feeling sorry for himself. The police radio was blurting tinny, staccato messages, and the car smelled like mouthwash. At that moment, *Agent* Porky walked by, looked briefly at the Doctor and nodded. *Agent* Becker nodded back more or less mechanically, and then the police cars sped off downtown.

FOURTEEN

"GRRR."

"Woof woof."

And up her slender ankles went . . . again, kicking at air.

"Hey! I think something's happening!" Winston was weighing on her. It used to be that just the sight of those slender, tapered ankles fired his instincts.

Dutifully, Gladiola widened the access route, mimicking interest through tedious labored breathing, hoping that might suffice to undo the knot.

Some minutes of fumbling and patient waiting, sweat collecting on the small of his back: "Oh, forget it."

Two bodies without words, afloat in separate universes and by chance supine on the same daybed in a house on the Riviera in Santa Barbara, California, USA, Planet Earth. From time to time, Winston let out a sigh. And each time, Gladiola reacted with hushed irritation. Demonstrations of his exasperation awoke no sympathy in her anymore.

Winston flopped his hands across his forehead and was playing with his fingers. "I swear, we're going to get that Empire of Chaos for this! You just wait!" His voice was quaking with mock bravado.

Gladiola did not react.

More silence.

"Hey?" Winston asked, the air chilling. "Are you in a bad mood?" He turned towards her. Tears were sliding down her cheeks, her face red, her mouth poised on the brink of a scream. Groan, he thought, not another bawling woman! "Aw, c'mon Gladiola, not you too. I've got enough problems."

And then the dam broke, not a dam of tears. Gladiola sprung up. "You've got problems?!" He had never heard her raise her voice before. "Winston Hewlett, your problems have hardly begun!" She picked up his clothes and then his sketch-book and began flinging them, piece by piece, at the lanky man on her daybed. "I'm finished playing your open-faced sand-wich, dammit! Get out of here! Out!! I never want to see you again!" Each imperative was accented by a hurled object. He ducked when she launched his shoes and sketchbook at him.

"What did I do? What did I do wrong?" The protest was weak and whiny and futile. Gladiola had locked herself in her bedroom, and it was obvious that she would not come out until he was no longer there.

When she was sure of that, she opened the door, cautiously at first, and returned to her front room. She collapsed in front of the wicker basket in which her mother, that desperate person unknown, had set her off into the rough sea of life so many years ago. Her sobs surfaced from great depths, narrating a tale of sadness not only about herself but about that helpless person who had launched her into this world in a basket like some mythic hero dispatched on an adventure. She hugged that wicker womb, wool, half-finished projects, knitting needles and all and rocked back and forth, her clothes still scattered on the floor, the contours of the basket leaving imprints on her skin. "Mama!" she wailed, "Mama."

❀ ❀ ❀

Later that day, she was sitting on a shady bench in Alameda Park, sketchbook in hand. She often came there when she needed to collect herself, like today. Her audition for the Santa Barbara Symphony Orchestra was fast approaching, and it was essential that she regain her equilibrium. She was making quick sketches of passersby as she usually did. That calmed her, took her mind off her problems. Then she caught sight of Porky.

This time he approached and sat down next to her. He did not speak. Nor did she. The silence was ringing in her ears like noon bells, but she had neither the strength nor courage to confront him despite the magnetic pull. No, there was no escape. Goodbye life, she thought.

Then Porky turned to her, pointing to a sketched face lodged in the corner of a page. "Look, Gladiola," he said calmly and cheerfully, "Do you know who that is?"

She shook her head.

"That's *Agent* Becker. He also lives in town."

Just what I needed to hear, a silent moan. *Agent* Becker's face was now staring mutely at her from her own sketchpad.

Porky smiled kindly, and she couldn't help smiling back. Why do people often smile in the face of danger? she was thinking. Just instinct?

FIFTEEN

T HE DOORBELL chimed.
"Just ignore it," Virginia said to Winston, "we're not expecting visitors." They were hunched over a game of checkers on the living room floor. It was Winston's move.

"Oh no you don't. You want me to move that one. Am I right?" He pointed demonstratively. "I wasn't born yesterday, sister. I know what you're up to. If I move there, you're going to jump me and get another king."

The doorbell chimed again.

"Ignore it," said Virginia.

A cozy evening at the Hewletts'. Winston had been home a lot these days, and his mood had been improving. Virginia liked that. Had he given up sketching? She hadn't brought up that topic. Nor had he. At any rate, she began hoping things were changing for the better. "Rejoice in hope, be patient in tribulation." That's what her parents used to say. She wished she could.

The board was pitched to a slant on the uneven surface of the shag carpet, Winston prostrate on the thick pile, his legs crooked upwards at the knees, elbows propped under his chin; Virginia was hunched squawlike, legs crossed under her muumuu which covered her like a teepee.

The doorbell chimed again.

"For crissakes, who is it?" Now Winston was irritated.

"Ignore it." A hint of alarm in Virginia's voice.

"Why don't you get it and tell em to go away, while I think about my move."

Virginia rose, ambling barefoot through the field of carpets that led to the door. She peered through the peephole and muffled a gasp. Immediately, she began securing a barrage of locks and chains.

Winston heard the clacking and rattling and snapped to his feet. Randomly, he grabbed for something he could use as a weapon—as it turned out, a Meissen rooster Virginia had once bought at Mr. Morris's. Then he bound towards the door. "Whassa matter!?"

"There's a maniac out there!" She was whispering urgently. "Call the police! Someone dressed like a spaceman or something!"

Again the doorbell. The Hewletts froze. Winston raised the porcelain rooster ready to strike.

"Winston!" The voice was muffled. "For the love of Pete would you *please* open the door!"

"Aha! Honey, it's just Doctor Pentius," and he lowered his arm.

"Call the police!" said Virginia.

But no, Winston turned the locks, flipped the chains and opened the door. Larez Pentius was wearing a baggy orange jumpsuit (today we would say "hazmat suit"). A gasmask dangling from his neck. He looked like a picture book alien.

"My boy, why are you holding a ceramic chicken? Hello, Virginia, nice seeing you again. Long time no see."

"It's Meissen porcelain and it's a rooster," Virginia curtly, her face somber.

"You're looking a little pale," said the Doctor. "I hope you're feeling well."

"Come in, come in," Winston cheerful and happy to change the subject. "And maybe you can tell me why you are dressed like that?"

"Have you forgotten? Tonight's the night. You said the room was very dusty, didn't you?" The Doctor raised a hand. "Wait, I'll be back in two shakes of a lamb's tail." Larez Pentius trotted back down the walkway to the sidewalk.

"I don't want him in this house!" Virginia stagewhispered.

"But honey, he's here to help."

Uh oh. He has that empty look in his eyes again. "To help?"

"Yes, I forgot. We were going to clean up the workshop and search for clues tonight."

"You're going to do what!?" Her mouth opened, but no words followed. Instead, her eyes turned to water. She made an about-face and stomped off. Winston heard the clatter of spilled checker pieces and then the slamming of a door.

Now the Doctor reappeared, a large satchel in one hand and a broom with an elongated broomstick in the other. "Something wrong, my boy? Where's Virginia?"

Winston did not answer.

"Well, she's always been a little over-sensitive, if you ask me. Not surprising when you consider her upbringing. Here, fellow warrior, I brought an extra broom, in case you don't have a spare. This time, we're going to make a clean sweep of it!" A broad sweeping motion and a toothy smile followed. "Hey, why so glum?"

Winston shrugged.

"If Virginia is on your mind, believe me, everything will be fine. I'm a shrink, I know about these things. Pouting, to paraphrase Churchill, is something up with which I shall not put!" He raised an index finger, the tone was cheerful, but Winston was not. "Here." The Doctor handed Winston the satchel . . .

❀ ❀ ❀

We leave the Doctor's patter now—he always came to life in company, and this evening he was especially garrulous, no doubt the anticipation. Winston was soon donning an orange jumpsuit very much like the Doctor's as well as a gasmask— meant as a prophylaxis against the dust. When all was ready, the Doctor grinned and then proclaimed, playfully ceremonious but definitely serious: "Let's get this show on the road!" To which Winston responded: "That's what Lily used to say."

Meanwhile, in another corner of the house, Virginia had changed into her nightgown and was propped up against a citadel of pillows in bed, reading glasses balanced at the end of her nose, feet tucked under the covers, a bowl of potato chips on her night table, and submerged in a trashie. The thumpity noises, the faint voices, sounds just a few walls away, hardly fazed her. She was a fortress festooned in a fortress and thankful for the gift of trivial literature. It had always been her solace. Besides, who could she confide in in a situation like this? There are some things that cannot be told. Not even to friends—if one has any. But why not? The question surprised her.

❀ ❀ ❀

The key turned effortlessly; the heavy steel door creaked plaintively. "Needs oil," the Doctor said as he reached for the light switch with familiarity. The neon lights flickered, as if stirring from a long sleep or awakening from an evil spell cast long long ago. Cold white light spread over the room revealing two long stainless-steel counters at the center of the oblong space. Orderly stacks of papers were piled on top like ruins of a lost city. "Pragmatic," "efficient." Those are words that come to mind. Nothing had changed. Everything was still in its place. Larez Pentius had almost forgotten those solid, steel shelves that lined the walls below the tinted windows; the swivel chairs, and the pair of high, metal stools, that once bore their weight. Yes, there we used to sit, work, talk . . . A ceramic mug was visible on one counter and a coke bottle. Leland's last drink, a cola he had poured on the day of his murder, the content long evaporated, the molecules still hovering somewhere in the dust or part of that dust, chemicals crusted on the walls of the mug and the bottle, both coated in dust as was everything else: floor, walls, furnishings, even the light fixtures so that the cold light was muffled in grey snow. All this enhanced the tomblike atmosphere. A grey mist hung in the air. It was a place of no shadows.

One might ask where all that dust came from, when you consider that this room had always been hermetically sealed behind the steel door leading to the kitchen. One source: the air currents, as silent as a whisper, as light as a cloud and invisible like the wind that most certainly wafted fragments of cooking, pollution, dander—young Winston once had a parakeet— and assorted other kitchen micro-detritus swept into that sanctuary whenever the door between the two worlds was opened or closed. And then there were most certainly the dead cells we the living shed continually. In this case, of course, we are especially referring to the dead cells, dandruff etc. that had once been a part of Leland Hewlett's own body. Yes, he was most definitely the main source of the dust that covered his sanctuary, he as well as Larez Pentius and of course to a lesser extent Winston himself and probably even Lily . . . and ultimately, Winston's beloved mother too.

The Doctor's living cells swelled with succulent nostalgia as he entered this holy shrine of his own past. His orange jumpsuit was one size too large, Winston's one size too small. They fastened their state-of-the-art gasmasks in place and proceeded.

"You can see my footprints from last week," Winston uttered hollowly through the mask while thinking: had it only been one week since all this began?

"Let's get this show on the road!", the Doctor's muffled voice. "Time to clean up!"

※ ※ ※

Clouds of grey were soon billowing, visibility approaching zero. It was a malevolent fog, and the more it was stirred, the more defiant it grew.

"Ow!"

"What?"

"You just hit me with your broom!"

"Sorry, I couldn't see."

"Never mind."

No need to describe the process in detail. Through patience in tribulation the dust was growing increasingly compliant, sinking to the floor as if in defeat where it was then compounded into neat piles, swept up and sealed in large paper sacks. Progress could be measured in the visibility of things, the orderly contours, the sheen of the polished steel, and soon that space began resembling that pristine venue of days gone by.

Finally, the Doctor removed his gasmask. "It's just like . . . it used to be." Then he sneezed.

"Gesundheit."

"Thank you. A few damp rags and the place will sparkle like new."

And it did. Larez Pentius was meandering up and down the aisles, his gaze reverent, tender, his fingers lovingly touching familiar objects visible on the stainless-steel shelves: analyzers, synthesizers, catalyzers, oscillators, voltammeters, pencil cases, drafting kits. Here and there, he'd tug on a counter drawer, and it would respond smoothly though neglected for decades; he was casting an interested eye on old batteries (some in dry pools of acid), wires, lightbulbs, photos. Photos. "Here's one of your father and mother, she was so pretty, and you as a baby in her arms!" And then he stumbled on some spiral notebooks. "Obviously they overlooked these! That proves they must have been in a hurry." He picked up one and then another, leafing through them randomly. "Ha! Look! Finally, you get to meet your father, the *real* Leland Hewlett. No wonder they wanted him dead. Just imagine! Any one of these ideas might have revolutionized life on this planet. If he had had enough time, he might have discovered the secret of immortality!"

"My father?"

The truth be told, there were wonderous things in those spiral notebooks. For example, his "homeostatic equalizer," the formula for a tonic for maintaining and strengthening the immune system. "Potentially indefinitely!" said the Doctor. In its unfinished state, as confirmed in Leland Hewland's notebook, it consisted of a mixture of cranberry juice and echinacea angustifolia. This combination was, according to the inventor, capable of producing such a homeostatic effect. Leland Hewlett did note, however, that there were still ingredients missing. "Simple and yet so elegant!" said the Doctor. "If he had lived, it might have become as popular as his POP-IT!" Or then there was a sketch of a diving mask that produced oxygen by electrolyzing ambient water, potentially allowing a person to remain underwater indefinitely. Perhaps the key to colonizing the seas! "I was there when he had the idea for the POP-IT. We were sitting right at this counter. All of the sudden, he began writing feverishly. The prototype was complete the next day. Can you imagine life *without* the POP-IT? Of course not. Nobody can." Or Leland Hewlett's radiometric energizer, consisting of a paddlewheel whose blades are black on one side and white on the other. In a vacuum, and exposed to light, that paddle might revolve eternally: in other words, a functioning perpetual motion machine! "According to these sketches, your father must have envisioned a ring of radiometers orbiting our planet and radioing cheap solar energy back to earth."

Exciting prospects, but Winston was quickly losing interest in these inventions of his brilliant father. Occasionally he'd nod politely, but frankly, his mind was elsewhere. After all, he had his own problems. Idly, he ran his fingers lazily along the rim of the sleek steel counter and remembered doing the same as a boy. In fact, he was about to mention this reminiscence when he noticed an unevenness at one spot on the otherwise smooth surface. Hmm? An imperfection? In my father's workshop? He crouched down for a better look. Something seemed to be engraved in the metal. "Doctor Pentius, I've found something."

It was a Deltagon! the Doctor immediately fetched a compass from a drawer—its location recollected effortlessly—and began taking measurements. "By Jove you certainly did!"

"I don't understand," Winston said.

"Just as I suspected," said the Doctor. "This Deltagon is tilted to the vertical at an angle of twenty-three and a half degrees." He stared at Winston meaningfully: "The same angle as the earth's axis to the sun."

"What does that mean?"

"My boy, not only is that angle responsible for the paradox of the seasons, it is also the cause of all irregularity in the measurement of time and space on our planet. There's no more fitting symbol for earthly chaos than this!"

"But we have no seasons in Santa Barbara, except when we're teasing tourists."

Larez Pentius's expression grew serious. "My guess is that the Empire of Chaos has somehow tilted our very souls—at least symbolically—to this angle to forever keep us prisoners of their anarchy. I cannot think of a crueler manipulation nor a more pertinent clue. Thank you for discovering it! I knew I could depend on you. You're a chip off the old block after all!"

Now the Doctor wheeled a swivel chair to the rim of the counter as close to the engraved Deltagon as possible and sat down. At first his look was pensive, and then, he fell into what seemed to be a trance. That is the only way to describe it. His eyes remained fixed on the mysterious symbol etched into the metal. He grew totally immobile, somehow inert.

"But Doctor Pentius, how did it get there? This room has always been locked. Doctor Pentius? Doctor Pentius?!" But the Doctor was somewhere far away. We can't know where. For he too had become a fortress festooned in a fortress, impenetrable, unreachable . . . at least for now . . .

SIXTEEN

"ALL RIGHT, Tony, once more from the top."

My God, no one had called him Tony in years! And when *she* did, the blood would burn his cheeks and his limbs caught fire . . . Hush, sweet memory, this is not your hour. Still, this wasn't what he imagined a third-degree would be like. No glaring flood lamp tilted towards his face, no backlit figures in the shadows, no cigarette smoke snaking towards the ceiling. Just humdrum overhead lighting. He could make out the faces with facility, and they were all lacking in sympathy. The walls of the room were institutional yellow. In one corner someone was hunched at a desk writing. The others, sitting and standing, commented and questioned at random. From time to time the scribe—or whatever he was called in their jargon—raised his head to punctuate the laughter. The oldest in the group, officially the arresting officer, must have been about twenty-five. The one with the red face and bad skin couldn't have been more than eighteen, though probably he was older. There were others there he didn't recognize. All were wearing tan uniforms and toting bulbous pistols in prominently displayed holsters. A couple sported shoulder holsters in addition. One of them, a corpulent guy, was straddled across a chair, elbows propped over the back. He was asking the questions at the moment. When he opened his mouth, Doctor Becker mainly focused on the gap between two bottom teeth.

"I've already explained," he was gesturing with exasperation, " I did not rape anybody. I have never raped anyone . . . ever."

"Don't you worry, we've got time, plenty of time. When you're ready to confess, just let us know." The plump cop with the missing tooth removed his hat, scratched his crew-cut head and began fingering the badge above the visor.

The door opened. Another teenaged law enforcer entered, a tall boy with a large, hard chin, the kind usually associated with classic criminal features. His shoulders were broad, and he was clearly enjoying what he was doing. "The license plate checks out. This is the same customer that tailed the lady from the antique store."

"Lemme see that report," the fat one grunted.

"Hey, you're one busy feller, ain'tcha?" the one with the bad skin said and smirked. He was stroking the barrel of his pistol lovingly.

"Put that damned service revolver away, Snyder!" the cop at the desk snorted, "You damn near blasted my foot off last week. Go play with something else!"

The others laughed.

Doctor Becker was squeezing his cupped hands together and compressing his thin lips very tightly.

"Why were you following Mrs. Virginia Hewlett?"

"Why did you rape that woman tonight?"

"What were you doing on that property behind the Mission?"

"I've already explained. I did *not* rape *anybody!*"

"Then maybe you can explain to me why the victim claims she was raped by some clown wearing a monkey suit like yours and with a kisser to match."

"Coincidence."

"Look, Tony," the fat one said, "according to the records, you're an MD. That can only mean you went to school for a long time. So you must be smart. So why don't you just smarten up and tell us about it. It'll make it a lot easier on everyone."

"Hey Doc!" the one at the desk called out, "what's an *ee-rot-o-stim-yu-lastics institute*? Sounds kinda sexy."

"Ee-rot-o-stim-yu-lastics?"

"Yeah, that's what he calls what he does."

"Holy shit! We sure picked a doozy tonight."

"Hey, that's like *erotic*, right?" the boy with the bad skin asked.

"Jesus, how come we never canned this one before?"

"I got a mind to beat the crap outta the bastard." The boy with the bad skin suddenly rushed towards Anthony Becker and raised a hand over him. The Doctor flinched.

Another officer rushed over. "Hey, put your motor in park, Snyder."

"Yeah, but that guy's spreading filth and smut in our city, corrupting children. I don't want him to get away this time."

"Tell us why you raped that woman, Tony," the fat one with the missing tooth asked calmly.

"We know you were lurking there in the shadows. Why?" said the arresting officer.

"Why were you tailing this Mrs. Virginia Hewlett?"

Doctor Becker took a deep breath. "I did not rape anybody." Then he raised his eyes as if imploring heavenly aid. "I do not know a Mrs. Hewlett." Admittedly, if they had asked him to take a lie-detector test, he would have failed on that one. "And if you must know," now he fixed his gaze on his main interrogator while tightening every muscle in his body, "I was out there meditating. I'm a meditator." He wasn't sure where that came from, but the way he said it somehow sounded reasonable.

"That's one I've never heard before. A meditator!" The fat cop was rubbing his brow.

"Who knows? Maybe he is," the tall one with the criminal chin remarked. "My sister's husband does that stuff too."

"Shut up, moron!" the fat one snapped.

"Lemme slug him," the one with the bad skin barked, "that'll get him talking."

"Hold your horses, will ya!"

"I promise I won't leave no bruises, okay?"

"Or maybe we should just plug him and say he attacked us and tried to escape. There's enough scum like him out on the streets. No reason for taxpayers to have to spend good money to feed him."

"No, no, no!" The fat one rose from his chair, raising his arms like a referee and grinning so broadly that the gap between his teeth looked like the open gate to a place of secrets. "This jerk is going to get his day in court like everyone else. Remember, this is the United States of America not some communist country. Jenkins, get me a baggie."

"Comin' up." The large one lumbered off and returned with a cellophane bag, reaching out to the fat one who now handed it to his prisoner.

"Here, Tony, now you get a chance to prove your innocence."

Doctor Becker took the cellophane bag. He asked no questions.

"Okay, Tony, now you get to whip it out and milk it."

There was a long, long silence.

"I'm sorry," Doctor Becker said, he was looking skeptical, "but I don't quite understand what you're trying to say."

"C'mon, smart aleck, don't play dumb. Flip it out and do it into the baggie. Or am I not being clear enough?"

Another long, long silence.

"Do you mean, m-masturbate? Into this . . . re-ceptacle?"

"That's right. Fill 'er up with regular . . . or super if that's more your style. That's the only way to prove your innocence.

We're living in the twentieth century. We've got semen samples of the pervert who committed the crime. If yours don't match, you're a free man, and you'll get to sleep in your own bed tonight. Understand now?"

"But there are more professional ways of extracting seminal fluid!" the Doctor protested meekly.

"Look Tony, if this is causing you problems, we've got plenty of faggots in the tank, and they'll be just de-lighted," he made a limp wrist gesture while the others guffawed, "to help yank on your tool."

"I refuse."

"Okay Jenkins, lock him up."

"Wait! Wait!" the Doctor interjected.

Immediately, the sheriffs formed a semi-circle of chairs around him.

"Can't I do this . . . in private?"

"Sorry, that ain't in the cards, Tony. You're gonna need reliable witnesses."

Again, a long, long silence. All was still. As if they were posing in a photographic studio, waiting stiffly for the photographer to snap the shutter release. Finally, understanding that he had no recourse, Anthony Becker slipped his jogging suit and his jockey shorts down to his thighs in one crisp movement and grasped his penis. He was determined to see this through now, the only course left for a man who had lost all hope, and began stroking . . . courageously, closing his eyes while filing through his stock of eroto-stimulastic hologram images, hoping through the power of imagination to find refuge in a less hostile environment. The semicircle of spectators was laughing, then giggling and ultimately, eyes fixed, their mouths dropped in silence and awe at the splendor of this spectacle, like a swarm of cobras swaying hypnotically to the piper's song, and wonderstruck by the utter mass of the Doctor's tool. He was stroking forcefully and increasingly unperturbed, a single willful goal in mind. Shortly before he reached the point of liberation, it occurred to him that he had completely forgotten his right to call an attorney.

SEVENTEEN

(S TEWART, played by *Agent* Porky, is seated next to **MAR-GOT**, played by *Agent* Gladiola Freytag. Their straight back wooden chairs represent the front seat of a car. **STEWART** is in the driver's seat)

STEWART: (eyes fixed ahead, shyness in his voice) It sure is nice up here. You can see the whole city below. Look, isn't that the courthouse?

MARGOT: (coy, a silly smile on her face) Uh huh. I think so.

STEWART: (sighs)

MARGOT: Did you say something?

STEWART: (his eyes still focused straight ahead) Uh uh.

MARGOT: Oh.

STEWART: What?

MARGOT: I thought you said something.

STEWART: (frozen in place) Uh uh. (The silence is growing increasingly uncomfortable. Finally, he turns slowly towards her) Say, that's a nice jacket you're wearing! (He slips his arm over her shoulder as if feeling the material)

MARGOT: (edging ever so slightly towards him) You really think so? It's new.

(They are face to face and eye to eye. More unbearable silence)

STEWART: Hey, and it's reversable! Wow! That's neat!

MARGOT: Uh huh, I can wear it on both sides!

(Silence again. Now, Stewart embraces Margot and kisses her awkwardly)

MARGOT: Oh Stewart! (She giggles)

STEWART: (shyly) Margot. (She lays her head on his shoulder. Silence)

(Enter **SEX MANIAC**, played by Nathan Weiss. He is wearing a raincoat down to his knees. His legs are bare, and he has heavy, black combat boots on. Wrap-around sunglasses over his eyes)

SEX MANIAC: (prancing wildly, his back to the audience, flashing his raincoat open at intervals) Momf slobber sloobber slurp.

(Stewart and Margot are eyeing each other dreamily)

MARGOT: Oh Stewart (sighs).

STEWART: Oh Margot (sighs).

(The Sex Maniac peers into the car window. They do not notice him)

SEX MANIAC: (excitedly) Oooeeee. Slobber momf momf.

MARGOT: (suddenly attentive. She sits up) Did you hear something?

STEWART: Just the beating of our hearts, my love.

MARGOT: No really, I heard something out there.

STEWART: Oh, it's nothing. (He turns to kiss her again)

MARGOT: No! Stewart, look! Look out the window! (She points) There's a man out there! He wants to get me! Help!!

SEX MANIAC: Harrrr, wompoo, slurp, slurp. Ooooeeee Ooooeeee! (He is yanking eagerly at the door).

MARGOT: Oh, help me, Stewart! I'm afraid! Look! He's opening the door!

STEWART: Go way! Go away! Do you hear me? Leave us alone!

SEX MANIAC: Momf momf oooaah ooooaah! (He flings open the passenger seat door)

STEWART: Margot, he's opened the door!

MARGOT: He's opened the door! Help!!

SEX MANIAC: Mmmm. Slurp. Momf. (He reaches across Margot and grabs Stewart)

STEWART: Margot Margot!! He's got me! Help me! He's pulling me out of the car!

SEX MANIAC: (dragging Stewart across Margot and out of the car) Homf, homf slobber, slobber.

MARGOT: Oh Stewart, I don't know what to do!

STEWART: (being dragged away) Help! Help!! Call the police!! Call my mother!! Help!!!

SEX MANIAC: (disappearing into the off with Stewart) Slurp slabber monch monch!!

APPLAUSE

A full house at Baudelaire's, Santa Barbara's one and only cabaret. With the added tables and chairs, the aisles were barely navigable, and the waiters were straining through labyrinthic passageways in the darkened, smoke-filled room. In a far corner, a platform had been erected and served as a stage. Word had spread; Nathan Weiss's new group, STAGE FRIGHT, starring Nathan Weiss and *Agents* Gladiola Freytag and Porky, was currently the talk of the town.

Tonight, Mr. and Mrs. Winston Hewlett were in the audience applauding with the rest. They had even managed to pony up a ringside table. Although Winston and Virginia had been leading reclusive lives the past few years, the name Hewlett still commanded a certain respect in town thanks to the reputation of Winston's father, the inventor of the POP-IT.

Winston and Virginia were smiling a lot, not only because STAGE FRIGHT was so entertaining. The serene, glazed expressions on their faces were likewise due to the generous doses of valium that had made this evening possible.

Each harbored a slew of private reasons for wanting to forget . . . something. One problem, however, they did share in common: Larez Pentius. The Doctor had been their uninvited house-guest for a week now, and both, albeit for different reasons, were growing impatient having him under their roof. From the moment he had fallen into trance while studying the Deltagon Winston had discovered engraved on the rim of the stainless-steel counter in Leland Hewlett's workshop, the Doctor had not budged. Not a shiver. It was difficult to determine whether he were still breathing! You might say, he was a man on a sabbatical from biological realism, neither consuming nor excreting, neither taking nor giving.

Winston and Virginia were helpless in their exasperation. Finally, they decided they needed this evening out.

"Having fun, hon?" Winston turned to Virginia. Seeing Gladiola up there barely fazed him. Perhaps he hadn't recognized her in costume.

"Sure, babe." She smiled, unwilling and unable to stop smiling.

And then came the sound of a flute performing a catchy melody, something Gershwin-like.

"Hey, I think they're starting up again," Winston was grinning. "They sure are funny."

"Uh huh," Virginia nodding slowly.

A single spot, and Nathan Weiss, in a bear costume, stepped into a circle of light. He waited for the laughter to die down and then began singing *recitativo*:

> It was love from the first moment,
> from the moment we first met.
> We were meant to be together,
> you were surely heaven sent . . .
>
> It happened in the winter,
> my eyes were filled with tears.
> I thought the spring would never come,
> but fi-na-lly you're here . . .
> I've . . . found . . . you . . .

Another spot, this one illuminating another bear played by *Agent* Porky, a pink ribbon visible between its ears. A few snickers from the audience. *Agent* Gladiola is trilling on the flute as the melody glides into the refrain:

> My point of view,
> now you've become,
> my point of view.

(*Agent* Porky's bear eyes blink coyly, and he hops gleefully)

> I wonder how . . . I lived so long . . . without you.
> There's something so . . . considerate about you. (three beats)
>
> My point of view,
> O honey bun,
> sweet little you!

(*Agent* Porky's bear eyes flutter, and he hops)

> We're two peas in a pod
> two bugs in a rug,

(The rhythm is growing livelier and at each rhyme Nathan and *Agent* Porky bump behinds)

> pull on the one and the other will tug.
> Nothin'll stop us
> no mamas or papas.
> We got our direction
> and need no correction.
> It's you for me and me for you

(They clasp hands)

> be-cause you're . . . MY POINT OF VIEW!

APPLAUSE. The stage lights go bright. *Agent* Gladiola puts down her flute and joins Nathan and *Agent* Porky who have removed their bear heads. She stands between them. They are all holding hands. When the applause finally dies down, once again the singing begins:

(*Agent* Porky)

> When the caravans plod by us in the sand,

(*Agent* Gladiola)

> and the camel driver dreams of far-off lands,

(Nathan)

and the sheikh's unwieldly gaze
is particularly ablaze . . .

(together)

we snuggle up together hand . . . in . . . hand.

(*Agent* Porky)

When the stars begin to fade before the dawn,

(*Agent* Gladiola)

and the desert air grows rosy in the morn . . .

(Nathan)

then we open sleepy eyes . . .
to the light of sunny skies . . .

(together)

and we break into our . . . merry . . . morning . . . song . . .
CAUSE . . . we're . . . the . . .

(lively)

Assholes on the edge of the oasis,
waiting for the sun to dry our bums.
We're tired of just living in a stasis
We're sick of always twid-dle-ing our thumbs.

(*Agent* Gladiola)

So round and round we turn.

(*Agent* Porky)

So what if sunshine burns!

(together)

We're done with being worms!
We want a little sun!
We're the assholes on the edge of the oasis,
kicking at the sand and at the trees . . .

(ritardando)

and we'd like to let you know,
what it's like to stub your toe
on an o-a-s-i-s you see,
oh yeah,
on an o-a-s-i-s sirreeee!

They bow. The stage-lights go out. The lights go on and the audience breaks into rapturous applause.

Winston and Virginia, eyes glazed and serene, were also applauding.

"That was fun, huh?"

"Uh huh."

"Thank you, thank you, ladies and gentlemen," Nathan bellowed over the roar of the applause, he and his cast bowing deeply, again and again. "Thank you," booming over the din, "We're STAGE FRIGHT, here to serve all your laughter needs, your humble servants!" Another deep bow. "A hand for Gladiola Freytag," his arm sweeping in the direction of *Agent* Gladiola who curtsied coquettishly. More enthusiastic clapping. "Porky O'Keefe," *Agent* Porky bowed at the waist to the applause, "and . . ." Now his hands were fumbling as if searching for a pocket in his bear costume. Finally, he reached into a cuff, pulled out a piece of paper and took a quick glance at it, " . . . yours truly . . . Nathan Weiss!"

Applause and whistling some stomping, a few hurrahs.

All at once, Winston and Virginia both went pale. Something had pierced their chemical armor, each reacting to the same two words, echoing painfully in some shadowy inner space: Gladiola Freytag.

At this moment, Gladiola spotted Winston and the woman seated beside him. "My God," she whispered to *Agent* Porky, "There's Winston Hewlett, and that must be his wife Virginia!"

Nathan managed to pick up the words "Winston Hewlett" which *Agent* Gladiola had just spoken and reacted visibly mortified: That letter! Dammit! I forgot to deliver that damned letter!

EIGHTEEN

WINSTON WAS A FACE without a mouth. A gloomy face. No other way of pinpointing the hole he had fallen into. He awoke with a headache, which boded no good for the hours to come. Not once did he consider the likely cause of his dolor might be the mega-doses of valium he had been consuming to dull the . . . *pain* (his word). He was lying in the conjugal bed which had developed a musty, saccharine odor slowly turning to pungency, like rotting meat. The meat in question was Winston and Virginia's, spoiling on living bone while all they managed was to look on helplessly as it happened. Virginia was already up. The whole night, she lay there beside him bundled into herself, an unfriendly wall, a border he dared not approach, let alone cross.

"Where are you going so early?" he said dully, somewhere on the edge of an emotion, as he watched her dress. A cold spell had settled over the room.

"Out," her terse reply. Seconds later she was gone.

Alone in bed, a long, somber Saul with no bright-faced David to assuage him with song. He slid his fingers under the covers, slithering towards the still warm center of the problem. But not even in solitude could he find the solace he was so desperate for. Comfort was on the lam, hotly pursued by a private police force he was unable to identify. He never saw it or them. But they were there. They were there.

A murky ache rose from his solar plexus, and then, briefly, a face flashed in his mind's eye, its identity very nearly unrecognized. But he caught it. It was Gladiola's. Had she really performed at the cabaret the evening before? She looked so different. A stranger. Pain, pain. She had been singing, dancing, holding hands with the others, frolicking. Life A.W., after Winston . . . and she was clearly mastering it, damn it, while *his condition* continued deteriorating. He had never seen her so, so carefree. Pain, pain.

To be fair, Gladiola was only part of his *problem* . . . but enough introspection for now. Time to rise, lazy bones. Lazy . . . *bones*? Bones are *never* lazy, only muscles and minds are. And up he got, stepping barefoot into the day . . . Ow! Dammit! How do those pencils keep winding up on the floor?! Sabotage, I say. Some subtle psychological warfare, a plot of the . . . dark forces . . . the . . . Empire of . . . *Chaos*? Whoops. No. He wasn't that far gone yet. Some less radical explanation was most certainly forthcoming. But off into the day now! A wash, some breakfast, bad mood and all, and then that daily sojourn in the workshop. Who knows? Maybe something had changed . . . for the positive? Nope. There he was . . . as ever, in that . . . that . . . *state* . . . or whatever it was.

Winston contemplated the Doctor's inert form on exhibition in that futuristic, metallic Museum of Hewlett Family History, the glazed gaze as ever fixed on that Deltagon engraved on the counter rim. Had it been eight days? The Doctor's talents as a fakir were truly impressive, and somehow Winston had grown accustomed to the sight of that preternatural reality, odd as it was, of that man able to control the input and output of his body so radically, a willing suspension of disbelief, you might say. Fortunately, Winston was also still able to ask the most salient questions: Is this really happening? And if so, why?

He also began imagining various ways of murdering the Doctor. Granted, all that *still* just a harmless dalliance to pass the time.

Scenario one: he affixes a pulley to the ceiling above the Doctor, feeds a rope over the wheel and ties a noose at one end which he slips around the Doctor's scrawny neck. He pulls on the rope slowly but steadily till there is no slack. Then, with a swift jerk, he yanks the Doctor up out of his seat. Immediately, Larez Pentius' arms and legs spread-eagle as if electrified. A few gurgling sounds and the body goes limp, swinging silently—albeit twitching from time to time but only for a short while. Enter Virginia, in slow motion. She is graceful and thin, her long hair, shimmering and rippling to the waist, the way it did when she was young. Her bright eyes radiate. She is smiling and looks so pretty. She pushes the hanging body playfully as if it were a pendulum, then falls into Winston's arms. They embrace.

Scenario two: It begins as in the first scenario, but here, the rope snaps or the pulley breaks free of its anchoring when he yanks on that rope. Apparently, the force of gravity has too great a hold on the Doctor's body. Larez Pentius is an immovable object, a dwarfed sun metamorphosing into a black hole. In a slightly different version of this fantasy, it is possible to raise the Doctor from his seat, but his position remains unchanged—as if he were some seated Buddha made of stone.

Scenario three: Winston fetches a shotgun (his father's shotgun) and holds it to the Doctor's temple; then he pulls the trigger. When the smoke clears, the head is gone, and the Doctor's neck looks like a tree stump someone splashed with red paint. After a period during which time seems to have stood still, the headless body finally topples over quite dead etc. etc.

But the truth be told: not even murder fantasies were able to relieve the boredom as Winston waited for this incorporate stasis to end. What more potent image of impotence than that of a person in a desperate state dependent on help from a catatonic psychiatrist!

He had never liked this workshop, not even as a boy. Too sterile and slick for his taste. No warmth, no cozy corner for a child to play with his Lincoln Logs or draw. A fitting tomb for his father, the inventor of the POP-IT and whatever other wonders he may have concocted in this cold venue. It was probably a fitting tomb for Larez Pentius as well.

That day fifteen years ago when he had found his father dead in the workshop came to mind now, a memory he evoked to combat the tedium of his vigil . . .

He was eating breakfast in the kitchen. The radio was on, and he was listening to pop music like most young people do, loud music. The door to the workshop flew open and Leland Hewlett, impeccably dressed in his spotless white labcoat, burst into the kitchen, shoulders hunched. "Hotter 'n hell in there," he was muttering half to himself and maybe half to Winston, a substitute for conversation. "You call that music?! It's just noise! Turn it down, dammit!" Then somehow, he tripped over Winston's long legs which seemed to be stretched halfway across the floor and caught himself on the sink. "Clumsy bastard! Why don't you watch where you park those stilts!" He flung open the refrigerator, grabbed a cola and reached for a POP-IT. "Lazy dreamer. Nothing'll become of him," he was grumbling, and then he chug-a-lugged the brown contents of the bottle without stopping for a breath. He belched loudly and sharply and then disappeared back into the workshop with a second bottle in hand, leaving a sweet-sour wave of cola molecules behind in his wake. Winston had never forgotten that smell. Maybe that's why he stopped drinking cola.

Around an hour later, Doctor Pentius phoned. Winston went to fetch his father and found him lying on the polished floor, arms and legs askew, so flat he seemed to have half sunken into his own reflection. Blood was trickling from his ears and nose and a small pool had collected around his mouth like a speech bubble in a cartoon, but red and without words. Winston imagined there had been a violent struggle in there, but he had heard nothing. He raced to the telephone, more shocked than sorrowed, and informed Larez Pentius. "Don't call the police," the Doctor commanded. "I'll be right over!"

Hotter 'n hell. That's what his father had said. And now it occurred to Winston, seated across from Larez Pentius in that gloomy steel space, that it was pretty hot in there now too. It was then the air-conditioner came to mind. Of course, the air-conditioner! There was no ventilation in this workshop! No wonder Leland Hewlett had had it installed. Why hadn't the inventor of the POP-IT etc. figured that one out himself? He stood up, stepped past the figure of Larez Pentius turned to stone and snarled with little respect: "In case you're interested, I'm going to turn on the air-conditioning. I can't take the heat."

"The air-conditioner . . ."

Winston started. Had the Doctor's spoken? "Did you say something?" Now, Larez Pentius began stirring like some life form evolving *ex nihilo* in fast forward, quickly growing animated—maybe it would be better to say reanimated. He was clearly excited. Could this be the same person who moments before had been in that faraway state of Catatonia?

"The air-conditioner! Of course! Of course!" The Doctor leapt to his feet, mincing faunlike, dust particles from the cleanup still clinging to his orange jump-suit. "Why didn't I think of that immediately?!"

"You're back!" Winston was reaching for the switch.

"Don't touch that switch!" Larez Pentius snapped urgently, very urgently.

Winston stopped in mid-motion. "Why? What is it?"

"The angle of this Deltagon," the Doctor was speaking in fast-forward while brushing the dust from his jump-suit, "that twenty-three-and-a-half degree tilt points directly towards the air-conditioning unit! See what I mean?"

"I'm afraid not."

"No time to explain. Whatever you do: don't . . . touch . . . that switch!" The Doctor had already bounded to the door.

"Aren't you hungry?" Winston queried.

"No time to think about food! This is war!" And Larez Pentius was gone.

NINETEEN

"No, HONEST. I really gotta go, important business, real important business."

"You just don't know how to relax," said *Agent* Porky. "That's why people like you get ulcers." He was lolling on the daybed in *Agent* Gladiola Freytag's front room, fingering a knitting needle he had plucked from the wicker basket, arm's length from him. Nathan was standing at the window looking fidgety.

"Thanks, Porky baby. You really know how to hit a hypochondriac where it hurts."

"Come on, Nathan, stay a while. We like your company. You're not feeling awkward, are you?"

"Awkward? Dear brother in sin, I'm tickled pink that things have worked out this way. No offense, you're real cute and all that, but to tell the truth, I'm very happy our little, um, experiment has ended in this convenient manner. I mean, at first, I thought it was just my bourgeois upbringing that made me believe our rubbing noses was getting indecent. But now I know. Our gonads are, well, how shall I put it?, just too similar for us to set up house together and make babies. All that belly to belly stuff may be okay for some people, but when I get hot and bothered and there I am snuggling up to you, well, frankly, I just don't know exactly where to *put* it! Bottoms up is not my style. Let me convey that in the language of the theater: the orifice in question is—at least for me—better suited for exits not entrances."

Agent Porky sighed.

"Some people may have no choice in these matters, but honestly, I just saw no future in us yanking at each other's you-know-whats every night in the dark, even if, well, like I say, you're a real cuddly guy. I don't know about you, but after a while, and I hope I'm not hurting your feelings, it starts getting, well, repetitious. Now I know why they invented girls. Besides, your beard itches—even at your tender age. Anyway, old pal, it's not as if I've lost a friend. Now I've gained a slave to help me achieve the heights of my theatrical aspirations— and a pretty little piccolo player to boot."

"Has he been saying rude things behind my back as usual?" *Agent* Gladiola Freytag entered, a pot of tea and three cups on a tray. She was looking impish, and the short shorts T-shirt combination she was wearing only served to emphasize the impression.

"Nathan says he's got some important business to attend to. He keeps insisting he has to leave," said *Agent* Porky.

"You're not going to leave before tea?" She set the tray down on her desk and sidled onto the daybed next to *Agent* Porky whose hand she clasped. "I thought we wanted to discuss the new skit?"

"Look, why don't you lovebirds just turtledove a while. I mean it's a real nice day. Make hay while the sun shines and all that. But I really gotta go. I mean it's urgent. Who knows? Maybe a matter of life or death."

"I think Nathan's just racing downtown to see if there's something about us in the new *Variety*."

"You just keep it up and I'm going to tell Gladiola where your ticklish spot is when you're in samadhi."

"I think I've already found it," *Agent* Gladiola grinned; she was looking very pretty.

❁ ❁ ❁

A matter of life or death? What Nathan meant is that he had
been imagining various methods that bulldozer of a biker with
the six-fingered hand could use when tearing body and soul
asunder as punishment for Nathan's negligence. Like the Lady
used to sing: Unless there's magic, the end will be tragic. And
he was certainly not one for sad endings, especially at a time
like this when he was having such a good time. Had he been
a Barbareño, as the natives called themselves (he preferred
"Santa Barbarian"), the name Winston Hewlett, son of the inventor of the POP-IT, probably would have rung a bell. He
would have had a face to associate with that name on the letter and delivered it—as promised—straightaway. When he finally understood who that guy in the first row was during the
STAGE FRIGHT performance, the one with the mindless grin
on his face, the alarm went off. What if that big bozo on the
bike comes back and ruins my career?

Nathan climbed into his car and off he went on that short
journey from one hill to another. He took no notice of the red
compact crawling slowly past him as he drove off, the driver
obviously hunting for a parking spot. By the time he turned the
corner and headed downhill, wending his way through time
and space, Virginia Hewlett was already marching resolutely
towards *Agent* Gladiola Freytag's house. She was feeling too
numb to be nervous. As she climbed the steps, she set the spider plant hanging by the door emphatically in motion with a
push of her hand and then rang the doorbell as if ending an
assertive sentence with an exclamation mark.

Her thought factory had switched off as she waited tensely
till the front door swung open. All at once she was standing
face to face with her rival. Noting the mixture of fear, embarrassment and relief in the younger woman's eyes, Virginia
quickly perceived her advantage. She was primed now for an

attack, for which reason it surprised her that she found that face very likeable. "May I come in?" she asked, her tone businesslike but with a hint of warmth *Agent* Gladiola Freytag could not miss.

"Of course," Gladiola answered as graciously as possible. The front door closed behind them.

❀   ❀   ❀

A few minutes later, another car was rolling slowly down *Agent* Gladiola's street: Winston's. He too was looking for a parking spot. It used to be so easy, he was thinking. There are just too many cars these days. Parking spots. That's what my father should have invented, not a way to make it easier to produce more cars. Finally, he caught sight of one. As chance would have it, it was the space Nathan Weiss had just relinquished, not far from where Virginia's car was. Without taking notice, he walked right past his wife's compact (under normal circumstances, he would have recognized that bright red car immediately) and forged on towards Gladiola's front door. His thought factory was *not* empty. Maybe because he had just seen Larez Pentius lugging a ladder to the outside wall of the workshop and then scurrying up to the roof. The Doctor had not volunteered an explanation, nor did he address Winston, and Winston made no inquiries.

Winston was aching for solace in body and soul, and he was certain that Gladiola was the only person left who might garnish that need, even if just out of pity. Virginia had stopped communicating altogether, and the Doctor was obviously unhinged and bent on luring him into an insane conspiracy about some final showdown between the forces of Good and Evil. Winston was clutching a few flowers he had hastily plucked at the edge of someone's garden. They were meant to symbolize his desire to reconcile his differences with Gladiola. Okay,

I've been selfish. I'll tell her that too. Step by step, his world was losing its sense of order, disfigured by a quiet panic that was seizing him in increments. He knew that his grip on reality was as fragile as cloud shapes on a windy day, and that worried him.

As if his plate were not full enough, shortly before reaching Gladiola's house, Winston saw the front door swing open. Someone, obviously in a good mood, was skittering down the porch steps. It was *Agent* Porky. Winston immediately intuited that the battle for Gladiola was already lost to that long-haired person. Wasn't that the guy from the cabaret act? He looks like a girl with a scraggly beard. Winston's cheeks flushed with the heat of panic, anger, jealousy and disappointment. He had no doubt: they were lovers. A quick fantasy of Porky's potency flashed before his eyes, and he hated him, envious as a vampire. Winston paused, and *Agent* Porky strode past him, the two men briefly exchanging meaningful or meaningless glances, depending on your interpretation. Winston sniffed deeply, as if hunting for a message in the other's scent. Sure enough, he caught a familiar fragrance: Gladiola's—mixed with sour male molecules he took to be Porky's. Oh yes, oh yes. It was clear, very clear what was going on. But wait. Had he caught Virginia's redolence in those molecules as well? Now I know I'm really going crazy. He was fidgeting with the pilfered flowers. I'm sure I've lost my sanity. I can't ring that bell. I'm afraid. He climbed the porch steps, slipping into a dizzying round of shall-I-shall-I-not. Bang. "Ow!" His head had been on a collision course with the hanging snake plant. The snake in the Garden? Checkmate. Nowhere to go. I'm alone, all alone. He about-faced and stomped back down the steps, his imagination busily producing images of Gladiola and her friend in intimate poses, scenes worthy of Doctor Becker's porn show. At last . . . his thoughts were exploding into chaos. Loneliness had emptied his belly of identifiable feelings, and the hollow smarted. He flung the flowers onto the sidewalk where they lay, orphans of love. What else could he do? So helpless. Should he leave a note "I was here" and sign it "Just a Friend"? No, he was not one for silly expressions of hurt. Maybe he was just jumping to conclusions? Inventing something that wasn't real? If only he had the courage to ring that bell, he'd find out the truth. Once and for all. But he was too proud—or scared. There was a time when he had power over Gladiola. She loved him. Yes, she had *loved* him, had been in his thrall. And he hadn't noticed! It would never be that way again. That is what his intuition was telling him. For one brief moment, he attempted to hold fast to the last memories of a tenderness once shared.

❀ ❀ ❀

Nathan rang the doorbell of the Hewlett house vigorously. No buzzer but some awful bing-bong chime. He tried again . . . and again but no response, just bells bells bells. Now his mind entered the impatience zone. He circumambulated the house till he reached the garden, hoping to find someone in that very private place and praying it wouldn't be a watch dog. "Hello-o!" the thespian warbled, "Anyone ho-o-me? Hello-o?" Silence. By now, he was beginning to feel uncomfortable like a trespasser. His eyes panned over the cliff-front property, catching a magnificent view of the ocean. Hmm, rich people. Then he saw a ladder propped up against the side of the house. "Hello?" tentatively. A head darted over the edge of the roof. It was Larez Pentius. Nathan and the Doctor locked eyes. "Hi. I'm looking for Winston Hewlett." Nathan was making an effort to sound harmless, all the more so because the Doctor's eyes were radiating pure insanity.

"I'm hunting for mountain lions," the Doctor stagewhispered.

"Oh," said Nathan benignly. "Well, perhaps you could . . ."

"They're somewhere in the air-conditioning."

"I see. Well, maybe you could tell Mr. Hewlett that . . ." But before he finished his sentence, Larez Pentius had jerked his head back and vanished, leaving Nathan a lone intruder in a stranger's garden. My luck. What now? Maybe I should put the envelope into their mailbox? But what if it gets stolen? Should I just wait? Return later? He reached the sidewalk, pondering these choices and others, when suddenly he was startled by the roar of an engine. A vehicle had come screeching to a stop in front of the house. Sensing danger, Nathan took cover behind a tree and peaked cautiously around the barky trunk. Now he clearly saw a Winnebago backing into the Hewlett driveway. He was almost expecting that fat biker to tumble out of that camper and demolish him on the spot for not keeping word. Yes, guilt grows its own appendages. But no. What he was witnessing was more outrageous than Nathan's most intrepid fantasy: the back doors of that Winnebago were slowly swinging open as if by remote control. Later, when he related the incident, he would recall having heard something like music, otherworldly music, shrill strains that raised the level of suspense even higher than what he was experiencing. Half an eternity seemed to pass before the doors stood totally agape. A blue glow, cobalt blue, emanated from within the wagon like a mist engulfed in a veil of music. "Holy hooligan," Nathan muttered to himself, "I think I've been overdosing on Porky's incense."

In the midst of this cobalt blue haze he could have sworn on a stack of Bibles that an odd shape, a symbol maybe, was floating weightlessly like a hologram:

"What the hell . . .!" And then that man he'd seen on the roof, a spunky old guy in an orange jump suit, appeared as if in trance and was marching slowly and deliberately into that blue haze. He climbed into the back of that Winnebago, his body passing through that floating symbol till Nathan was not sure which of the two was more translucent. For a brief instant Melanie flashed through his mind. Once that man had entered that space, the doors of the camper began closing, slowly, very slowly. Meanwhile, the music was growing ever fainter and finally went silent. With that, the spectacle was over. A moment later, the Winnebago was varooming down the street and disappeared around a corner.

Awesome, Nathan was thinking, but only briefly. And then: Hmm. There must be some rational explanation. Maybe a performance. You never know these days. But weird. I wonder if we could incorporate something like that into a skit? Gotta tell Porky and Gladiola.

He was about to return to his car when another car drove up and pulled into the Hewlett driveway. This time, a tall man with a serious expression climbed out. It was Winston. Nathan recognized him. His eyes brightened. "Mr. Hewlett?" he asked.

"Yes?"

"A letter for you," and he extended his arm towards Winston.

"A letter? From whom?"

But by then the envelope was in Winston's hand, and Nathan had scurried off to his car. He did turn his head once to say: "Sorry it took me so long to deliver. Hope it won't cause you any inconvenience."

"Who are you?" Winston called out. "Haven't I seen you before?"

"Just a friend of a friend," Nathan answered and drove off.

Winston was scrutinizing the envelope attentively, as if to confirm that it was really addressed to him. Mistakes do happen. Or is this . . . another one of those DROP IT notes? Isn't one enough? Finally, he did what he had to do. He opened the envelope and slipped out the folded sheet:

MEET ME AT THE BIRD'S NEST
IN HOLLYWOOD
MUST SEE YOU URGENTLY
FINGERS

—
—
—
—
—
—

Fingers. He knew that name. Yes, from Gladiola. No need to ask if this trip was necessary. He was already back in his car and turning on the ignition. Okay, it's time to get to the bottom of all this. Let's get this show on the road! Without stopping for lunch, he headed for Hollywood.

TWENTY

THE BIRD'S NEST was a no-nonsense bar behind an unspec-
tacular facade on Hollywood Boulevard. Winston had no
difficulty finding it. After all, this was the second half of the
twentieth century. He stopped at a phone booth, looked up
the name in the Yellow Pages and *voilà!* Finding a parking
spot was far more trying . . . as usual. When the door fell shut
behind him with a thump, a loose spring yielding to the force
of gravity, he sensed at once that he was far afield from all that
was familiar. Long after his eyes had adjusted to the degree of
light that distinguished this cavern from the bright California
afternoon he had stepped out of, darkness was still enveloping
him. Outdoors, Hollywood Boulevard was bustling with the
usual traffic and harried pedestrians, all heading somewhere
or nowhere. In the Bird's Nest, equivocation was the rule of
law. No motion apart from the bartender's and an occasional
hand raising a glass to silent lips sharing no secrets. If there
were music playing, it is not important to mention it, because
no one would have been paying attention anyway.

Winston settled into a high bar stool at the dark wooden
counter. Briefly, he radiated the scent of daylight. When he
caught the reflection of his face in a large mirror behind the
bar, glasses racked up between him and his self-image, he recognized the fresh look of a country gentleman, accented by his
neat khaki pants, snappy white shirt and beige cotton jacket.
But gradually, the darkness swallowed him as it had the oth-

ers, and soon, he too assumed his place in the obscurity, observable even in his slouch, shoulders hunched over his beer and generating a look of outward equanimity. From time to time, he'd peek down the counter and peer at hands, seeking to count the number of fingers clasped around the beer glasses (as were his own). A voice broke the silence.

"Hey bub," someone was talking to him, "What do you think about historical continuity?" The voice was treble and nasal.

"Pardon?" Winston's response rang instinctively aloof.

"I said, what do you think about historical continuity?"

Winston turned briefly towards the person who had addressed him and saw that he was a dwarf. He had never spoken to a dwarf before, and for a moment, he was jarred. He wanted very much to get an eyeful of that exotic presence, satisfy his curiosity but managed only a few stolen glances.

Frankly, it might have been more appropriate if Winston had asked his interlocutor what he meant by that question, for in all honesty, Winston had no idea what his neighbor had asked or why. And so, he peeked at the small man from the corner of his eye fleetingly and shrugged his shoulders, "Not very much," as if hoping the conversation and the questioner might now disappear.

"I don't believe there's such a thing." Now Winston turned to him again. The dwarf was portly, bushy white hair erupting from the top of his head, and a grey walrus moustache half covering his lips. Something about him made Winston think of a frost gnome. He glimpsed quickly at the short legs dangling over the edge of the stool and wondered how the man had negotiated the climb. "And y'know why?" the dwarf continued, "Because try as I may to perpetuate my own kind, I've failed! Get this. A dwarf cannot produce a dwarf. Did you know that? I've got twelve kids, each one from a different mother, and I still gotta crane my neck to see their noses. And to top it off, their mothers were all dwarfs just like me! How do you explain something like that?"

Winston shook his head.

"Well, I can't either. I mean, if there WERE such a thing as historical continuity—I mean all that cause and effect stuff—you'd figure I should be able to breed my own species so to speak, don'tcha think?"

Oh, that's what he means. Winston's mind clicked into gear. *That's* what historical continuity is. I see.

"But I can't. So, I'm living proof that what people call historical continuity is bunkum. Listen, I'm not telling you this just to chew your ear off. This stuff has implications. Take Hitler. Yeah, I know the old joke, and you're probably thinking: *you* take'm. Well, I don't wan'im either. He didn't like dwarfs one bit. But you know all that stuff about the treaty of Versailles and the inflation crisis in the Weimar Republic being the cause of Hitler's rise to power? Well, I'll tell you. It's all unadulterated horse manure. And d'ya know why? Because events are like dwarfs. Whatever they produce looks nothing like themselves!"

Winston was now taking a good look at the dwarf, trying his hardest to appear attentive.

Meanwhile, the dwarf was scanning him from head to foot. "God, you must be a big one. Stand up a second. I want to see how tall you are."

Winston shook his head ever so faintly, but his "no" could easily have been interpreted as coyness which it was.

"Come on, let's get a gander at you."

"No, I don't want to," Winston demurred.

"Jeezus Krist, it's only for a second. It's not like I'm asking you to pull your pants down. Just stand up a second."

"Well . . ."

"Just do it."

And so, Winston stood up. He felt ridiculous, especially as the dwarf's mouth fell open in astonishment. He had never felt so tall before. It was as if he kept rising and rising, ever higher.

"Wow. How big are you anyway?"

Winston shuffled back to his seat, his heart thumping as if he had just performed a feat that demanded great effort. "Six foot six."

"How many meters is that?"

"I don't know."

"You know that someday we're going metric, don't you? I tell you, your grandchildren probably won't know what a foot is. Imagine sitting here and saying to Ed, Hey gimme another two hundred milliliters. Jeez, it sounds like a chemistry lab."

Winston smiled politely.

"D'ya know how tall I am? C'mon, guess."

"Well, I . . ."

"One hundred and thirteen centimeters. You must be a good two hundreder."

Why was this conversation making Winston nervous?

"Ya better start gettin' used to it, pal." The dwarf cupped his beer-glass in both hands and took a long gulp. "Y'know, you probably don't have any idea what it's like to be a dwarf. I mean sure, you're a big fellow and maybe people stare at you sometimes on the street. But me they gawk at with x-ray eyes, and then they turn away real quick like they didn't notice me. That hurts. I bet you don't know this but, well, we've got an organization to protect our civil rights. 'Little Power' it's called. We got consciousness-raising groups too. Wouldn't hurt you to come by either, big fella. I mean, do you think we get any real respect from society? Have you ever heard of a dwarf doctor or lawyer or painter or poet? Have you? Of course not. Cripples maybe, but not dwarfs. Do you know what my claim to fame is?"

Winston shook his head.

"Well, I'll tell you then. I was one of the Munchkins in the Wizard of Oz. Honest. What? Don'tcha believe me? You gotta imagine this . . . thousands of us swarming around the MGM studios, all wearing those funny little costumes. Make-up people and costume people surrounding us like cattle drivers. D'ya think even one of them was a dwarf? Nosirree. I'll tell you though. There's one thing we got that'll stop anyone from thinking of us as cutesy little kewpie dolls, no matter how they dress us up. And that, my friend, is our reputation for . . ." He leaned over and pulled Winston towards him by his upper arm and winked: "*Potency.*"

Winston smiled nervously.

"That's right. Some guys may have problems getting it up. We've got problems getting it down. Did you know that the royal courts of Europe used to keep dwarfs for private sex shows? That's like saying we invented the porny flick. Whaddaya say to that? Rumor has it that we can go at it for hours. And d'ya know what?" He tugged at Winston again and pulled him down, whispering into his ear, "It's true, we can!" Now the dwarf gave him a serious look. "Whaddaya say to that?"

Winston nodded. He was clearly feeling uncomfortable, but all he could manage to say was "Look, why don't you let me buy you a beer."

"Say, thanks, pal. But let me tell you something else. Let me tell you why people believe we actually are who they think we are. Because, to get back to the point, most people DO believe in historical continuity, or want to at least, because without it, well, there'd be no such thing as tradition, and without traditions, there'd be nothing to lean on! And you know what that means?"

"What?"

"That means even a lotta dwarfs want to believe in historical continuity. Can you beat that, huh? But I guess it's okay. Sometimes people *do* need a crutch."

Winston was not enjoying this conversation. In the first place, talking to strangers always made him nervous. Secondly, he still wasn't convinced that this *was* a conversation, and thirdly, he had something more important on his mind. He was looking for Fingers, his liaison to the Empire of Chaos and, hopefully, a solution to his impotence. "I hope you don't mind if I change the subject . . ."

"Of course not. You know why?"

"No, why?"

"Because there's no continuity anyway! You can say anything you want, whenever you want. Marzipan. Creole. Loop-dee-loop."

"Well, I don't know how to put this, but, you see, I'm looking for someone, a fellow named Fingers. I wonder if you might know him. He's probably easy to recognize because . . ." he pointed to his hands, "Well, he's got six fingers on each hand."

"Fingers? Hmmm." The dwarf raised a stubby hand to his chin, "I don't think I ever met anyone by that name. Is he a dwarf?"

"I don't think so."

"Hmmm . . ."

Now the door flew open. Street sounds and a few rays of unbearably blinding light briefly penetrated the comfortable darkness, snuffed out quickly and gratefully as the door thumped shut again. Winston turned in time to see the outline of a plump woman, fortyish, lumber past him. He could not make out any details in the murky light, but for some reason he had the impression she must have been a prostitute. As she was passing the dwarf, Winston saw him lunge purposefully and goose her.

"Arnold!" she teeheed.

"Pardon me, bub," he turned to Winston, "but business before pleasure." He gave Winston a playful jab in the ribs, which caused Winston to jolt reflexively. Deftly, the dwarf shimmied down the barstool and toddled off. As he waddled behind her, she quickened her step. There was giggling, an exchange of words. A door slammed somewhere in the rear and the two disappeared.

Winston imagined hearing sexual sounds from behind that door. Maybe they were, maybe they weren't. Thumping, laughing, moaning . . . And all at once, he was feeling lonely, very lonely, a man without a friend in the world—which was more or less the truth. He had a sudden urge to cry "help." But at that moment, a voice accosted him in the dark, face still obscure in the shadows.

"I don't mean to eavesdrop," the figure said, "but I couldn't help overhearing that you were looking for Fingers."

"Why . . . yes." Winston was having difficulties making out the features of this new acquaintance.

"Well, you won't find Fingers here."

"No?"

"Come with me," the person gestured. Winston paid. The two of them rose from their barstools and headed for the door.

❁   ❁   ❁

In the blaze of light that was Hollywood Boulevard, the stranger soon came into focus. Winston was relieved to see that the five-fingered man, apparently a go-between, was about his own age, dressed as conventionally as himself though perhaps a tad nattier with the top two buttons of his shirt open, a tuft of chest hair peeking out. Together, they climbed into a taxi. Winston heard his companion say "Century Hotel" to the driver.

They rode through town silently. From time to time, Winston attempted some small talk. The stranger remained taciturn.

"Will I see Fingers at the Century?" His timidity was fading, and he was certainly curious.

No answer.

"Who *is* Fingers?"

No answer.

"Are you from Los Angeles?"

No answer.

"It's pretty here but smoggier than in Santa Barbara, and the traffic's worse."

"Yes, that's true."

Finally, they reached their destination. Winston's guide ushered him into the hotel, polite but perfunctory. They trekked down two or three long, red-carpeted corridors until they reached a door marked "PRIVATE." There they stopped.

"Here, put this on." Winston's factotum handed him a blue rimmed, semiglossy white tag fixed to an adhesive back. His name WINSTON had been printed on it in neat black magic marker letters. He peeled off the back and stuck the tag on the breast pocket of his jacket. He asked no questions. The stranger did the same on his own jacket pocket. His tag read HERMIE. Afterwards, he held out his palm solicitously, and Winston passed him the peeled off back of the sticker.

"Hey, Hermie, how did you know my name?"

Hermie shrugged minimally, then slipped a key into the heavy metal door and pushed it open, clearly with effort. They proceeded down a narrow passageway flanked by what seemed to be heavy velvet curtains. The space was illuminated but dully, and Winston could not determine the source of the light as they penetrated the passageway ever more deeply in stillness. He did hear murmuring up ahead. None of this was frightening him. Quite the contrary, he felt an excitement as if he were anticipating something important and followed willingly.

There was a clearing at the end of the curtained passageway, a windowless space, it too cordoned off by a wall of high dark red curtains. A group of men and women were milling there. Counting Hermie and himself, they were twelve, and indeed, twelve plain wooden chairs were lined up in a neat row parallel to the curtain wall, obviously one for each. The floor was polished to a spit shine. There was something familiar about this setting.

"Ah good! They're here," a man with a twangy Australian accent spoke. "Just in time. All right, why don't we b'gin. Everyone please tyke a seat. Hermie, why don't you and Winston sit et thet end."

Very curious, Winston was thinking, he knows my name too!?

All were seated now except for the Australian. Winston peered down the long row of chairs, then at the high curtains . . . curtains? It was then he caught sight of the bright spotlights high above. Why, it's like in a theater! He felt excitement in the air, a tinge of anticipation. Not unpleasant. As if they were waiting for something or someone. Was it *him* they were waiting for?

"O-kye!" the Australian called out, and then slowly the curtain began to rise. Winston gasped. Dazzling lights. What now? And there, before his eyes, were rows and rows and rows of people, thousands of people, and all were applauding wildly! Why, he was on a stage! Now, the Australian stepped forward to a podium.

"What's going on here?" Winston whispered to Hermie.

"Shh, you'll see."

The Australian raised his arms high above his shoulders. He was handsome and athletic and wearing a shirt and trousers that emphasized the V-line of his torso. His shirt too,

like Hermie's, was unbuttoned at the top. He was the image of
health and virility. In fact, upon closer examination, Winston
determined that the entire crew radiated an aura of after-hours
at the tennis club.

As the crowd settled down and the last hushes went mute,
the Australian began to speak. "Good evening! Good evening!
lydies an gennelmen and welcome t' our guest seminah. Before
we fill your ears with the gobs of goodies we've prepared for
you this evening, I should like you to know that we have a
very . . . special . . . guest . . . with us . . ."

Murmurs percolated from the audience.

Does he mean *me*? Winston was thinking, a hint of panic.
What am I supposed to say?

" . . . because, dear lydies and gennelmen, t'nyte our
beloved founder . . ." At this point a hysterical applause exploded from that sea of people, so deafeningly loud, that the
speaker had to bellow into the microphone to be heard, "Yes,
our very dear friend, beck from his recent trevels, is here
to share with you the rare treat of his company! Yes, lydies
and gennelmen, mye I present . . . WYATT AMA-DYE-US
ROSENBLOOM!"

There was no orchestra present, but the excitement generated by that name might have been mistaken for blaring fan-
fare. A roar of enthusiasm erupted from the rows of spectators, wild and uncontrollable. Thunderous applause, screaming, whistling, arm waving, weeping and fainting, as down the
center aisle, a dark-haired figure, as sportily dressed as those
on stage, his arms raised in a victory pose, ran up towards the
stage and leapt effortlessly up and over to the podium, his every gesture accompanied by further outbursts of appreciation
until the applause transmogrified into a rhythmic thumping of
hands and feet which only went mute when that man raised his
arms in a gesture calling for silence. He was broad-shouldered,
forthcoming, not particularly tall, a headful of jet-black hair

neatly coiffured. His face was rugged and masculine, and a smile was stretched across it. He was wearing a herringbone jacket, a sport shirt, naturally with the top two buttons open, his pants meticulously pressed. Authority spumed from his pores.

"Thank you. Thank you. Thank you. And I want to welcome you, dear friends, to our guest seminar tonight. Tell me, isn't it great the way Marsy flatters me?" SIXTY SECONDS OR SO DURING WHICH PEOPLE STAND WHISTLE AND WAVE ENERGETICALLY. "It makes me proud to know that I have friends prepared to say such nice things about me . . . even if I do pay them so well." LAUGHTER. "And I'm so happy to be with all you lovely folks tonight, that's right, all three thousand of you times two hundred dollars." LAUGHTER AND APPLAUSE. "Yes, people are always criticizing me for taking money to teach you lovely folks how to think for yourselves, but what they don't know is that you ENJOY giving me that money! Isn't that right? APPLAUSE. "Because once you've been suckered by me, you KNOW that no one will ever be able to sucker you again! Right?" APPLAUSE AND WHISTLING. "That's why I especially want all you new folks, WITHOUT HESITATION, to sign aboard tonight. Join us, yes, become QUID PRO QUO graduates. Just wait till you see what's in store. And you graduates, you know it doesn't have to stop there. Why, we've got plenty of other things for you to spend your money on too. Hundreds of marvelous seminars. Because what are the real facts? You come here to get it. Right? And we do the best we can, just so you CAN get it. Isn't that so? You lovely suckers!" LAUGHTER AND APPLAUSE. "Let them laugh at us. We know we're getting it, right?" APPLAUSE. And how about this. Now, QUID PRO QUO courses are being offered in New York, Chicago, New Orleans, San Francisco and Tuscon, Arizona—as well as here in L.A. of course." APPLAUSE. "You see! They're starting to

GET IT all over now! We've even started Spanish language classes under the supervision of our own Manny Cabronez, a great guy. Where is he? Hey, Manny, stand up and take a bow." THUNDERING APPLAUSE. "Manny, how do you say GET IT in Spanish? DI-NERO, huh?" LAUGHTER AND APPLAUSE. "What a guy. And what a night. And what wonderful people you are. I love you all." THUNDERING APPLAUSE WHISTLING WAVING. "But I'm not here just to talk about love—though what else is there really? I also want to tell you a little about the European tour I've just returned from. Well, I managed to get to lots of countries on your money and stayed in some of the nicest, most elegant hotels in the world thanks to you. And let me tell you, they sure know what elegance is over there. Why, do you know that in some of those places you're supposed to leave your shoes in front of your hotel room door at night? And the next morning, you find them there polished to a spit shine. I was so thrilled by that quaint custom that I decided to try it out after I returned to New York. I put my shoes in front of the door to my room overnight, and what do you think I discovered in the morning?" WHAT? WHAT? "The door was gone!" LAUGHTER. No, but all kidding aside. There are some great people over there in Europe, and lots of them are desperately in need of our help. Do you know that in Germany, people are so well trained they won't cross the street till the light turns green. One place I visited, the traffic signals were out of commission—or *kaputt* as they say over there. The whole day, nobody crossed a single street until they got written permission from the mayor. And you can't imagine the paperwork it took for that. Here in L.A., of course, we wouldn't have that problem—even if people were that disciplined. I mean, when was the last time you saw a pedestrian? Let alone someone crossing a street!" LAUGHTER AND APPLAUSE. "But I want you to know that next summer the entire Lichtenstein Philatelist Union is coming to our New York office to take the training. When they saw the energy of our QUID PRO QUO team, I tell you, they were ready to pay the postage!" APPLAUSE AND LAUGHTER. "And I hope you're all prepared to pay the postage too, especially you first timers at this guest seminar. Dig generously in your hearts and pocketbooks—unless of course you're happy with those useless worries you carry around and don't know how to get rid of. We want to relieve the weight a bit, so when those lovely hostesses come around asking you to sign your name on the dotted line, be generous. Your generosity will help us all. And before I forget, I want to let you know that we were followed all through Europe by camera teams, which means that our message, GET IT BEFORE IT GETS YOU is going to be broadcast on TV throughout Germany, France, Italy, Switzerland and Austria. Isn't that great!" APPLAUSE. "Soon, all of Europe is going to GET IT too! And then Asia!" THUN-DERING APPLAUSE. "That's right! We want everyone to get it just like we did! Right?" THUNDERING APPLAUSE WAVING AND WHISTLING FEET STAMPING. "But what about you who haven't gotten it yet . . . be honest: haven't you had enough? Can you really stand all that bullshit, yeah, all that garbage that stands between your space and mine? Aren't you tired of IT happening to YOU? You shove things in one end and they come out the other. You're more than a tube, don't you know that?" YEAH YEAH YEAH. "Why not stay up around the clock when you want to. Why eat every day? Why piss and shit like housebroken dogs? My friends, YOU can learn to take control. You DON'T have to live a chicken-hearted life! That's right. YOU DON'T HAVE TO HESITATE! If only you just got it—GET IT?—most of those things you call your problems and hang-ups would DISAPPEAR! Don't you know that? YEAH YEAH YEAH APPLAUSE. And we CAN help you to get it, so you can help yourself! And it doesn't take long. Ask your friends and neighbors who have graduated. They're the ones with the blue name tags. And you graduates, if you see someone wandering around looking lost and wearing a green name tag, go over and speak to him or her. Tell them what you've experienced and what it's done for you. For so much freedom, the price is really pretty low. Am I right?" THUNDERING APPLAUSE WHISTLING WAVING STOMPING YEAH YEAH YEAH. "It's never too early, and it's never too late to get it. But listen, you don't want to hear me blabber on . . ." WE DO WE DO WE DO. "No, no, I'm going to let Marsy, that Tasmanian tiger, carry on from here. I think he's got a whole program planned for you. And he won't try to sell you a used car the way I do. Marsy's going to tell you folks just what goes on during our training sessions, so you'll know that we're selling you the steak and not the sizzle. Isn't that right, Marsy?"

"Rightie-o, Wyatt."

"But ya know, folks, no words will ever replace the real thing. So, when you're listening to old Marsy and our various speakers here, don't forget for one instant that every word you hear is pure, unadulterated sourdough unless you decide to get it yourselves. D'ya understand? Ah, I love ya!"

Wyatt Amadeus Rosenbloom threw a kiss out to the audience, and the entire auditorium exploded into a pounding, thundering tremor of applause, screaming, waving, fainting and even some falling into convulsions. Flowers were hurled from all directions, hundreds stood and wept. A few even vomited from the excitement as he walked off into the wings.

"Isn't he gryte! Isn't he gryte!" Marsy cried into the microphone, unable to restrain his tears. "Is there anyone like him in the world?" The crowd was screaming "NO NO NO NO NO!"

And while this rumble was quaking across the auditorium, Hermie nudged Winston. "Come on, let's go," and the two of them slipped off unnoticed into the wings where Wyatt Amadeus Rosenbloom was waiting.

"This is the one who wants to see Fingers," Hermie said in a voice loud enough to be heard above the din.

"So, Mr. Hewlett, at last." Wyatt Amadeus Rosenbloom said, extending his hand and shaking Winston's firmly. "We've been waiting for you . . . for quite a while."

❀ ❀ ❀

"But what is this QUID PRO QUO?" Winston and Wyatt Amadeus Rosenbloom were sitting in the generous back seat of a Mercedes limousine while driving down Wilshire Boulevard towards Santa Monica. Hermie was hunched behind the steering wheel and so silent that Winston soon forgot he was there. The car was coasting smoothly, and soon Los Angeles too seemed to disappear. Wyatt Amadeus Rosenbloom flipped open a built-in bar.

"A screwdriver, Mr. Hewlett, or have your tastes grown more . . . sophisticated?"

"A screwdriver! Jeez, I haven't had one of those since I was a kid . . . Wait, don't tell me you know . . ."

"There's a lot we know about you. But not to worry."

"What, me worried? Haha." And it was true. He was enjoying the new faces and experiences and eager for more.

"Well then, let's just go for a Remy," Wyatt Amadeus Rosenbloom gestured theatrically. "That is, if I can find the cognac glasses." He was fumbling in the dark in that bar which seemed to have various compartments; flashes from passing cars and streetlights were flickering against the seats. Winston looked on with interest . . . that is, until he began feeling carsick, an unwonted condition he attributed to the excitement or the flashing lights, or maybe to the fact that he hadn't eaten all day. Virginia was always the one who suffered bouts of carsickness, especially on winding roads. Sometimes he would tease her in those situations. Now he understood that it was no laughing matter and swore he would be more considerate in the future. A sour taste rose up from his stomach, and he was afraid he might not be able to keep himself under control.

"Ah! There they are!" Wyatt Amadeus Rosenbloom raised his head cheerily and clinked two glasses. "Mr. Hewlett, you're looking pale. You DO need a drink."

"I'll be all right." Winston belched quietly.

"Now, back to your question." He poured the cognac and handed Winston a glass. "Cheers. Oh, come on, Mr. Hewlett, just glug it down."

Winston stared at the glass with disinterest, fearing he was really going to be sick. After a moment's hesitation, he gulped the contents down. The cognac burned, and he gagged, thinking that what he least wanted, i.e., to make a spectacle of himself, was about to happen. But then, the warmth of the alcohol reached his stomach. He heard the gurgle and smiled apologetically. Wyatt Amadeus Rosenbloom didn't seem to notice any of this. He was too busy sipping at his own glass. Winston felt himself relaxing.

"How shall I put it, Mr. Hewlett?" Wyatt Amadeus Rosenbloom leaned against the cushioned seatback, his hands cupping a knee. "You were at our Guest Seminar tonight. You saw how enthusiastically the people reacted. Perhaps it would be simpler if I said QUID PRO QUO means *something for everyone*. Hmm, I see you don't get it. Let me put it this way. Five years ago, It might have been me out there in that crowd, looking for a way out of some private misery. In those days there *was* no Wyatt Amadeus Rosenbloom and no QUID PRO QUO. There was just me, Jack Smith, a John Doe among John Does. I had sold encyclopedias, used cars, insurance . . . even women, Mr. Hewlett, and do you know why?"

Winston shrugged and held out his glass for a refill.

"Because I didn't get it, just like those people out there tonight."

"Get what?"

"That's the point, Mr. Hewlett." He refilled Winston's snifter without missing a beat, "and perhaps I can best explain it by sharing a bit more autobiography with you."

Winston took a sip of his cognac. He was feeling fine now, as if they were floating in an airship through fields of sparkling stars.

"You see," Wyatt Amadeus Rosenbloom was mugging flamboyantly as if being interviewed in front of running cameras, "Let me be completely honest with you. I've done some pretty, well, criminal things in my life—no, I never snuffed anyone, if that's what you're thinking, but the way I was heading, that could have happened too. And do you know why I was that way? Because I wanted to 'get somewhere.' And I'm not talking about traveling. I wanted to *get* somewhere, but all I was doing was marching in place, and getting, as they say, nowhere fast. In those days, I could think of nothing more desirable than having money, fame and a big car. I know what you're thinking: that I have all those things now. And you're right! But the truth is: I may have them, but I don't need them anymore! Anyway, let me get to the point." He took a sip from his glass and smacked his lips. "Ah, that's good. Nothing like a fine, satiny cognac. Come on, Mr. Hewlett, drink up, drink up. So, where was I. Oh yes, let me get back to the point. Well, about five years ago, I was involved in some pretty illegal business. To put it bluntly, I was dealing cocaine. I'd buy the stuff in Mexico and smuggle it across the border into San Diego to unload it. I don't know if you've ever dealt drugs, Mr. Hewlett, though looking at you, my gut feeling says you probably haven't. Well, to put it mildly, it's a very risky business. On the other hand, the risk you take is actually part of the payoff. In fact, it's one of the few businesses left that still smacks of adventure. And believe me, I was *very* good at it. I could get past the most ornery and attentive customs agent where others wouldn't've dared. Also, I could smell a frame-up fifty yards away, because I have another talent: people can't lie to me. I don't know why, but they just can't."

Uh oh. Does he know *everything* about me?

"Well, with qualities like that, you'd expect business would go well for me. And it did. And that was a problem too because I knew I'd never get caught. Do you know what it means to realize you can lead a criminal life and never get caught? Believe me, it's not a nice feeling, Mr. Hewlett, although you might think it ought to be. And do you know why? Because nobody commits crimes to get away with them or just for profit. Anyone who says that is a liar. The real reason people are criminal is to get caught. You may not believe that, but no matter. Explaining why that is so gets extremely complicated, and we don't have that much time to talk now. Let's just say it has to do with interconnectivity. That's a big word, I know, but if you're interested, we have a QUID PRO QUO brochure that goes into that subject in great detail. But back to the point. The date was September 13th, a day that will live on in my personal memory forever. I was in a hotel room in Tijuana, planning to smuggle my load across the border the next day. Suddenly, I had this . . . strange sensation—that's the only way I can describe it. I felt it in my whole body. Every pore and every cell was vibrating with it. It was like sheer panic and perfect joy in one, if you can imagine that. Then, as suddenly as it occurred it was over, and I still didn't understand what it was, except that afterwards I was completely exhausted. But one sentence kept racing through my mind at a thousand miles an hour: 'Drop your load and go to San Diego.' I should add that I had thirty thousand bucks worth of stuff with me. But I didn't care. I just picked myself up, left everything behind in Tijuana, crossed the border clean as a whistle and checked into a hotel in San Diego. I lay there for three days not eating a thing, just staring up at the ceiling. And that, Mr. Hewlett, is when I *got* it. There's no other way to put it. Everything was suddenly so clear, so simple, if you know what I mean. Even my ambition was gone. There's no other way to describe it. I also knew that if *I* could GET it, others could too. It didn't even have a name at first. I just picked myself up and headed for Hollywood, where I rented another hotel room—nothing as snazzy as the Century, mind you. That's where I first met Marsy and Manny and Hermie and some of the others. They were drawn to me immediately and wanted to learn how to get it too. And once they saw how easy it was, it began to spread. Just like that. So, we gave it a name, QUID PRO QUO, concocted a program and pretty soon, people came flocking to us by the thousands. And do you know why?"

Winston shook his head.

"Because we tell them the truth, *always*. There's something for everyone. I make no secret about *anything*. Not even about my past. You can read the story I just told you in a QUID PRO QUO brochure, free for all to see. But here's the rub. Getting it is so easy that most people won't believe they have gotten it unless you make them suffer. What I mean is: we had to disguise our product in order to sell it. Can you imagine that? People feel cheated unless they suffer a little! Then we found the perfect solution. We devised a program that lasts two weekends and called it a 'seminar.' The candidates—that's what we call them, it puts them in the right mood if you know what I mean—come to us early in the morning. They sit cooped up in a room until late afternoon, and then, after a short break, again until about midnight. But here's the rub: during the training, they're not allowed to leave the room under any circumstances. We call this a 'contract,' and everyone has to agree to that contract before we allow them to become candidates.

Most of them love the idea because people are suckers for discipline and authority, Mr. Hewlett, things they've been hungering after for years. You can't imagine how chaotic many people's lives are. Anyway, sitting together in one room for so many hours during the training has a certain effect on people, especially because of the novelty of the situation, and pretty soon their bladders start bursting, and you've got a room full of people, all with the same excruciating urge to run off to the toilet. But that tension, that conscious feeling of suffering associated with having to quash that need for so long gives them, each of them, the feeling that they're experiencing something *very* intense. And so, by the time they finally do get it, they're really convinced that they've gotten it. Our job is easy. All we have to do is fill the time with a few simple exercises we've lifted from theater workshops and yoga courses and allow some time for candidates to make their silly hysterical confessions about one stupid tick or another. By the time they finally get it, they're completely satisfied. Do you get it now, Mr. Hewlett?"

"I have the feeling I'm beginning to get it, Mr. Rosenbloom."

"Please call me Wyatt. I've chosen my name very deliberately. It includes all my heroes: Wyatt Earp for courage and corruption, Mozart for genius and Slapsy Maxy Rosenbloom for pure chutzpah."

❀ ❀ ❀

They pulled into a dark street in an older part of Santa Monica with an ambient seediness and parked. Winston had been feeling safe in the company of Wyatt Amadeus Rosenbloom. This unexpected adventure had brought him to places so out of the ordinary, that he was already looking forward to the next episode. He and Wyatt Amadeus Rosenbloom climbed out of the car chattering away like old friends, Hermie trailing discreetly behind. The street was eerily quiet, and their footsteps and voices echoed from brick wall to brick wall. The air smelled of dead fish and crustacean rot, an indication of their proximity to the ocean.

As they reached the sidewalk across from where the car was parked, a door flew open and a body lurched out, dropping onto the pavement in front of them. Wyatt Amadeus Rosenbloom held an arm protectively before Winston, and Winston halted. A barstool followed and thunked against the sprawled body, striking it at the base of the skull, causing the miserable creature to emit a husky "oof" before collapsing into unconsciousness. It was all happening in slow motion. Above the door, Winston deciphered some barely legible words on a faded sign: KITTY'S CORNER. Then he focused on the motionless body. It had short-cropped hair, a smooth snarled face and was wearing a white T-shirt, black leather vest, blue jeans and black engineer boots. "Why . . . it's a woman!" he exclaimed. "Is this where we're going?"

"You wanted to see Fingers," Wyatt Amadeus Rosenbloom was grinning broadly. He opened the door. "After you, Mr. Hewlett."

❀ ❀ ❀

Kitty's Corner was jumping that night. Loud music, dim smoky light. The hardest edge of the female sex among its own. Winston, Wyatt Amadeus Rosenbloom and Hermie pressed through the thick crowd of fems and bulls and others who formed the fabric of mixed humanity that filled the room to capacity and maybe beyond, cutting through comedies, tragedies and melodramas alike. There were the loners, the groups, the clinging lovers, the foresaken, the brooders, the laughers, the fragile, the goons, the loud voices, the whisperers, the gang around the pool table, the parents, the children, the stars, the star worshippers, the ex-stars, the philosophers, the story-tellers, politicians, virgins, profligates and of course, because it was a Saturday night, the gang on the dance floor.

> Oh we're dancin',
> shimmy shimmy shimmy bop.
> Oh we're dancin',
> and we're never never gonna stop.

Miraculously, they found three chairs at a corner table and sat down. Soon, a waitress was shoving her way over to take their orders. She was attractive and young, her face expressionless as befitting a slave, and the buttons on her blouse were undone, so that when she leaned over, Winston saw *everything!* Being well-mannered, he tried not to stare too conspicuously. When he did peek, he hoped no one noticed.

"Nice tits!" Wyatt Amadeus Rosenbloom was leaning over to him, "hmm, Mr. Hewlett?"

Winston laughed good-naturedly. He liked Wyatt Amadeus Rosenbloom's impertinence. "Is this a *lesbian* bar?" he whispered.

"That's right."

"And this is where we're going to find Fingers?"

"I see you've never met Fingers before."

Wyatt Amadeus Rosenbloom nodded to Hermie who rose and disappeared into the crowd.

Now a fresh wave of anticipation rippled through Winston's nervous system.

"Mr. Hewlett, or may I say Winston, as I see that you are still wearing your name tag from the QUID PRO QUO meeting . . ."

Winston made a gesture to remove it.

"No, no, leave it on. You never know when you may forget your name. Anyway, as you know, I can't help but tell the truth, and as you also know, I think the truth is a marketable quality, so I hope you won't be offended if I give you a little practical advice . . . You see, I know why you're here to see Fingers . . ."

"You do!?" Now Winston was feeling the sharp sting of embarrassment. Do they all know? Is impotence written on my face? Wyatt Amadeus Rosenbloom had said he could see through anybody's lies. Would he, Winston, be forced to blurt out his shame?

"Yes, Winston, I know all about you and your friend Doctor Pentius . . ."

"Doctor Pentius?!"

"And I tell you, Winston, drop it, because, frankly, you don't know the facts . . ."

"But you don't understand . . ." And now it dawned on him that he was in *Maenad* territory. Then it was true. The Empire of Chaos *did* consider him a co-conspirator with Larez Pentius and his father because of some fabled invention. That, however, bothered him less than the fear that at any moment he would be forced to divulge the horrible secret of his impotence to Wyatt Amadeus Rosenbloom. Oh well, he probably knew anyway. After all, weren't *they* the ones who'd struck him impotent in the first place? Were they playing cat and mouse with him?

"I do understand, Winston . . ."

"No, Wyatt, this time you've really got it wrong . . ." He was about to say more, but at that moment Hermie returned.

"Please come along, Mr. Hewlett. Fingers will see you now."

"Winston rose. He was a head taller than his guide, soaring, in fact, high above all heads at Kitty's Corner.

"Good luck, Winston," Wyatt Amadeus Rosenbloom smiled cheerfully, "And don't forget: the truth! Always the truth!"

A funny thought crossed Winston's mind. If he managed to survive all this, he would love to draw these things he was seeing and maybe share them with the world.

❀ ❀ ❀

Winston and Hermie cleaved their way through the wall to wall female bodies, pushing aside one hard luck story after another with a simple "Excuse me, may I get by," until finally, they reached a door at the rear of the club.

"This is as far as I can take you, Mr. Hewlett," Hermie raised his otherwise soft voice so he could be heard over the background din. He was pointing at a door.

"Winston looked into Hermie's serene face with affection. "Well, I want to thank you for everything you've done," he said bashfully. "I've barely exchanged a word with you, but somehow I have the feeling I know you."

"You feel that because we have something in common, you and I."

"Are you . . ." Winston began.

"Yes, I also challenged the course of history once."

"Challenged the course of history?"

"You shouldn't tamper with things you don't understand, Mr. Hewlett."

"But . . . all I want . . ." But how could Winston say what he really wanted at a moment like this?

"I know the consequences. I was once overzealous too."

"I'm sorry, I'm afraid I don't . . ."

"Please don't play naive, Mr. Hewlett. You have no idea what you are sabotaging."

"And what would you suggest?"

"Drop it, Mr. Hewlett, drop it. That's what I would suggest."

Before Winston could respond, Hermie had been swallowed up by the crowd, and Winston was opening that door . . . slowly . . .

❁ ❁ ❁

"Don't just stand there like a fly on the wall, sweetie," a voice boomed, "Shut the door behind you! Yes! You're right where you want to be! So, don't worry your bitty self about anything. We've been expecting you. Isn't that right, girls?"

It was a spacious room with a high ceiling, like a ballroom, everything in some shade of red: the plush carpets, the furniture, the wallpaper. Even the steady quiet pulsing of the music was wafting into his consciousness on something like a red cloud. Bodies were strewn carelessly across the vast carpet like flowers in an English garden, most reclining on puffy satiny cushions, red of course. Others were slouching on velvety chairs and sofas or ensconced at long tables decked out with heaps of platters overflowing with chunks of meat, raw and cooked, salads, fruits, mountains of beer cans, never-ending columns of wine bottles, punch bowls, mounds of red jello, and at the center of the buffet, a model of a Harley-Davidson chopper molded of what from the distance seemed to be—and smell like—chopped liver. The plethora of bodies was "yeah-yeah-yeahing" in response to that question posed by the incredibly corpulent figure, hair cascading down in black, curly locks and seated in a custom-made, generously over-dimensional armchair, upholstered in red velvet and gold brocade, throne-like in Winston's proximity while chewing on a dark, moist Brazil cigar. Is that a he or a she? Winston was not sure. The only certainty was that the hand conveying that fat, black cheroot to and from the thick sucking lips had six fingers. He counted them twice. There was no mistaking. It was Fingers. He would not have been more amazed had that person had four arms or two heads. Furthermore, he or she was surrounded by what on closer examination appeared to be the most unappetizing and unsavory assortment of thugs, goons and slobs imaginable: glubbering, blubbery females in various states of dress and undress, some looking like they needed a shave, unbelievably ugly tough guys, slovenly biker types, fat and slobbering, mouths wide open in stupefied laughter, teeth missing, some kissing each other in ways that Winston instinctively found revolting, if only for aesthetic reasons. Meanwhile, pretty nymphettes and slender smooth-cheeked serving boys, barefoot and clothed in translucent smocks were flitting about the room, carrying trays, bottles or glasses to those motley, wriggling piles of undulating flesh. Some he saw being yanked down by one guest or another, then muffled in one lap or other. Women with red henna'd hair wearing tight outfits of gold and silver lamé were smoking cigarettes in long holders, their lips as red as Winston imagined his face must be, creatures that looked like mass escapees from institutions for the insane, a collection of idiots and morons. He would have liked nothing better than to slowly backstep and exit that room as if by mistake he had entered the wrong restroom, excusing himself with a simple "Oh pardon me," and how nice it would be, he thought, if I suddenly wake up and find that I am only dreaming all this, that none of it is really happening, just some long, complicated nightmare, the noxious result of eating pizza too soon before going to sleep, and I would swear never again to eat pizza after midnight. He pinched himself as unobtrusively as possible, only to find that he was awake indeed. And the motorcycle posters on the walls were real, and the tables and chairs where some of the mob were lounging were real, and there was nowhere to go but out cold, and he was too scared to do that. Now, for the first time during what he was calling his adventure, he was feeling seriously frightened.

"Oooh, what a big one," Fingers was moaning, looking him up and down, "just the way I like them. Mmm."

Winston was standing there like a pillar of salt. Or he wished he were one.

"Come on girls, a drink for the gentleman!" Fingers roared and snapped his or her fingers in a complex way Winston could not quite follow. Immediately, four stunningly beautiful nymphettes shot to attention. They stood in a row facing him, teeheeing and swaying like cheerleaders at halftime. Beneath their translucent crepe smocks Winston briefly eyed their firm breasts bobbing up and down to the rhythm of their innocent sounding laughter, but he did not feel at leisure to gawk. Not at all. In no time, they had fetched him a chair, a drink and some food, and before he had a chance to document both the motion and the change of altitude, he was sitting opposite Fingers on a raised platform, potentate and impotentate, a drink in his hand, a warm girl on his lap and surrounded by a sea of merrymakers, many of them, to his great displeasure, gaping at him with interest.

The girl on his lap was tickling his ear with a flirty finger, but all that fidgeting was patently irritating Winston.

"Shoo! Can't you see he doesn't like you?" Fingers scolded and swatted the girl off Winston's lap with a long peacock feather, whereupon she landed on the blubbery girth of a female creature with sores on her lips, a spider who immediately snapped at the pretty little fly, rapidly secreting her in the folds of her flesh where she began vampirizing her, the girl managing to emit but a few muffled screams.

My fault, Winston might have protested, but he was unable to utter a word.

"Well darling, let's drink to something practical. Your health, for example!" Fingers batted an eyelid coquettishly and raised a can of beer, clutched tightly in all six digits, high

into the air. Winston watched that hand with enduring fascination.

He was smiling weakly. What else could he do? And he
hoped the content of his glass was only wine. Meanwhile Fingers chugalugged his or her beer in what seemed to be a single gulp, then guffawed and sprayed those nearby—except for
Winston—with beer and laughter before tossing off the empty
can which ricocheted off the forehead of a bearded biker who
laughed dully.

"Do you know why I've got the biggest sissybar in the
world, sweetie?" Fingers giggled.

Winston was afraid to ask.

"Because, haha, because I'm the biggest sissy in the
world!!" He or she yucked uproariously, and that laughter was echoed by deep thundering guffaws resonating from
the other red-faced celebrants.

Well, you've met your match in me, Winston was thinking
though too frightened to share this bit of irony.

"So tell us, hon," Fingers said, after the laughter died
down, his or her hands cupped around his or her crossed, blue-
jeaned knee, "What exactly do you want from us?"

Instantaneous silence, the kind that needs a chisel to break.
All eyes and ears were waiting for Winston to speak. Not
a breath to be heard. "I . . . I . . . don't want a-anything,"
his meek answer. How could he say what he *really* wanted?
"You're the one . . . who . . . wanted to see . . . me." He was
relieved to have found those words at least.

"Of course, sweetie, of course! How could I have forgotten. He's cute, isn't he girls? And what a *big* one says my
radar!"

A low hungry growl rose up from among the merrymakers.
Winston could feel their eyes burning holes in his clothes. He
pressed his knees together and crossed his hands over his lap
as if fearing for his innocence. Could it be that they *all* knew

his problem? What if they made him . . . take his clothes off? Or stared at it? Or laughed at it? O God, he would die! He was feeling helplessly transparent. "Why did you want to see . . . me?" he peeped.

"Well, actually, I didn't *want* to see you, sweets, but now that I have, I can give you . . . one . . . gooood . . . reason." Fingers winked and blew a kiss in Winston's direction.

That did it. Winston's lower extremities immediately turned to jello. He was feeling as wobbly as the red stuff he'd caught a glimpse of on the nearby serving table, and now, he was fearing the worst. Something dreadful was going to happen. He was sure. Ugh. Just then he heard strange groaning sounds in a far corner of the room and turned to look . . . Oh my God! Two people were . . . doing it! Actually doing . . . IT! Winston had never seen other people . . . in the *act* (except in Doctor Becker's holograms), and he grew as red as the interior decorations around him. He wanted to turn his head away—embarrassed that others might recognize his curiosity—but for the life of him he couldn't take his eyes off of them. Seeing pictures of things like *that* was one thing, but *real* people—that was different. Mesmerizing. They were bumping around rapidly and making moaning sounds. He was hypnotized. They, by the way, were an unwashed (at least from his looks) fat biker with a week's growth of beard, wrap-around sun-glasses over his eyes, a leather vest, heavy boots and filthy dungarees, rolled down to his knees, and a serving girl, one of those pretty, nymphetic creatures. He had mounted her from behind. Her smock thrown over her shoulders, and Winston's attention was homing in on the lovely roundness of her hips and buttocks tapering at her slender waist. From time to time the biker's red ithyphallus slipped into view. Winston was awed by its dimensions. As for the girl, whose breasts strained downwards as if she were a she-wolf, she had an angel face, twisted now, grimacing. Was that pain or pleasure? They were pumping rapidly. The sounds exiting that angelic throat were gritty and loud. Why, she seemed to be having . . . an orgasm! Surely, that's what it was, Winston assessed. She was blubbering indiscernible syllables, hurling herself against the biker forcefully, groaning and then crying out even louder as if electrified. Then at last, she collapsed to her elbows while continuing to moan. Meanwhile, he was still going at IT, huffing and puffing, pushing and shoving, grunting hard and fast, and look, could it be? Had she reached yet another climax? Two in a row? Because, yes, she was wailing again, louder this time, crashing buttocks to groin rhythmically and faster still, so that sparks began shooting about the room like fireworks, and soon all and sundry were infected by the explosions and grabbing randomly at neighboring bodies or passing servants, phalluses shooting out like switchblades, buttocks and female genitals opening like flowers, serving girls and serving boys yanked down, swallowed by the masses, the air smelling of salad oil, sex juices, sweat and excrement; mammoth dykes, dildos strapped strategically to warm stimulated clefts, greased to mazola slickness, riding up and down on white thighed teens, genitals proffered like furry little animals, servant boys (specially selected for their proportions) engaging the oral appetites of red-faced bikers, beards scraping against red, irritated, hairless bellies or pushed into pungent saggy skinned, aging orifices, hysterical laughter, heads sloshing, white firm rear-ends flexing and dimpling, flexing and dimpling, faster and faster, and there two large-membered toothless scarfaced bikers consuming each other unabashed; and then Winston's buggering eyes began focusing on a lone figure, her back to him, beautiful, slender waist, rounded flowering hips, lovely tapered legs and ankles, smooth skinned, hair rippling down her back, serving girl image, in total solitude, a cat o' nine-tails in her hand, and she was flagellating herself, cackling, flagellating, cackling.

Winston is shivering, fixated on her, fascinated, not knowing what to do, not daring to do what he might have liked to do, a hint of sexual desire suddenly warming his belly, yes, warming HIS belly, his eyes fixed on her and continuing to be fixed on her as the room is transformed into one seemingly unified slime of mucous membranes and swollen sexual parts and moaning and crying, sperm shooting past his eyes like rockets on the Fourth of July. He wasn't aware *it* could travel such distances—the smell of ammonia and sex. And then a glob lands on his hand. O horrors! Sperm! O unwanted intimacy! How disgusting! Unable to move, not knowing what to do now. He can't touch it, and he can't stand it. Sperm, slimy stranger secretion, viscous, slithering warm over his hand, an amoeba, and he is frightened of it, helpless, as if death itself had crash-landed on the back of his hand. And then, that lone, lovely figure, rhythmically flagellating herself turns towards him. Stepping over gyrating, shimmying bodies, approaching Winston. She is the ugliest woman he has ever seen. Her features are boney, angular, hairs sprouting from her nose and chin. Her breasts are flat, milkless, empty pockets, hanging lifeless against her bony chest. Her naval is sunken and hollow, and her labia hang down like bat wings. She smiles at Winston. It's a broad smile, full of longing. She is missing teeth, and the corners of her eyes explode into avenues of crow's feet. She takes his hand, the hand on which the sperm is beginning to liquify and licks it up. Her tongue is milky white and slimy. She smiles at him again, her lips are chapped, and she says to him, "I am lonely," whispering those words, inaudible to the others. Winston hears them but doesn't want to believe what he is hearing. He smiles back nervously, flushing. He wants to run away, but where to? His heart has almost stopped beating. "I am lonely," she repeats. His head is a jumble of frightened thoughts colliding like a crowd panicking in a burning theater. She is still touching his hand; and he is afraid and disgusted. Her hand is cold and skeletal, and he is afraid she will steal his soul or want him or need him and never let him go. He is afraid she will continue telling him that she is lonely, that he is lonely. What if she DID need him, and what if he needed *her*? She is so ugly. Oh, and ugliness can never free me from loneliness. Winston pulled back his arm, freeing it from her grip. A wave of guilt washed over him. A wave of fear. A wave of relief. A storm of waves. He did not know what to feel anymore. She grinned sardonically, just standing there, not moving, just staring at him. He was nervous, paralyzed. Meanwhile, the orgiastic tremor around them was gradually dying down, the smell of sweat predominating now over all other odors. The decibel rate drifted back to a normal level. She was grinning still, an inscrutable look, and Winston could not escape her eyes no matter how he tried.

"Come, come, Doreen, sweetie, can't you see that Winette doesn't want to play. How often must I tell you, hon, you can't force people to like you." Fingers came back into focus, still enthroned above the crowd. Not participant but watcher, he or she leaning towards Winston, the space between them reduced to a crack. "Honestly, Winette, I see you've got a real serious streak. Well, no matter. That's why you're here in the first place."

Doreen was slinking off with sunken head, and Winston— how surprised he was—thought his heart might break. Tears were welling up. Cry in public? No, not that. *Please* not that!

"Nasty children, aren't they, hon? Really, sometimes I think all they have in their heads is nonsense. All right girls, button up your play suits. It's time to . . ." Fingers stopped in mid-sentence, face turning red as if he or she had gagged on something or was having a seizure or had been befallen by some terrible cramp. "Oh! Oh! Oh!" he or she was gripping the upholstered arms of the chair as if for dear life.

"Is there anything . . ." Winston was asking discreetly but clearly with genuine concern . . .

"Oh! Oh! Oh! Oh girls! I feel . . . I feel . . . I feel . . . a P O E M coming on. I can't stop it. Oh! Oh! Oh . . . it's (pant, pant), it's (pant) it's oh, it's . . . CO-O-O-ming . . ."

> Don't underestimate wishes,
> they're inscrutable mutable things.
> They never let go,
> not a thousand times, no,
> though one begs and bargains and sings.
> A friend of mine once had the need
> to fondle a chimpanzee.
> He prayed to escape
> from this lust for an ape
> till he met the chimp of his dreams.
> Now he lives in the jungle
> in simian marital bliss.
> He swings on a vine
> from five until nine
> and comes home to a sweet hairy kiss.
> But this I'm afraid's the exception,
> the one to every rule,
> for sadly I say,
> when wishers get their way
> they're doomed to play the fool.
> O how clean you would feel,
> If you could glean what is real
> and be rid of those wishes you hid
> and know what they actually mean . . .

"Oh dear. Oh dear!" Fingers raised his or her palms to his or her smooth fat cheeks, pressing them and shaking that large round head from side to side so that the curly black locks bobbed about like so many cork-screws. The long fringes on the sleeves of his or her black leather jacket gyrated like Christmas tree tinsel in the wind, and the ample flesh beneath seemed to be doing the same. "I'm getting so philosophical! I'm going to have to stop right this second before I ruin everything! Don't you think, girls?"

Snickers and giggles rose up from tangles of spent bodies, stretched out like seals on a beach at Fingers' and Winston's feet.

"Heavens to Betsy!" Now Fingers placed a six-fingered hand over his or her mouth in what seemed to be an expression of dismay, "I've almost forgotten! Look, Winette, d'ya remember asking me if there was some reason I wanted to see you? Well, there is, hon. I DO have something to tell you. Dear me, how could it have slipped my mind! And now we won't be able to have any more fun this evening. Oooh, what a shame, because, well, I was just getting to like you. Sigh. Yes, I do have something for you: a message from Headquarters . . ."

"Headquarters?" Winston palely.

"Oh sweetie, don't you worry your pretty little head. It's just that those sillies down at Headquarters want to see you . . . and pronto. Here." Now Fingers fumbled in a pocket and handed Winston a paper slip.

Winston scanned it quickly. What he saw was a phone number . . . and that symbol again:

"You just call this number, hon, and you'll get your instructions."

Winston was not concentrating on numbers. That wave of anticipation was back. For he knew he was getting closer to solving the mystery.

"Are you with or without, hon?"

"What do you mean?" his voice defensive.

"Wheels, silly!" Fingers flapped his or her wrist limply.

"My car's parked in Hollywood near a bar called the Bird's Nest."

"Ooooh, that rat's nest! I hope a nasty midget didn't say bad things about me?"

"Only that he didn't know you." Hmm, talking to strangers was getting easier.

"Well, *that's* bad enough, don't you think? Anyway, sweetie, Iris here," Fingers pointed to a man as conventionally dressed as Winston, an inconspicuous figure Winston had not noticed before, "Iris will drive you back to your car. Then, you go call up the girls down at Headquarters. And listen, anytime you like, you just come visit us, okeedokee? Right, girls?"

A chorus of goony voices roared out in assent.

"And remember, Winette, if there's anything you really want, all you have to do is *ask* for it."

Winston followed Iris out a backdoor he had somehow overlooked. He was feeling like a character in a fairy tale. Indeed, he was having such a good time, he was hoping this adventure would not end just yet, even if it did seem full of uncertainties . . . and—who knows?—perhaps dangers to come!? One thing he was sure of: he still did not understand *what* they wanted from him. Had Fingers just given him advice? Did he look like he needed advice? But now he tossed caution to the wind and followed his latest guide, Iris, into a waiting car.

❊ ❊ ❊

" I still don't understand," said Winston, streets whizzing by in a blur, "Is Fingers, well, a he or a she?"

"There's a lot you don't understand, Mr. Hewlett," Iris's gaze was fixed on the road, "So why not that too?"

"Yes, but, oh, how should I put it? I mean, what does Fingers have, well, you know, under his kilt?"

"I know what you mean, Mr. Hewlett, but there's only one way to find out."

"How?"

"You've got to look."

"Ugh. No thanks."

Iris shrugged. There was silence.

"Have you looked?"

"What if I have, would that give you a better idea?"

Winston stifled a response. He saw it was useless.

"If I gave you an answer, you wouldn't believe it anyway," said Iris.

"Try me." Winston sounding dauntless and enjoying the feeling.

"Soon enough, Mr. Hewlett."

✻ ✻ ✻

Night was several hours old when Iris dropped Winston off near the Bird's Nest. The tinsel had faded on Hollywood Boulevard, and the street was baring its tired face without make-up. A sea breeze funneled down the street tossing litter into a swirl. There was a slight chill in the air. As Winston watched Iris drive off, he felt something like nostalgia, as if the party was over. His eyes were following the car as it faded beyond a distant street-light. Then he moved on. Now what? Was his adventure over? Had he reached a dead-end?

He was still clasping the slip of paper with the telephone number of Headquarters, contemplating it like a souvenir from an exotic vacation. Should he call? Or should he just drive home and enjoy the memories of an extraordinary day? Increasingly, he was thinking that not even the Empire of Chaos could solve his problem.

As he was mulling over plan A and plan B, his feet had already made a decision independent of the rest of him! They were heading resolutely towards a nearby telephone-booth, his hand reaching into a pocket for a coin. 'What the hell.' Those were the words that floated into consciousness, followed then by a silent playful chuckle . . . and that was the moment *they* grabbed him from behind. Someone was pressing a damp, cold cloth against his mouth and nose, holding it firmly in place. No possibility of resisting. His world was turning grey and white, and the grogginess set in within seconds. Sweet noxious vapors, nothing pleasant about that smell, and off he dropped into blankness, barely noticing that he was sinking.

It was day when he awoke, probably drifting from a drugged sleep into natural slumber with no transition. His head was throbbing, and he felt hungover. A whirring sound filled his ears. His mouth was dry, and he was feeling queasy. He opened his eyes and the world started coming into focus: a reduced world, an empty room, maybe seven by ten feet, the ceiling low, the walls metallic. Like being in a box. In one corner there was a steel chest which seemed to be riveted to the floor, in another a heap of rags. Behind him were two small windows, cheap frilly curtains over them. The light entering through the curtains was diffuse and grey.

Moreover, and this puzzled him as he was coming to his senses: the room was vibrating. At first, he suspected his own body was the source of that quavering, but no, that wasn't it. Was it on a conveyor belt? On a track? Floating on water?

All this, of course, perceptions of a fogged mind. As the grogginess abated, he rose, intending to approach the window. "Ow!" He banged his head against the low ceiling. With shoulders hunched, he went to the window and pulled the curtains aside. Aha! Now everything was clear. He was in what seemed to be a camper or Winnebago, roaring down the San

Diego Freeway at around 60 mph. The sky was blue, cars were pulling by at high speeds that seemed like slow motion. Relativity, of course. Gas station masts loomed from behind shrubbery. What is going on? Where were they taking him? *They?*

By now he was fully conscious and perceived the swelter. Stifling. No fresh air. He rattled the door handles of this prison in motion, but they were locked. And even if he had been able to jar them open, he most certainly would not have leapt onto the freeway at 60 mph. Waving for help would have been equally fruitless. This was Los Angeles, and he knew how *he* would react if he saw someone waving at him frantically from the rear of a Winnebago.

He sat on the steel chest above the left rear tire, his only furniture. The heat was growing intolerable, and he opened the top buttons of his shirt like the QUID PRO QUO people did, though he was sure he could not pass for one of them. That's when he noticed that his WINSTON name tag was still in place on his jacket pocket. At least I'm still me.

Then something like a groaning became audible. What was it? The creaking of metal? Whatever it was, it was growing louder and more treble in pitch. It seemed to be coming from under the pile of rags, old blankets, oily shirts and scraps of assorted cloth. A ghost? He didn't believe in ghosts. But the whining intensified. Hopefully nothing wrong with the brakes or the wheels. And then . . . could it be? Was that heap of rags . . . moving?!

Panic! Inexplicable, irrational, like when a large hairy spider suddenly skitters over your feet. The fear of fear invading every cell. He started, instinctively fleeing to the point furthest from the source of menace. Shallow panting.

Again movement, a loud smacking sound, a groan. "Oooooooooh!" moaned the pile of rags.

"Aaaaaaaaah!!" ululated Winston.

"Ooooooh!" groaned the rags.

"Aaaaaah!!" Winston cried out, half embarrassed by his hysteria.

Panic of course is always short lived. Everyone knows that—or should—including Winston who now began analyzing this odd situation . . . yes, rationally. When you have nothing to lose, you fight—or at least you look. Anyway, what demons would be fool enough to hide under a heap of stinking rags? Now he approached those rags, first cautiously and then boldly! And then he tossed them aside defiantly. Yes, he wanted to get to the bottom of this mystery.

"Why . . . Doctor Pentius!"

The Doctor resembled a fetus in a jar, still in his dusty orange jumpsuit and smelling of those rags he had been buried under, his knees drawn up to his chest. He was cupping a pipe, the one Leland Hewlett had once given him, broken in body but not in spirit. He looked up at Winston, first weakly . . . and then . . . a toothy smile cracking across his gnarly old face, and his eyes illuminating, "Why Winston! What a nice surprise!!" The voice wearied quickly, and the Doctor closed his eyes as if asleep. He was breathing with some effort. After a few moments posing as eternity, he opened his eyes again. "Still on the trail, eh, my boy?" he muttered drowsily. "Good for you! I guess I underestimated you. You're a chip off the old block after all!"

Winston helped the Doctor into a sitting position, propping him against a wall like a truss of arrows with poisoned tips. The whirr and whoosh of traffic was filling their ears. The world was nearly back in focus.

"Oh, my head," said the Doctor, "I think I have to lie down again.

"Can I do anything?" Winston was crouching beside him.

"No, no, my boy, it'll pass. It's just the after-effects of the ether. Nasty stuff."

Ether. Aha.

Silence. Two soldiers on the way to the front. Then Winston rose, this time careful to duck his head, and began pacing. He pushed the curtains aside.

"Relax, Winston. Save your energy."

"Just look at all that traffic! Just imagine the smog it's causing. What a horrible town!"

"You're talking like a typical Barbareño." There was some color in the Doctor's face again.

"Where do you think they're taking us? I have the feeling we've been driving in circles for hours."

"You may be right, my boy." The Doctor was fondling his pipe. "If my theory is correct, this vehicle is from their smog division. That metal chest in the corner is filled with a potent mixture of lead, cadmium and other heavy metals, in concentrations, if my sources are correct, hundreds of times more toxic than in ordinary exhaust fumes. They've got hundreds of these campers, posing as Winnebagos, on the road pumping poison into the air to slowly strangle our air supply. Pure evil, my boy."

"How do you know that?"

"I have been researching *them* for years. There's a lot more I know as well . . . for example, how they murdered your father." The Doctor's eyes had regained their familiar vehemence. "It was the air-conditioning."

Likewise, Winston's skepticism had returned, but the Doctor didn't notice that.

"A vile and pernicious instrument of destruction, Winston. They installed a device in the air-conditioning that vibrates at a frequency of exactly seven Hertz. Do you know what that means? Seven vibrations a second is a wave-length that interacts directly with theta wave signals in the human brain. At low intensity, it interferes with concentration and disturbs sleep patterns. Turn up the volume, and it will convert a brain into pudding. Increase the amplitude any higher and you can destroy entire cities, continents—the entire planet!"

Aha! That's what they did to my potency! But that thought Winston kept to himself.

"Now I expect you understand the urgency of our mission."

"*Our mission?*"

"Of course. Don't you understand? They've taken the bait. We are not THEIR prisoners. They are OURS!"

This time, the Doctor did take note of Winston's skeptical expression.

"Winston, people like you and I were born to be outsiders. It's our fate. Our challenge!"

Winston's eyes were fixed on his.

"Life can get lonely when you battle for the truth, Winston, very lonely, and yet, without heroic action it loses its meaning."

The Doctor was waiting for a reaction. Winston was looking deeply into that tired old face across from him. The jowls were drooping in a dumpy kind of way. And finally Winston did speak: "Look, I'm a pretty good-natured guy on the whole, and I also know that lots of people think that means I'm an easy touch, but frankly, Doctor Pentius, I don't buy what you're saying."

A shadow crossed the Doctor's face, like when a cloud passes in front of the sun, sadness filling the Doctor's eyes. Winston looked so tall, maybe for the first time. "Then, why are you . . . here?"

"Because . . ." Winston had to muster up all of his courage, "Because of my . . . impotence."

"Wouldn't it have been easier to seek professional help?"

"Live and learn," Winston shrugged. Why was he feeling sorry for the Doctor?

"But, your father . . ." Larez Pentius had barely spoken those words when it occurred to him, the psychiatrist, that he had just used the wrong tactic.

"My father!" Winston's voice was resonating at at least seven very loud vibrations a second. "My father! Damn him! Damn him! Damn him!" Suddenly he was kicking the walls of the camper in time to the litany of damns so that the vehicle began quavering like a Chinese gong. "Damn! Damn! Damn!"

God, what an amateur I've turned out to be, the Doctor was thinking.

Winston was not letting up. Something in him was feeling good, and he wasn't about to stop. "Damn! Damn! Damn!"

Larez Pentius grew invisible, as any mental health professional might at such a moment.

And then, suddenly, Winston went silent. He grew fiercely attentive. The Doctor too cocked his ears. Briefly, their eyes met conspiratorially. Something was happening. The Winnebago was slowing down. Winston drew back the curtain. "Look! We've left the freeway! I think we're going to stop!"

"They're probably wondering about the ruckus," said the Doctor.

"Now's our chance to escape!" Winston grabbed Larez Pentius by the arm.

The Doctor gazed at him, wide-eyed, even sympathetically, but silent. He knew he was dealing with a Winston he was unfamiliar with, a man who would make his own choices.

Winston too was reading the Doctor's thoughts. "You don't want to escape?"

The Doctor shook his head.

"Why not?"

"Let's put it this way, my boy. I've made it this far; I wouldn't want to miss what happens next."

Winston shrugged his shoulders. And then the vehicle came to a stop. They heard the cabin doors opening and the sound of footsteps. A key clicked into the lock.

"This is your chance, my boy." The Doctor was smiling broadly.

Winston smiled back. Yes, they had made their peace. He focused on the doors as they swung open. A shock of California daylight filled the cabin. In a nonce, he was soaring through the air, his large frame kicking down two figures standing in his way. "UFF!" He had taken them by surprise. In an instant Winston was yards away. "Love to Virginia!" Larez Pentius called out, and Winston heard no more.

He was running ferociously, a human locomotive but somehow off track, when it finally dawned on him that the thugs he had just stampeded over ... were wearing costumes! More precisely: they were dressed like Beagle Boys, those masked jailbirds he remembered from Mickey Mouse comics. An odd thought. Well, maybe not, because now he saw where he was: in a parking lot at DISNEYLAND and heading for what seemed to be the main entrance, a pale, flat tinsel backdrop under the hot midday Anaheim sun. He looked back briefly. The Beagle Boys were locking the doors of their camper—Larez Pentius obviously still within—and then they began pursuing him! He raced unwaveringly towards the ticket booth.

TWENTY-ONE

VIRGINIA WAS CONTEMPLATING the room with calm curiosity, her eyes moving from object to object, focusing on something, then continuing to the next. Nothing out of the ordinary: a music stand, a drafting table, two armchairs, plants, a sewing basket, a daybed, daybed, daybed. Yes, she recognized the pattern on that slip-cover. Gladiola was standing at attention studying her unexpected guest with cautious interest. Their eyes had still not locked, and Virginia had no playbook, no plan of attack. Anyway, at this point, words seemed superfluous, and she saw no reason to make a scene. She did however sense her advantage thanks to the element of surprise. She was also aware that nothing could go wrong. "Nice apartment," she said graciously, smiling in Gladiola's direction. Gladiola smiled back, perhaps a little sheepishly. Finally, the two women began exploring each other directly, head to toe examinations as well as deep into the eyes. Virginia was wearing an elegant—and tasteful—pantsuit; Gladiola was feeling practically naked in her T-shirt and short shorts and considered that a disadvantage. I must start considering how I dress, she was thinking.

"Won't you sit down?" Gladiola said politely. Virginia nodded benevolently and lowered herself into a nearby easy chair, folding her hands on her lap. She was silent. Gladiola sat across from her, straight-backed at the edge of the daybed, waiting for the unknown.

A pretty girl, Virginia was thinking, intelligent, polite, well-bred, cultivated. "At least my husband has good taste," her voice serene, a hint of sympathy and a portion of triumph.

There was a long silence, but it wasn't icy.

"I suppose I should get to the point, though perhaps you are already aware. The truth be said, I've known about you and Winston for some time, my dear, but I preferred not to interfere, that is, till now."

Gladiola nodded painfully, like a little girl who had been caught doing something naughty; she was also relieved. She eyed Virginia's self-assurance with fascination.

"Winston, as you've probably observed, is not very good at keeping secrets, nor is he, as I'm also sure you've noticed, a very orderly person. He leaves his sketchbooks anywhere and everywhere for all to see. At first, I ignored them. To be honest, I was not particularly interested in what he was drawing. Then one day, I decided that I *should* take an interest in his hobby, that he would appreciate that. That's when I discovered the reams of sketches he had made of you in the most . . . *varied* . . . poses. In fact, I became quite familiar with this room through those drawings." She gestured broadly and with dignity. "I will admit; his skills surprised me . . . positively. He really does have talent—though frankly, if you don't mind me saying this, I think you are prettier in real life, softer in my opinion, than in his renditions." Gladiola blushed. "Mind you, it wasn't the sketches that got me thinking. All artists have fantasies, and why shouldn't he be free to give form to his? It was when I found drawings in his sketchbooks that *you* had made of *him* that I began suspecting that something was . . . out of the ordinary. Your drawings are quite good. My compliments. It was, shall we say, the *nature* of the poses that led me to believe that sketching was not the only interest you shared."

"Mrs. Hewlett . . ." Gladiola interrupted.

" . . . No, no. Please let me continue. You'll have plenty of opportunity to talk. You see, once I got over my initial shock, frankly, I had nothing against your . . . affair. I figured maybe Winston needed something like that now. He'd become so irritable, and I imagined a little adventure might be beneficial for a man drifting into midlife. And so, whenever he said he was going out to do some 'sketchin',' I was happy for him. You look so incredulous. But believe it or not, I *too* was a beneficiary of your trysting. He would come home relaxed and friendly. All in all, we were getting along much better.

"But then something started changing again. He was growing moody. He'd ignore me. Something was disturbing him, and I didn't know what. It was nothing I could put my finger on, that is, until it occurred to me that he, well, must have fallen in love with you."

Gladiola's eyes widened. "In *love* with me?"

"You look skeptical. But really, it was the only explanation for his change in behavior I could come up with. I imagined he was caught up in some awful conflict of interests. By then, unfortunately, I was feeling too insecure to confront him with the facts directly. And, to be honest, I was afraid he was going to leave me. And I didn't want that. Sometimes, I'd hear him on the telephone: 'Hello, Gladiola, how 'bout some sketchin'?' It was not difficult for me to guess what he meant by that."

Gladiola smirked bashfully.

"I felt him slipping away, and I was too powerless to do anything. And so I decided to write him a note . . . anonymously, mind you . . . that's how vulnerable I was feeling. It was silly of course, but I didn't know what else to do. I wrote two words on a small card and was foolish enough to believe that would bring him to his senses: *drop it.* I slipped that message into an envelope and mailed it to him."

"*You* wrote that note!?"

"And I regret I did. Because I think the shock somehow made him . . . impotent . . . at least at home . . ." She eyed Gladiola interrogatively.

"Yes, the same," Gladiola nodded, "but . . ."

" . . . And then he began raving about some secret sect and some plot to destroy the world and God knows what. I still don't understand how those two words . . . I just wanted him to get the message as obliquely as possible. Which is why I didn't write 'drop her', imagining he might figure out the note was from me. Trying to avoid confrontation is often a mistake . . ."

"But why . . ." Gladiola interrupted, ". . . why did you use that . . . *symbol* in your note?"

"I suppose he ranted about that too. It's all so ridiculous. You see, after I had written those two words, I wanted to end my message with a period, but I thought that would look silly after the 'it' and maybe weaken the effect. Three dots didn't seem right either. Too mysterious or vague, I thought. So I placed the period below the words, I guess for emphasis. Probably an exclamation mark would have been better. Anyway, that period looked lost there, and so I added two dots below it to form a triangle. But I still wasn't satisfied, and so I added another row with three dots and finally a fourth row with four—I guess for the symmetry. Then I decided that was enough."

"Mrs. Hewlett, I know there's no way to apologize for the suffering I've caused you . . ."

"Dear girl, I didn't come here for an apology. I just wanted to get to know you. I was very curious."

"But I owe you one, and I guess you ought to know, I did fall in love with Winston. Though maybe love is not the right word. Maybe I was addicted to him. I needed him. You see, when I came to Santa Barbara, I had no one. I was lonely. Then I met Winston in that figure drawing class. He was good-natured and easy to talk to. I knew he was married, but I never intended to take him away from you. I suppose that after a while I did figure out that Winston was using me, just the way you imagined, but once I did, I ended the relationship. And now I regret it ever began at all."

"Please don't blame yourself, my dear. I just wanted to, well, clear the air. Things happen. Those are the facts, but it's all ancient history now. People make mistakes. When I was younger than you, I made a mistake I have never stopped regretting. It was so painful that I have never shared it with anyone—not even Winston. I was always too ashamed. But I'm going to tell it to you. Somehow, I like you very much, and I trust you. I guess I'm just like you. I too need a friend. I need to tell someone . . . finally. You see, when I was sixteen, I got pregnant and had a baby. Can you imagine? I was a child having a child, and I didn't know who to turn to. In those days, finding someone to sympathize with a situation like that was very difficult. The world was different, and my parents have always been, well, what you might call 'Bible beaters.' They would have imagined some union with the devil. And then, all by myself, in my room—my parents had gone out to a meeting, which was my luck—I delivered my baby myself, a little girl. I was terrified, but I had gone to the library and read up about how it's done. I've always liked to read. Thank God there were no complications. But do you know what I did then?" Tears were visible in Virginia's eyes, and her voice began to break. "I washed her and dressed her in a tiny pajama I had bought for the occasion. Then, I put her into a basket, pinned a note to the blanket and deposited her in front of a church—not the one my parents attended. God knows, she may have died of exposure! I abandoned a newborn baby to fend for herself!" Virginia's mouth was tightening, a final attempt to suppress the sobs that were no longer suppressible.

But now Gladiola's voice was cracking too, and her eyes were turning very liquid. The words came out shakily, "Was it in Woodland Hills?"

"Yes," Virginia nodded, weeping, "But how did you know?!"

"In a basket like this one?" Gladiola was blubbering.

Virginia took a very long look at Gladiola's sewing basket.

"Did the note say 'Give this baby a good home'? And did you put the same symbol on it like on Winston's note?"

Virginia continued nodding, her mind knotting up out of control.

"MAMA!!"

"MY BABY?"

The two women locked eyes, and for one instant time and space disappeared. They fell into each other's arms and embraced long, tears flowing amply, kissing, caressing heads, arms, shoulders, backs, sobbing loudly and laughing—all in a complex unity of voice and body. "Mama!" Gladiola cried out again and again, and Virginia rocked her in her arms.

"My baby! How often I have dreamt of this moment," she was whispering sweetly.

It took a while for the two women to regain their composure, and when they did, they were both sitting on the floor holding hands. Yes, there was much to talk about . . .

"It was at summer camp," Virginia was explaining, "That's where it happened."

"And you really delivered me by yourself?"

Virginia nodded. "I was terribly frightened. I thought I would die or that you would die. You were such a pretty baby." She started crying again.

"But I don't understand. How did you manage to conceal a pregnancy?"

"Well dear," Virginia was smiling, "I've had slimmer days, but when I don't watch my diet, I always tend to land on the thicker side of thin. I wore muumuus all the time. Back then they were all the fashion in the San Fernando Valley." Now Virginia took hold of a bare leg and examined Gladiola's ankle. "Thank God you inherited your father's ankles. Take a look at these." She raised a pant leg. "See. Piano legs!"

Father? "Who *was* my father?"

"I'm sorry to say, there's not much I can tell you. His name was Tony, at least that's what I called him. We met at Bible Camp. He was seventeen and had bushy dark hair. He was such a serious boy, and I had a terrible crush on him . . ."

"Dark hair? Your hair is dark too. How can I be blond?"

"Runs in the family on my mother's side . . . One night, Tony and I pirated a rowboat and paddled out to the middle of Bear Lake. And that's when it happened. I don't know why or how anymore. But the very next day, his parents came and took him home. They didn't think the camp was right for him, something about it not being intellectually challenging enough. I never saw him again, and I never found out his last name. I only remember that he was very romantic and very polite. I'm sure you inherited very good genes."

TWENTY-TWO

"**O**NE PLEASE!" The words were addressed to the blond woman behind the cashier's window, her hair ratted and stringy. There was urgency in his voice. Before him a turnstile . . . which seemed to be his only escape route.

"One what?" The words slipped lazily from the painted red lips, not a shimmer of compassion in her green eyes. A look of boredom. It was clear that she had been waiting for someone like Winston, someone in a hurry.

"One ticket! One ticket!"

"Adult, junior or child?" her tone blasé, her painted countenance vacant and cold.

"Adult! Adult!" Winston caught on quickly what this was about and was sorry he couldn't come up with a smart-alecky answer that might irritate her the rest of the day. Unfortunately, he had no time for that. A brief glance back: the two Beagle Boys were tramping across the parking lot like an army. Moreover, he had his first real glimpse of them, and were they ever big!

"Simple admission, Big 11 or Deluxe 15?" Sales patter rattled off mechanically, her lips barely moving.

"Please, all I want is a ticket!" Too late. Winston immediately regretted that he'd said *please*. Now she really knew she had him.

"Simple admission is $4.50," she continued eyes half closed, hands fidgeting with a ticket book. (To be fair: she was barely aware of the sadistic pleasure sweeping through her extremities). "With a Big 11, you get one "A" coupon, one "B" coupon, two "C" coupons, three "D" coupons and four "E" coupons. An $11.15 value for only $6.00. With a Deluxe 15, you get one "A" two "B's," three "C's," four "D's" and five "E's." A $13.35 value for only $7.00. Is this your first visit to Disneyland?"

Now he noted that she bit her fingernails. "Yes! Yes!" The Beagle Boys were closing the gap.

"Then I would suggest a Big 11 for starters." Her voice was sounding cheerful and helpful. Something like a smile unfurled over her lips.

"Okay! Okay!"

"What'll it be then? The Big 11?"

"Yes, yes!"

"That'll be $6.00, please."

He fumbled in his pocket and fished out a ten dollar bill which he slapped on the counter. The counter girl snapped it up like a dog getting a treat, pushed a ticket book in his direction and began counting out his change. But Winston had already grabbed the tickets and was dashing into the park.

"Hey!" she called after him, "Your change!" No response. Winston had already faded into Main Street U.S.A. without looking back. He was too distracted to think about change. She shrugged and shook her head as if indicating to the person next on line that that guy who'd just ran off was crazy, and then she pocketed the money.

Main Street U.S.A. was packed with a dense milling crowd, and Winston did his best to avoid head-on collisions. The general pace was slow. and soon he too was trying his hand at conforming and blending in, though he was most definitely a visitor from another dimension. Deftly he weaved through masses of flesh, past the Guided Tour Garden, the Disneyland City Hall, the Information Center, cutting a path (as unaggressively as possible) through the gaps between the warm bodies and scents. "Hey! Don't push!" someone chided.

From time to time, he'd glance back, checking whether his pursuers were still on the trail. And then he saw them entering the park, and if his eyes weren't playing tricks, it looked like they hadn't had to pay! There they were, inside the front gate, conversing with a group of Goofys and Mickeys and Donalds, all shaking hands, patting each other on the shoulders with familiarity. Yes, and you could see that those unshaven masked Beagle Boy faces were smiling. "Look out, you jerk!" a coachman in frock and top hat blurted out just loud enough for Winston alone to hear. "Whassamatter? Lookin' to get your puss stuck up a horse's ass?" Winston jumped out of the path of the horse drawn streetcar, then dodged a putt-puttering horseless carriage and whisked past a fire engine and an omnibus at the Disneyland RR Train Station, beyond the Penny Arcade and the Main Street Cinema where the Keystone Cops were playing round the clock, then down he went past the Town Square Cafe, the Carnation Ice Cream Parlor, the Sunkist Citrus House, the Coca Cola Refreshment Corner, where he crashed into a line of people waiting on line for Great Moments with Mr. Lincoln. He dodged the cannonade of cokes and french-fries, cotton candy and curses that followed and charged on, curving round the Mad Hatter Shop, Rings 'n' Things, the Glassblower, the Flower Market, the Hallmark Communication Center, the Silhouette Studio, the China Shop, jostling unexpectant passersby at every turn. His breathing was heavy, half from exhaustion, half from fear. He turned his head and saw that his pursuers were rapidly narrowing the gap. Why had no one noticed his plight? He took a sharp right and crossed the border into Tomorrowland.

The border between the two Lands was not clearly marked, and so only gradually did he determine that he was now in Tomorrowland where the milling crowds were equally dense as on Main Street U.S.A.. How dearly he wished he could have faded into that somnolent crowd and disappeared! But he was just too tall for that. He stood out everywhere, and now he was desperate for camouflage. It was then he caught sight of a vast, cordoned-off area where under a shaded awning winding rows of visitors were waiting patiently (or impatiently) for admission to some ride. He joined them and hoped the Beagle Boys would oversee him.

The queue kept lengthening behind him like some never-ending hungry serpent, the anticipatory excitement of the crowd growing ever louder, children chattering in high, hysterical staccatos; adults laughing and cracking silly jokes, anything to pass the time. Anyone who cared to analyze the makeup of that line would have recognized a veritable cross-section of the U.S. population: male, female, minorities, old, young, middle-aged, opulent and just-getting-by. Some had saved long for this day, others had deeper pockets, but all shared the same eager interest: to experience the thrill of this ride. To this end, they were prepared to wait in orderly, cordoned off rows, protected by a linen awning from the inimical Anaheim sun.

Winston may have looked as dull as the others, but his mind was a heavily trafficked freeway. He had still not identified what exciting adventure he and the crowd were waiting to experience. Indeed, he was just about to ask his neighbor that very question when he caught sight of *them*. Fear immediately began rippling beneath his skin. One Beagle Boy nudged the other, pointing menacingly towards Winston. They were smiling cruel smiles. Now they were in focus in their blue brimmed caps, black half-masks that covered the top half of their faces, blue trousers, red long-sleeved cotton pullovers, a prison-number on white background plastered across their chests, just like in the comics. Both were corpulent and unshaven, and their mouths had those same nasty expressions as in the comics. Only a few roped-off rows of hungering human-ity separated pursued from pursuers.

"Look, Mom, the Beagle Boys!" a small boy yelped excit-edly, pulling at his mother's arm and hopping up and down. He was a little fellow, maybe about eight, eyes wide open hun-gry for experience, and separated from Winston's pursuers by a single cordon. The Beagle Boys smiled benevolently at the youngster who with lightning speed kicked both in the shins. They were howling in pain.

"Marvin!" And the surprised mother slapped the boy matter-of-factly on the cheek and apologized to the Beagle Boys as they rubbed their shins, probably wondering whether the child had iron taps nailed to his shoes.

"Hooo!!" the boy wailed, "Whydja hit me?! Hoooo!! I was jus' gettin' back at em for what they did ta Unka Scrooge! Hooo!!"

Winston approved.

"Ya see," the man behind Winston, short-sleeved, pale hairy arms, saggy skin, sixtyish, was muttering to his wife, "It's just like I always tell ya. It's television. It makes em vio-lent."

"So whaddaya want?" said his wife, a red head with a polka-dot blouse, thin lipped, arms crossed, "Throw all the TV's out the window?

"For starters, why not?" He was jingling his keys.

The woman's expression was pained, and she waved a hand at him disparagingly. "And stop playing with your keys!"

"It's all staged," a young man with a scraggly beard sprout-ing inofficiously from his chin was telling his girlfriend, "all of it," his arm tightly gripping her waist.

"Even that?" Excitement and adulation in her voice.

"Uh huh. I read it somewhere."

"Hit em again! Hit em again!" some teenagers in chorus.

Then the line began moving, really moving, and the next thing he knew, Winston was handing someone a "C" ticket. "What ride *is* this?"

"Adventure thru Inner Space." The ticket-taker winked as if sharing a secret with him.

In a nonce, Winston was cupped into an acoustic shell, seat-belted and, lickety-split, conveyed into, yes, inner space; the cushioned shell in which he nestled chugging gently down an invisible track into palliative darkness.

For those, like Winston, who haven't experienced it: in the confines of *Inner Space*, voyagers pass progressively by and through a series of crisply illuminated polished polyethylene models representing atoms, each a power larger than its predecessor, until one is gradually dwarfed in the winding course of this "adventure" by the gigantism of these constructs feigning the most minute indivisibility in the material world. The space is cool and unemotional, and the models are pristine white. For Winston the experience was like wafting through the soothing molecules of a valium crystal. The speaker boxes in the acoustic shell emitted eerie pentatonic harmonies in whisper tones, and the shell glided effortlessly through the illusion of infinity, all motion nearly imperceptible.

Weightlessly, he was floating through the gaping monumental white girders representing invisibly miniscule atomic entities, bathed in utter black space, other monster atoms glowing in the distance, the illusion of something perceived. Willingly, Winston was relinquishing control over his body till he was a mere extension of his acoustic seat in a posture of eternity. Increasingly he ceased being a brain, existing solely as a pair of seeing eyes; and he was glad to be that. Maybe it was the music, or the darkness, or the coolness or all the above; whatever the cause, he was a happy denizen of this impersonal land where savoring the moment was all that was required of him.

You might say the laws of gravity no longer applied. If a voice had whispered to him, "Come, Winston, fly with me!" he would have followed, hesitantly perhaps, like someone leaping from a springboard for the first time, but he would have risked it and not have been surprised to discover he really *could* fly, like in dreams. Tall Winston was savoring his smallness, dwarfed by something minute, a pilgrim in a cosmic cathedral under an unvaulted ceiling, a lone traveler. It didn't occur to him that he was alone. That was good.

But alas, in space and time good things always come to an end, and soon the atoms began growing smaller, ever so imperceptibly at first, but ineluctably. Perceiving the loss, Winston's awe began deflating as well, and the memory of where he was and what he was escaping—namely, from two Beagle Boys who were probably on the lookout for him at the end of the track out there in the Anaheim sun—returned. Yes, he was reaching the end of the track, was about to be banished from the cool garden of oblivion, cast back into the finite. Serendipity was crumbling outwardly and within. How many "C" tickets did one need to reclaim that world as one's own? Did a cleaning crew enter this realm of superlatives at night, switch on a floodlight and scrub the stiff white particles till they were whiter than innocence?

Now the atoms were fist size, slick table models on black velvet, then, sparkling white marbles, then strewn salt. He was feeling the warm dry Southern California air scratching at his face. The shelled cocoons ahead had already vanished into daylight around a bend. The atoms had regained their invisibility and he his visibility. Shell by shell, Winston's fellow travelers (they too invisible till now) passed through the gateway that separated the worlds. Inevitability was the last station.

Winston was thrust into day. The light blinded him, but only briefly. With the instincts of the desperate, he located his assailants. They were standing at the foot of the steps by the exit like parents waiting for an eager child. He tensed up the way any threatened animal might, his eyes in partnership with his will to survive. A single flight of steps and six or seven fellow voyagers from Inner Space, all plodding lazily down those stairs, were all that separated him from the Beagle Boys.

Thought quickly turned to action. He reached out to the nearest back and shoved the mass of slow-motion bodies down the steps into the Beagle Boys like standing dominos. Assassins and victims began forming a pinwheel of limbs and colors, screams of surprise and pain, curses and even a few trickles of blood and scraped skin. To be sure, Winston regretted weaponizing others, but he had no time to consider the consequences. He did hear someone call out "That's him! He did it! Someone get him!" But before his pursuers could untangle themselves from this knot of unexpected intimacy and before anyone had time to figure out which "him" to "get," Winston had already circled the Rocket to the Moon and was high above Tomorrowland in a bright Skyway Bucket heading for Fantasyland.

He took a brief moment to congratulate himself for having eluded those miscreants on his trail (of course still regretting his appropriation of innocent bystanders). And then the nausea struck . . . again; way up there in his Skyway Bucket. Just like that! But why should he be getting motion sick? That was Virginia's specialty. And yes, he did enjoy teasing her. Sometimes people can be so cruel. To distract himself, he began scanning the Disneyland panorama, slowly turning his gaze—how often would he have such an opportunity?—but alas the relentless swaying of the bucket in the hot dry wind and all that open space only made him feel worse, the sun bleaching and blurring everything with aggressive intensity, even the eagles circling above. From this vantage, the Magic Land seemed a hodgepodge of jerry-built architecture with no thought to composition . . . *chaotic*, you might say. He was not pleased to have used the word "chaotic" so carelessly. Moreover, he hoped he would not be forced to rain down vomit on that place—though that possibility struck him somehow as biblical. No. Forget it. He had already transgressed enough against the innocent. His attention was focused on Sleeping Beauty's castle. They say that locking your eyes on a fixed object is a useful aid in combatting motion sickness, but the tacky gaudiness of that structure irritated him. He knew that only one thing would help now: returning to good old *terra firma*.

If only he could feel weightless like in a dream. If only it had been a dream! Now the swaying bucket disappeared into the hollow bowels of the polyethylene Matterhorn, that mountain-shaped construction that dominated the park's skyline, and briefly ever so briefly, Winston closed his eyes and felt the calm of the solacing darkness.

What he couldn't know was that the Beagle Boys, equipped with field-glasses, had been tracking his course from below.

At the far reaches of Fantasyland, somewhere near the Frontierland border, he finally alighted. He was groggy and had a sour taste in his mouth but was happy to be on solid ground again. No time to loll around though or take in the sights. No time to indulge his vertigo. Off he went, as quickly as circumstances allowed. Negotiating the thick crowds at the Mine Train Ride and hastening past the Casa de Fritos, the Burrito Wagon and the Pepsi Cola Golden Horseshoe, he circumvented the Frontierland Camera Shop, the Oaks Tavern, the Wheelhouse, the Delta Banjo and the Oscar Mayer River Belle Terrace. And that's when it hit: the delightful smell of mustard reached his nostrils.

Could he be hungry? At a time like this? Hmm, when had he last eaten? No, sorry, no time for thoughts like that, and off he went, sprinting past the Tom Sawyer Island rafts, curving around Fowler's Harbor and finally crossing the border to

New Orleans Square. This time the coast really did look clear. This time, he was almost certain he had shaken his pursuers. But just as he was about to allow himself a sigh of relief and reward himself with something to eat, he spotted them again in the vicinity of the Sara Lee Café Orleans! And they had obviously noticed him too because they were heading towards him from the banks of the Rivers of America! Moreover, he could have sworn that a Peter Pan had pointed him out to them. Yes, it was true! They were shaking Peter Pan's hand before stampeding his way.

No, not him. He was no sitting duck at the Wild West Shooting Gallery. His mind was too sharp, at least he hoped so. He feinted a dash into the Café Orleans and exited via the back door, darting round the Cristal d'Orleans; and then, as desperation is also a mother of invention, he slipped into yet another line, this winding serpent of toe-tapping humanity queuing up for a sojourn with the Pirates of the Caribbean. He crooked his knees and hunched his shoulders, but it was a vain attempt at conformity, and, alas, the Beagle Boys homed in on him immediately. They too joined the line—just a few heads behind him! And now he had a very good opportunity to get a gander of them, and boy, were they ever mean looking—and big! This time, he knew he was trapped. Suddenly, the line began moving swiftly, and in no time, Winston had handed a faceless attendant his "E" ticket and was sitting in an open rowboat, alone and vulnerable. A cable clicked into gear, and off he went, chuffing into a green roofed Caribbean on a journey that promised to convey him from port to exotic port. The air was warm and humid and filled with the echoes of jolly pirate music. The water was lapping lazily around him, reflected, and tessellating blurrily on the hot-house ceiling and the cavernous walls. No warm-blooded Caribbean; this was the habitat of robots, servo-motor wonders, convincingly humanoid in appearance: pirate robots, sailor robots, police robots, robot

tavern girls pouring streams of beer into the seemingly bot-
tomless mugs of robot customers, robot chambermaids fleeing hotly pursuing robot drunks. A robot dog was wagging
its tail eyeing a group of robot pirate jailbirds who were cajol-
ing it with a bone that would forever be wiggled inches from
its snout, the pirates hoping the dog might fetch a key from
a sleeping jailor, a key which would always stay inches from
their fingers never to free them from—how else to describe
it?—from the illusion of imprisonment! They put in sixteen
hour days, these robots, a small dose of electricity and an occasional dusting their only remuneration, smiles and frowns
fixed permanently on their faces, bodies shaped into unalter-
ing stoops or set on stools or upright, positions without relief,
no promise of change, passive prisoners, barely watched over
by their makers, their obedience a given. Sexless creatures cre-
ated in their masters' image, ageless icons of good and evil, put
to work in the entertainment industry, golems of playful spontaneity whose antics mirrored secret cravings of hundreds of
thousands of real-life spectators.

In this feigned Caribbean danger zone, only Winston's danger was real. He looked back and there they were! Sitting only
three boats behind! One was raising to his mouth what looked
like a tube. No, not a tube, a blowgun! In an instant PHHH-
HHHHWWWWAT! A dart whizzed by Winston's ear, its tiny
quill piercing the drinking hand of a robot pirate. But what's
this?! The robotic motion halted immediately. The robot paralyzed! Paralyzed? A robot? Winston wanted so much to cry
for help. But alas, yet again he was too inhibited to scream.
Why? Because he did not want to make a spectacle of himself
in front of strangers. It also crossed his mind that he could
leap into the water and swim off or wade away, depending on
the depth. But what if the water were electrified?

PHHHHHWWWAT! Another one sailed by him, lodging
in the wooden stern of the boat ahead. PHHHHWWWAT!

This one whizzed past so close that Winston felt the whoosh on his cheek. PHHHHWWWAT! Another one—and what's this?—it struck a corpulent woman, piercing her polka-dot blouse and into her adipose triceps. A brief jerk, and her grey head slumped against her husband's short-sleeved shoulder. Damn, another innocent victim. PHHHHWWAT! Again. He ducked. Once more, a robot was out of commission. Short circuited? PHHHHHWWAT! Again. Winston feinted to one side. The projectile missed him by inches. Music honky-tonking about him, the air heavy and humid, he was sure he was suffering from a lack of oxygen. He dared not turn back to look. Superstition in action. No place to hide, a sitting duck after all—and in a small pond. PHHHWWWAT! Another one. PHHHHWWWAT! PHHHHHWWWAT! PHHHHHWWWAT! The seconds passed like minutes, the minutes like hours, the darts raining down like in mediaeval warfare. Ahead, a chorus of robots were singing "Yo ho ho and a bottle of rum!", frivolity that reached Winston's ears like a dirge. Had no one noticed Winston's desperate plight? Not even the man whose wife had passed out was stirring. Indifference? Fear? Were they imagining maybe that *he, Winston,* was part of the show? PHHHHWWAT! That one singed his hair. PHHHHWWWAT! Winston cowered into the horizontal as much as his physical geometry allowed. Choruses of robots were dancing, fat fleshy smiles and hyperthyroidic eyes catching an impassionate glimpse of Winston as he floated by. In the boat behind his, a small child was bobbing, "Look mommy, that man scared! Hee Hee Hee!" "Shh. Brendon! It's not nice to point."

And finally the light. The light! It's over! Thank God! The boats were chugging into the safe harbor of daytime. Quickly, the music and the humidity ebbed and vanished. The sky was menacingly blue, the sun beating down relentlessly on Anaheim. Winston returned to a sitting position but attentively, a returnee to the land of the *status quo*, the masses squirming under the sun's blinding pallor. Food smells filled his nose. He inhaled deeply. Air. Even if it were hot and dry. Ahhh! The woman in the polka-dot blouse was being carted off on a Red Cross stretcher by four straining medics dressed in Keystone Cop garb while parents wrapped tanned hands over children's eyes, and Snow White and a couple of dwarfs were interviewing the clueless husband. Meanwhile, the Beagle Boys had stowed their blowguns and were acting extremely well behaved. As for Winston, he sprung out of the boat and made a dash for it. A few eyes followed him. There was some laughter. Fun. In a nonce, the Beagle Boys were hot on his track.

Fun? Certainly not for Winston. He was earnestly consternated, for he no longer doubted that his pursuers were intent on doing him serious harm. And yet, he still did not understand what terrible transgression he had committed to deserve this treatment. In fact, in the course of his flight, occasionally he'd ask himself: what am I running from? He found no answer to that compelling question, but for the life of him, he couldn't stop now.

Next stop, New Orleans Square in the French Quarter. But what now? A quick look around and it was clear to Winston that there was nowhere to hide but in visibility itself, in this case the milling crowd. Always the crowd! Why must others suffer because of my plight? Maybe some people considered it a clever ploy to submerge into a throng like into a labyrinth and then exit at some unexpected oblique angle to throw a pursuer off the track. But tall men lacked this luxury. They were born to be seen. Enveloped in these thoughts and perhaps others, Winston hurried through the Square and, oopps! He oversaw a curb, was thrown off balance and stumbled against the burly tenor of the Royal Street Bachelors, a trio of musicians, tenor, baritone and bass, dressed in top hat and string-tie paddle-boat gambler garb and singing "Down by the Old Mill Stream" in the vicinity of the One-of-a-Kind-Shop, a lively audience semicircling them. There was no way to avoid the collision. Winston impacted with the tenor as he was blaring a *forte* "strea-a-a-m" a full fifth above the baritone's tonic. The man crashed to the ground with the expected "oof," his top hat propelled into the air, then tumbling earthwards in what seemed to all to be slow motion, eyes fixed hypnotically on it as it landed perfectly on Winston's head, imparting him with a rather roguish look. Without stopping to think or missing a beat, Winston lifted the hat and sang, perfectly in key, "Not the river but the stream," he too skillfully harmonizing a perfectly pitched fifth above the tonic. Then he tossed the hat deftly onto the dazed tenor's head, and to the accompaniment of generous applause dashed off in the direction of Cristal d'Orleans, past the Sara Lee Café Orleans and over into Frontierland.

Suddenly and unexpectedly, he found himself in a place without a crowd, no rush, serene, an open space, and more importantly, there was no sign of *them*. A caesura between the worlds, if there is such a thing. All was quiet, so quiet he dared to think: could it be that he had shaken them? An incipient resurgence of confidence and relief was stirring within. Moreover, the fact that an audience had applauded him had electrified him. If he survived this, he was eager to tell Virginia about that experience. He was sure she would not believe he was capable of something like that. And then, he caught the scent of mustard. Mustard? Where was he? That's when he saw that he was directly across from the Oscar Mayer River Belle Terrace. "Mmmm, what I wouldn't give for a hotdog with mustard." He was smacking his lips, and his stomach gurgled its approval. And why should he not be hungry? After all, when was the last time he had eaten? Pursuers or no pursuers, he was determined to get himself something to eat . . . and now!

He stepped over to the counter. Of course, there was a line, after all this was Disneyland, but it wasn't a long line. The peppy, freckle-faced young counterman, white shirt, white cap and white apron, was attending to customer after customer with witty panache, and Winston was fascinated by the way he had mastered his dull profession so creatively. Finally, it was his turn.

"What can I do ya outta, Winston?" the counterman snapped spryly, his bright freckled face looking so clean and impudent.

"What . . . you mean, you know my name too?!" Winston tensed.

"Hey, Winston, what can I say? You ARE wearing it on your heart. You must WANT us to know it."

Winston looked down, and sure enough, he was still wearing his name tag from the QUID PRO QUO meeting. He was about to peel it off.

"Wait wait! Hold on! Don't ruin a good thing now. Listen, my name's Bob, if that makes you feel better." They shook hands. So, tell me, Winston, what would you like?"

Winston leaned towards the counterman in a confidential sort of way, his stomach cueing him in anticipation. "Listen, Bob, right this moment, I would like nothing more in the world than a juicy hotdog."

"Sure thing, Win." Bob winked. "With the works?"

"No, no," Winston's eyes brightened, "just mustard, *gobs* of mustard."

"You bet," Bob smiled, looking so healthy and fresh, "I like someone who knows what he wants and can say it." And he plopped a redhot onto a roll, squirted a thick layer of bright yellow mustard on it and handed it to Winston. "Here, Winston, this one's on the house."

"Why, gee thanks, Bob!" Winston was smiling. Could it be? Was his fortune changing? Someone had been nice to him, someone who had nothing to do with some mysterious Empire of Chaos. He waved a cheerful bye bye and walked off, staring hungrily and with joyous anticipation at the tasty pleasure to come.

He was standing at the banks of the Rivers of America under the afternoon Anaheim sun. Sunlit sparkles twinkled on the calm ripples of that dark body of water. A cool breeze accented the river's edge with wavelets. The smell of mustard, so close at hand, wafted deliciously into his nostrils. The bustling traffic of Disneyland seemed to have slowed to pale, measured, rhythmic circumambulations. The chattering in the air was like the hum of the wind. For the first time Winston was feeling an aching as his muscles dared relax. He was tired, exhausted in fact. He would have liked nothing better than a hot bath and then to lie in a soft bed and sleep. He raised the hotdog to his welcoming mouth, the steam and the aroma already in contact with his tongue. The bun touched his lips, dry and soft, and he pressed it deeper into the cavity of his mouth, saliva flowing abundantly, his tongue touching the tangy yellow edge of the mustard and the smooth rounded greasy tip of the hotdog. His stomach gurgled gratefully as he bit into it. A wave of well-being rippled through him, but only briefly. For before he could bite through, he saw them again. And they had seen him. This was no time to think about food. He tossed his hotdog into the Rivers of America, where it floated like a soggy yellow ship on the murky surface. There was still the taste of mustard on his tongue, but it was a sad taste and soon a bitter memory on the go. He raced down to the riverbank, taking cover behind clusters of passersby. He glanced back . . . but wait . . . they were nowhere visible. Was it possible? Had he shaken them again? Twice in a row? Had his luck changed after all? And then he dashed aboard the Mark Twain Steamboat, hoping he had booked safe passage.

He slipped into a remote corner of the second level deck and eked out what seemed to be a secure spot at starboard. An artificial breeze was gusting off Tom Sawyer's Island. All was quiet, but frankly, Winston was just fed up. Better said, he was angry and frustrated and hungry and frightened. He seriously wanted this insanity to stop. He had had enough. Moreover, he still didn't know why they were after him nor how this waking nightmare could be taking place in broad daylight without anyone noticing . . . or caring!

The foot-weary were shuffling idly along in search of seats, but he paid little attention, neither to his fellow passengers nor to the shrill strains of the steam whistle nor to the drawl of the captain's voice over the public-address system. WELCOME ABO-AHD. THIS IS YAW CAPT'N SPEAKIN' . . . By the time he realized the Beagle Boys were flanking him, shoulder to shoulder, it was too late to react. Very sinister smiles stretched across those unshaven faces, beady eyes peering anonymously through black masks. One was raising a tiny blowgun to his lips, in all likelihood a close-range weapon, Winston surmised. Yes, right there, in a sea of oblivious, distracted faces, they were intending to assault him. The one with the blowgun was filling his lungs, preparing for the foray. Winston was drifting into the kind of paralysis every animal experiences when the predator's teeth and claws have penetrated the skin. The Beagle Boy set the blowgun to his lips. But then, THUD!! With all his might, Winston thrust an elbow into the Beagle Boy's solar plexus. Reactively, the Beagle Boy gulped, swallowing something. Then, nonplussed he stared at Winston. You could see the terror in those eyes behind the mask. Yes, the Beagle Boy had ingested the poisoned dart he had intended to use on Winston. He went pale and silent and collapsed at Winston's feet. A few people glanced over lazily at the small commotion. Winston had already climbed over the railing and leapt into the water below.

That's when the stir began. "Man overboard!" someone cried. "Help! Help! Someone's fainted! Is there a doctor on board?" BLEEP BLEEP BLEEP!!! The foghorn was blaring. Sirens were whining. Passengers were screaming. "Are we sinking!!? Are we going to die?!" Panic. But by then, Winston was swimming solidly towards Tom Sawyer's Island, full rudder ahead. He dragged himself, wet clothing and all, ashore and then crawled into the bushes, hiding like Odysseus on Calypso's island.

A wise decision. For in no time, search-parties were out looking for him. Goofys, Plutos, Captain Hooks, Mickey Mouses, Donald Ducks, Pinocchios and even the Disneyland Security in paramilitary uniforms. Regrettably for those in charge, they had designed this corner of the Magic Kingdom unwontedly too realistically, and Winston was able to stay out of sight in the thick underbrush until they finally abandoned their search. When he was certain the coast was clear, he found a sunny glade, stretched out lazily in the warm grass and spread out his clothes to dry in the afternoon heat.

Then he closed his eyes and tumbled into a brief, deep, dreamless sleep. When he awoke, his muscles were sore, the force of gravity was weighing on his body and his head was navigating through a cloud. He wrestled himself to his feet, no easy task when you're feeling groggy, before gradually experiencing the rejuvenating benefits of his short nap. As he distended his limbs, the warming blood began flowing into his extremities and into his brain. He filled his lungs with ample oxygen and sighed with pleasure. Finally, he was feeling safe, and this time reliably so. While dressing, he noticed what seemed to be a metal plate, half hidden in the high grass at the edge of the clearing. It was square and corrugated, slightly larger than a manhole cover and equipt with a handle, which made him think that it might be a trap door.

He was sure there would be no harm peeking inside, and so he pulled at the handle. It did not give easily; the metal plate was quite heavy. But with a little effort, he finally succeeded in raising it. Probably it hadn't been opened in years. A musty odor wafted into his nostrils as he peeked into the dimly lit maw below. The metal-rungs of a ladder nearly reached surface level and seemed to descend into something like a large space, maybe a room. Then he heard a humming sound, a motor or generator perhaps. Had he chanced upon the Disneyland power plant? Had it been dark down there, he probably would not have risked exploring, but a descent into what seemed to be a dimly lit chamber aroused his sense of palatable adventure, and so he climbed into the hatch.

It was not a large space, but clearly a room, and the ceiling was high, very high, like in a cathedral. It wasn't possible to determine the source of the dull light, but at least it was bright enough in there for him to easily make out the contours of the smooth walls and cool marble floors, grey and immaculate, reminding him somehow of his father's workshop. Well, not quite, because there were frescos on the walls, subdued colors in subdued light, and they depicted an array of Disney characters: Mickey Mouse, Donald Duck, Huey, Louie and Dewey, Snow White, Peter Pan, Tinkerbelle, the Seven Dwarfs etc. etc.—seemingly the entire Disney Pantheon—yes, even the Beagle Boys—in stiff profile, like figures in an Egyptian tomb. Never before had Disney characters impressed him with such formality, divine and menacing, larger than life. It was cool in that space (which was a relief), and dry. Moreover, everything seemed so impeccably clean and silent, incredibly silent—except for that steady hum. A generator perhaps? Had he stumbled onto a storeroom of this huge complex? Or maybe the machine room? Or who knows. Perhaps they were preparing a future ride—but what kind of ride? Hadesland? Or maybe it was an abandoned project.

Then, at the far end of the room, he noticed what appeared to be a portal, a wide, marble-veneered doorway that seemingly led into another chamber, this one—there was no mistaking—more brightly lit than the first room. As he proceeded in the direction of that portal, he could hear the tap tap tap of his own footsteps as well as the boom boom boom of his heart. He felt a tingle of excitement in his solar plexus mingled with fear, a fear of the unknown. He stepped cautiously, but his curiosity was relentless. Anyway, there was no place for him to hide.

This second room was at least double the size of the first if not more. Here too the walls were ornamented with the same stiff profiles of the Disney Pantheon. In contrast to the first, empty room, however, this one brought to mind a flea market or a second-hand store. There was a sheer endless array of things arranged in rows and lanes in this massive space— including three cars, *real* cars: a Rolls Royce Silver Shadow from an earlier generation; a Model T Ford; and finally some ancient roadster he couldn't identify, maybe a Stutz Bearcat. Then the furniture! Couches, chairs, a couple of large desks, a drafting table, an old sewing machine, a few early console televisions, various carpets rolled up and tied at both ends, filling the air with the harsh scent of camphor. There were lamps, credenzas, dresser drawers, consoles, paintings, a king-size mattress, tables, all of it set up like at some fabulous estate sale. Not to mention the stacks of sealed cartons, each marked with what seemed to be an identification number. Winston might have examined some of these items in greater detail, but the light, though brighter than in the first chamber, was still dim and a strain on the eyes. Meanwhile, that hum filled the air, was sounding louder in fact—as easy to forget (or remember) as tinnitus. Virginia would *love* it here, he was thinking. Anyway, she knows more about antiques than I do. In fact, she has a sixth sense and would home in on the best of it im-

mediately. For some reason he felt especially attracted to the
Rolls Royce. Maybe some boyhood dream. He approached it,
a little awestruck at first, but after a brief moment of hesitation, he opened the driver-side door. First, he peeked in shyly;
then, he climbed in and sat behind the steering wheel. It really was comfortable, just as he imagined it *should* be. He
sank into the thick upholstery and planted one hand on the
steering wheel while caressing the dashboard and everything
else with the other. Just for fun, he opened the glove compartment. There were some maps, a few old coins, a pack of
unfiltered cigarettes, matches, ancient looking, and a vehicle
registration in there. He held the registration to the light and
read the name: Walter Elias Disney. Why, heavens to Betsy!
This car must have belonged to Disney himself! Now he *really* felt like he was in Disneyland—and finally he had something to be *positively* excited about! Nor did he need a ticket
to get on this ride! Endless savored time passed, and when
he'd finally had enough of this experience, he slid out from
behind the wheel, stepping onto the running board (cars like
this one were designed with large people in mind!). Yes, he
was having *fun!* And now, he wanted to see *more!* But where
to begin when there are so many choices? Oh, I wish Virginia
were here. Hmm, something about that solid oak desk nearby
caught his interest. But what? No need to analyze predilec-
tion. He headed for it and opened a drawer at random. There
was what seemed to be a stack of letters in there. And now
things get strange: but trying to explain the difference between
chance and fate has never been easy. Maybe that is why the
Greeks had a single word for both concepts. You see, Winston picked an envelope from the pile without the least forethought and read it. It was addressed to "Walt Disneey Los
Angeles California" and written in the large uneven handwrit-
ing of a child. And then he saw the return address: WINSTON
HEWLETT 1234 EDGEWATER SANTA BARBARA. How

can this be possible? *Is* there some *plan* after all that I know nothing about? He slipped a letter out of the envelope: "Dear Mr. Disneey. I like your cartunes a lot. When I grow up I want to be a cartunist too. My dad says I cant draw, but I dont beleave him. Your frend, Winston Hewlett."

Well, maybe I can draw, but I certainly couldn't spell. At the bottom of the page, with a little effort, he was able to decipher a word scribbled hurriedly: "Answer?" Had Walt Disney written that? Had he intended to respond to Winston's letter? Winston had long ago forgotten that he used to draw as a child. To think, he had to jump off a boat in the middle of an amusement park being chased by two goons in order to resurrect this memory from oblivion. He slipped the letter back into the envelope and tucked it into his jacket pocket. No one will miss this, he reasoned with certainty.

Now he dropped onto a cushiony sofa. Ahhh. He leaned back and raised his feet, his attention fixed on nothing not even the hum of that generator or whatever it was. Time vanished quickly as a concept, and the minutes passed like hours. What a mess of things, he was thinking. I'm sure glad none of it belongs to *me*. He'd never liked clutter, neither in his brain nor in his surroundings. If ever he got to build his studio, it would be minimalist, utilitarian like Gladiola's apartment. The fact is, there was *nothing* here in Disney's land that he might remotely want to possess—not even the Rolls . . . well, except for that letter, but that was his own property anyway. All junk—no matter what the value. Stop. Never say never. That last thought was thought too soon. On a nearby desk, a marmalade jar filled with diverse pens and pencils caught his eye. Hmm. He got up and examined it more closely. Were *these* the pens that HE once used to draw those immortal characters the first time? Awe . . . struck. It was like cupping sacred bones or a saint's teeth in his hands. Larceny stirred in Winston—usually an honest man. His nape grew warm with unaccustomed craving. Yes, he wanted to POSSESS one of these pens that might have been used to capture the first vision of those holy hieroglyphs around him. His fingers were truly itching. That idiom wasn't just a figure of speech! He picked out a very handsome Rapidograph. It felt good in his fingers, a magic wand. He secreted it in his jacket pocket right over his heart. Indemnity, you might say, for damage suffered.

Soon after securing his just reward, he quickly began losing interest in that world of objects—enough!—and moved on to the next chamber, passing through yet another marble portal. This room was even more spacious than the one he had just left and brighter too, but with the exception of a single folding wooden chair at its center, on whose canvas back "THE CHIEF" was printed in large black letters, it was totally barren, that is to say with the exception of those frescos on the wall whose colors were especially vivid here. In his opinion this larger space would have been more appropriate for displaying the clutter of that rumble sale he had left behind. But there must be some logic to all this. Meanwhile, he was still unable to find the source of the illumination. The humming was louder here than in the other rooms, likewise the echo of Winston's footsteps. Naturally, he approached that lone chair and—as if drawn by some power unknown—sat down on it. It was a tight fit, and the wooden joints creaked under his weight. For a moment, he was afraid it might collapse beneath him. It did not. All at once, he was feeling strangely powerful, authoritative, and, yes, very confident. What was going on? Was that the ghost of Walt Disney at work? Was his luck changing? *Something* was happening. But what? All at once, *he* and not a generator began humming. He was humming a tune though: "When You Wish upon a Star . . ." Was he . . . becoming . . . a fan?

Nothing lasts forever, however (except for love of course), and gradually Winston moved on to discover that there was only one last chamber to explore. To reach it, he had to pass through yet another marble portal, this one more elaborate than the others, flanked by columns topped with, well, very kitschy Corinthian-style plinths. By now it was clear to him that he was definitely in the most secret land of the Magic Kingdom. This ultimate room was brightly lit, almost too bright, though it was still not possible to locate the source of the illumination. Here, the colors of the frescos were rich and satisfying. For a while he stood motionless before them, overwhelmed by their visual power. Finally, he turned his attention to the only object in this room: a massive steel locker (how else to describe it?) at its center. It looked like some rectangular silver rocket ship, sparkling and glaring in the blazing light and rising upwards towards the high cathedral ceiling. This chamber was the smallest, but Winston had the impression that he had reached the core of a precious jewel. It was an experience that dwarfed his recent journey to the center of an atom. And now at last, he knew that that droning he had been hearing in this underworld land was emanating from this slick, silver oblong. The pitch was constant but never irritatingly loud. He circumambulated the sleek silver box several times like some mysterious Kaaba, scrutinizing it ever more attentively. Except for a single hatch, bolted tightly and sealed like the entrance to a fortress, there were no visible seams on the surface. Through a small oval window, which seemed to be made from some thick armored glass framed by the top of the hatch, a few dials and blinking lights were discernible. Carefully, he placed a hand on the steel locker and detected a gentle vibration. Above something like a keyhole, a shiny metal plate was affixed, and here he read the words "Cryogenic Research Center North Hollywood California Patent Pending." Now Winston peeked into the oval window and to his surprise— yes, for a moment he started—he saw a *face*, blue-white in color like some ice gnome. There was no mistaking the identity of that face however. Yes, it was HIS. He remembered it from television. The master himself. Walt Disney. His eyes were closed as if he were asleep on his feet. Winston fixed his eyes on the frozen visage, almost expecting something might move. Nothing did.

When Winston finally decided to abandon this air-conditioned Orcus, two thoughts came to him. First: would anyone believe this story? That is, if he managed to survive this day, for he still couldn't be certain he had escaped his pursuers. And secondly: how did they manage to keep that mausoleum so free of dust? He was thinking of his father's workshop of course. Does a cleaning crew work down here too?

He surfaced into the still warm Anaheim afternoon. The glare made him squint, but he was glad to be above ground in this world of earth and sky again. He lowered the trap door and made a mental note of a few landmarks in case he might ever need to or want to return. Then he reconnoitered Tom Sawyer's Island, warily at first, until he finally located the wharf. There it was possible to hire a raft to taxi him back to the mainland. He handed a languid attendant a waterlogged "D" ticket and returned to Frontierland.

His pursuers were nowhere in sight, and so he decided he would finally do what people are supposed to do when they visit Disneyland: take in the sites. Naturally, maintaining an alert calm, like any animal of prey. By now he had concluded that the Magic Kingdom, despite its many lands, was crowded and small—too small, in fact. One could measure the distance between land and land not only in fantasies but in countable footsteps. Still, he was feeling fine.

In Fantasyland, he was lazily eyeing bunches of eagerly excited children as they scurried from ride to ride: from King Arthur's carousel to Dumbo the Flying Elephant, from the bob-sled down the Matterhorn to a spin on the Fantasyland Autopia in antique cars. The adults seemed no less gleeful. Yes, people were having a good time, and Winston was content, despite the bleached, sunbaked look of the place. In fact, if you scrutinized the surfaces, you could see that often the paint was more chipped than it ought to have been in a redoubt against cruel reality. But who needs to go into details?

Near the Matterhorn, he spotted a stretch of green lawn. It looked very inviting, and so he sat down under the shade of a magnolia tree. An afternoon breeze licked at his face as he watched the bustle from this calm vantage point. At first, he did not notice the tiny Mickey Mouse, perky and smiling, and hopping playfully towards him. But then Mickey danced right up to him. Winston grinned. Yes, now he was *really* feeling the spirit of the place. It *was* a wonderland after all. Then Mickey rubbed his cute mouse snout against Winston's ear so that it tickled. Winston felt like laughing.

"Listen, asshole," Mickey whispered, "Get the fuck off the grass. This ain't yer livin' room."

Before Winston could react, Mickey had stopped hopping gleefully. In fact suddenly the mouse seemed to freeze in mid-motion, tilting his large mouse head as if scrutinizing Winston.

"It's you!" Mickey exclaimed through his mouse head.

"Me?"

Then Mickey lifted his mask and revealed his face. A large, grey walrus mustache flopped out first from beneath the mouse head. And there was sweat on his forehead. It was the dwarf from the Bird's Nest. "Listen," he said, "you better get outta here pronto. They're *after* you. And I mean it."

That hounded expression returned to Winston. "But how?" he asked.

"No time for questions. Just follow me." Winston tailed after the dwarf via some circuitous route out of Fantasyland and back to Tomorrowland until they arrived at the Disneyland Alweg Monorail Station. "Do you have any "E" tickets left?"

Winston checked his wrinkled ticket book and nodded affirmatively.

"Hop on the monorail," the Dwarf said, "and get off at the Disneyland Hotel. From there you can catch a bus outta Anaheim, which I'd advise you to do *real quick*."

Winston shook the dwarf's little gloved hand and thanked him.

"Tell me, Winston," the dwarf winked slyly, "What do you think about historical continuity now?" And he hopped merrily away.

❋   ❋   ❋

The silver doors of the Monorail slid shut with a bang, and the elevated train whooshed silently down the track. Calm in the air, and many faces, including Winston's, were pressed against the windows taking in the sights, eyes sweeping over the busy network of waterways, painted domes, pavilions and bleached plazas. Unlike the others, Winston of course was inclined to see it as a venue of danger and not as a receptacle for dreams. Then he placed a hand over his heart, fingering Walt Disney's pen as if to verify that this had all really happened and that he had come out victorious. Moreover, he was seriously contemplating the question of historical continuity. In fact, it occurred to him what he might have replied to the dwarf. Dammit. Why did he always come up with good answers when it was too late? He might have said: if there is no such thing as historical continuity, then you wouldn't have returned into my life! Ha! Imagine that. The dwarf's own role in these events would have confirmed that the continuity he disclaimed did exist!

The Monorail rolled on, and sundry walkways, lawns, bodies of water, buildings, rides and restaurants as well as questions about historical continuity gradually slipped into the past tense. A deft hairpin curve and they whisked past the parking lot. Winston tried to reconstruct the exact location of that Winnebago, but the lot was fuller now, and there were hundreds if not thousands of campers down there. Larez Pentius came to mind and he wondered where he might be. But even that thought faded quickly. He was feeling as cool as Walt Disney's grave.

Finally, the Monorail arrived at the Disneyland Hotel. Last stop, and Winston descended. So far so good. No goons, no costumed Disneyites, which is to say, no potential collaborators. This time, it really seemed like he had escaped, and soon he was blending into the anonymity of Anaheim. From there he caught a bus to Bueno Park, eventually transferring to the Artesia Blvd. line, stopping at practically every dizzying traffic light in the townships of Lakewood, Compton and Torrance, until a couple of hours later he finally arrived at Sepulveda Blvd. The ride up Sepulveda was no less grueling, and by the time he got off at Santa Monica Blvd., he was feeling queasy for the third time since arriving in Los Angeles. At Santa Monica Blvd., he took a cab. By the time he arrived at the Bird's Nest, it was already dusk.

Traffic was racing by in the hazy pink-green sunset which was quietly shifting into California sundown purple. Headlights twinkled sleepily in the pastels. Pedestrians trudged by, shadows in the twilight. Neon lights and streetlights blinked on. Night was falling when Winston finally reached his car. Yes, it was still there. He fumbled in his pocket for the key (thankfully he hadn't lost it), noticed a parking ticket clamped into the windshield wipers flapping about in a gust of sea breeze. He shrugged stoically, pocketed the ticket and wedged himself behind the steering wheel of his car.

Now what? He was free to go. There were no further surprises to expect, no hit men, no new contacts, no messages. He
was free to start his car, turn on the radio, listen to the evening
news and head home as if nothing out of the ordinary had happened. In fact, soon he might not trust his own memory about
the events of that day.

Anyway, what had *really* changed in his life? He was still
as much in the dark about his impotence as at the beginning
of this journey. Nor did he understand why he had been so
hotly pursued. Had all this taken place in just over twenty-
four hours? And there were other unanswered questions. Like:
Why was this happening? *What* did they want from him?
What in heaven's (or should he perhaps say *hell's*?) name was
this Empire of Chaos? *Why* had they killed his father? *Where*
was Larez Pentius? Clearly, the most important question—
at least for him—was: What . . . did . . . they . . . want . . .
from . . . *him?!*

He was tapping his fingers against the steering wheel, a
kind of substitute for both thought and action. He was tired,
thirsty, hungry, irritable, in need of a bath and a shave. But he
was also curious, very curious . . . maybe too curious. Finally,
a decisive rap of the hand against the top of the wheel. He
climbed out of the car, locked the door (you never know; after
all, this was Hollywood), reached into his jacket pocket and
fished out the still damp piece of paper Fingers had given him.
He made a beeline for the nearest telephone booth, careful to
reconnoiter his surroundings in case of a surprise attack, and
then placed a call to Headquarters.

❀ ❀ ❀

The cordial voice on the other end of the line promised to
dispatch a "contact" immediately. It was like ordering a taxi.
And it was true: Within minutes, he heard the beeping of a

horn and a voice calling out: "Hey, Winston!" Hardly time for Winston to ponder the efficiency of this . . . *organization*—or whatever they were.

The voice was coming from a Winnebago, double-parked just a few feet from the phone booth and blocking traffic. Cars were honking furiously. "Hey, c'mon! Hop in! The natives are getting restless!" The voice was light, cheerful, downright friendly. Winston's first reaction: panic. He was rooted to the sidewalk.

"Hey, c'mon, we're holding up traffic!"

A Winnebago? Was that . . . a *Beagle Boy* . . . in there calling out to him? How many were they? Do they have ether? Indeed, serious—and, yes, justified—concerns. It took a while before he approached the cabin, prepared to run, punch, kick or scream . . . and then: "Bob!" That's what he said. Yes, there behind the steering wheel was the same Bob who had treated him to a hotdog at the Oscar Mayer River Belle Terrace in Frontierland. "What are you doing here?" Are you . . ."

"Listen, Win," a cheerful smile on his freckled face and still wearing his chef's uniform. "Lots of people gotta moonlight these days. I mean, you can't live from redhots and mustard alone."

Winston climbed into the cabin, and Bob shifted the camper into gear. In a nonce, the Winnebago was whining down Hollywood Blvd.

"Hey, Win," Bob turned briefly towards Winston once they were rolling, his look undissembling, his voice reassuring, "Couldya do me a favor and slip this on." It was a blindfold, not unlike the mask the Beagle Boys wore, but without eye holes. "I'm sorry pal, but they don't want you to know where Headquarters is. Something about security, and, well, orders is orders, huh?"

Winston obliged with no backtalk, adjusting the blindfold compliantly. For some reason, he trusted Bob, and now they swerved around a corner. He was certain they were heading east.

All was dark, at least for Winston, and they rode in silence, Winston feeling at ease, a little sleepy even. Maybe the exhaustion. Then they seemed to be on a freeway, the vehicle whirring through the night. Soothing monotony. Bob was whistling softly, maybe "When You Wish Upon a Star." The air was cool. Cars were sloshing by like waves at the seashore.

Finally, Winston broke the silence: "Say, Bob, d'ya think you could answer a question for me?"

"Sure Win, shoot."

"Why do you and your friends want to pollute the air?"

"Pollute the air? How do you mean?"

"I mean, this Winnebago is spraying poisons into the air, isn't it?"

"Poisons into the air? Where d'ya get that from?"

"Doctor Pentius."

"Who?"

"Larez Pentius." Pause. "You mean you don't know who that is?"

"Nope, I'm just a redhot guy, but whoever your friend is, he's got it backwards. These babies are specially designed to suck hydrocarbons OUT of the air. They don't spray poisons INTO it."

"Are you sure?"

"Posilutely, man. We've got thousands of these jalopies cruising around L.A. We call them the 'Smog Squad'. And another thing, but I'm not sure I can explain this. You see, they don't run on gasoline but, well, on carbon dioxide. And guess what: the exhaust from this mother is pure O two. Polluting the air?" He laughed. "Gee, Win, I hope you don't believe everything you hear!"

More silence and more motor sounds over long stretches, and then Winston sensed they were exiting the freeway and weaving through streets, making lefts and rights, obviously a residential neighborhood, till finally, they came to a stop. "Are we here?" said Winston.

Bob mumbled an affirmative.

"Can I remove my blindfold?"

"In a sec, Win. I'll be right with you." Bob climbed out of the cabin and stepped around the camper to Winston's side, opening the door and helping him out.

"Mmm," Winston inhaled deeply, "Eucalyptus." He was relaxed, a cheerful, intoxicated expression on his face, like a drugged sacrificial victim. Bob piloted him by the arm through the cool, medicinal air. "Watch the curb." A wrought iron gate creaked and shut behind them, and they continued along a flagstone path, plush shrubbery brushing against Winston's shoulder, then up a step and into a house. A door closed behind them almost silently. Hmm. Seems to be a pretty tony neighborhood. Wonder where we are.

No fear. He was sure he was nearing his destination—his *fate*—and about to receive answers to his questions, all of them. Winston was prickling with satisfaction. Would he be reunited with Doctor Pentius? Was the Doctor already there? He was feeling something like triumph—without a guarantee that things would turn out well. Granted, there was no escape. But so what? He would see this one through to the end, come as it may. That's what facing reality is all about. Right?

They walked a few paces and then stopped again. Another door opened as silently as the first, and they stepped into what Winston supposed was an elevator. Something about elevators. Eyes open or closed, it's a sensation of being confined. The descent was long and slow; they seemed to be traveling deep below the surface. More silence. Winston might have cracked a joke had he been able to think of one. Only afterwards it occurred to him he might have said, "Wonder what it's like here during an earthquake." They landed as if on cushions.

The door slid open and Bob piloted Winston, his hand on Winston's elbow, onto something that appeared to be an open cart. The air was cool on Winston's face, somehow reminiscent of Walt Disney's tomb. A soft hiss, and the cart was rolling noiselessly down what may have been a tunnel or a corridor. "I suppose you're going to say the exhaust fumes are pure oxygen," said Winston.

"You bet," said Bob.

"Can you buy these things anywhere?"

"Oh no, not yet for sure. That would be insane."

"Why?"

"The infrastructure, Win. You need the right infrastructure."

The vehicle rolled to a stop. Bob helped Winston out of the cart and shepherded him through yet another door. "Catch you later," he remarked cheerfully but was gone before Winston had a chance to say goodbye. The door fell mutely shut behind him—as if he were now in an airtight space.

"You may remove your blindfold now, Winston," a female voice, both kind and authoritative, intoned.

Winston lifted the mask. Once again, he was becoming a serendipitous dreamer negotiating the paths of some new Magic Kingdom, and again unencumbered by any thoughts of returning . . . returning to what? But where was he? Had he re-entered Walt Disney's tomb? Was this some chamber he had overlooked? The light was opaque; cool but not cold.

Soon his eyes were adjusting to the opacity, and he saw that the surfaces of this chamber, all of them, consisted of mirrors. A new experience for sure. The walls, floors and ceiling reflected everything manifoldly to the most intricate detail. It was as if he were standing at the hub of a kaleidoscope, a place where, well, everything was as it *really* is: infinite! But let's not wax too poetic. *He*, at any rate, was the epicenter—at least from his point of view. When first he looked floorwards, he nearly lost his balance. Then came a barely describable elation. Hey! Look at me! I'm a star! Suspended in eternity! I'm floating! I'm . . . free . . . !

But he wasn't free. He saw that he was facing something resembling a tribunal bench as if he were a man on trial. It was the color of a sunrise or sunset whose pale red gold intensity sent shivers through his body. He had never before seen a color like that, not even in his charcoal box. It was warm and cool at once, awakening a sense of awe rather than fear. Moreover, something best described as a steel blue translucent veil of light was wafting before his eyes. And at its center, he recognized that symbol he had become so familiar with: the *Deltagon*. It was suspended at some halfway point between himself and that golden tribunal bench. And it was glowing— like lapis lazuli! None of this is easy to describe, but somehow, at least at that moment, that Deltagon struck him as the solution to a complex mathematical question he hadn't asked. Sorry, no other words to express this. Was he back inside that atom in the Magic Kingdom? Had his imagination synched ineluctably with the Disney experience? And then *they* came into focus. They were standing behind the tribunal bench. They were seven, He counted twice. Heads of eagle, bodies human and cloaked in golden capes. They stood motionless, their reflections, like his own, replicated in sundry mirror castings. It was the eagle at the center who most caught his attention. Her eyes (at least he assumed those eyes were female) were fixed on his, not cruelly, but ever so intensely, as if she knew secrets . . . *his* secrets. There was nothing he could conceal from her. That was his impression.

A barely perceptible nod to the eagle at her right. "Mr. Hewlett," that one spoke, this time a male voice, the words enunciated with deliberation, "Why are you here?" The voice sounded nasal as if the eagle had a cold.

Anticipation swished along the length of Winston's spine, and he spontaneously interpreted that question as an admission of defeat. Had this journey perhaps *not* been in vain? Would he receive the answers he had been seeking? Yes, the time had come to demand the return of his stolen potency. His eyes assessed the standing forms before him. He was feeling confident. Were *these* his judges? Was there nothing else they wanted to ask? The silence had reached its farthest edge. Finally he spoke: "Why did you do it to me?"

"Do what, Mr. Hewlett?"

His hands transformed into blazing beams of light radiating from the glowing star he had become. The eagles were leaning expectantly—and with curiosity—towards him.

"Why did you make me . . . *impotent!?*" Yes, he was feeling a surge of release. It felt so good! Merely articulating that word energized him. Something volcanic was erupting from within. It was anger! That's what it was! And now it was bursting to the surface, emotional magma. He knew for sure he had asked the right question.

"Impotent?!" the eagles squawked in unison. They seemed unprepared for the force with which he had posed his question. "Forgive me, Mr. Hewlett, I don't understand," said one.

"You don't understand! That's a good one! Sowing the seeds of destruction, huh?"

"Sowing the seeds of destruction?!" an eagle at Winston's far left screaked.

Winston was standing broad and tall, very tall. "You know damn well what this is all about! That letter you sent me!" Chaos beware, there was no stopping this hero now.

"Letter? What letter?" Eagle feathers were fluttering; his judges were chirping with urgency in some staccato language Winston did not understand.

He reached into his pocket, the gesture dramatic, and soon he was gesticulating with that envelope he had received so long ago. Was it really *that* long ago? It was dog-eared and crinkled, and some of the ink had run thanks to his dip in the Rivers of America. Fearlessly he stamped over the mirrored floor, penetrating and passing through the blue Deltagon veil, his footsteps replicating like the rest of him, his defiance infinitely reflected. Then he slapped the envelope onto the red gold bench. "Here!" Boy, was he mad. "Read it yourself!"

They huddled around the crumpled envelope. The eagle at the center slipping out the wrinkled card and reading the message.

DROPIT

"Drop it??" the female voice exclaimed, "Drop what?"

"That's exactly what I would like to know!" Winston had lost all inhibition. "And while we're at it, maybe you can tell me why Virginia has gone off her rocker?!"

"Who? Mr. Hewlett?

"Oh, come on, don't play dumb! Virginia! My wife!" He was fuming.

The eagles were exchanging rapid glances, chattering in some whisper tone that sounded to Winston like the whooshing of wings, though on one occasion, he was sure, he had heard the word "Deltagon" and maybe his father's name as well. Vigorous gesticulating. Sparks were flashing through the lapis blue like heat lightning, though Winston took little notice of all that. He was waiting for a response.

Finally, they came to order again. A solemn silence settled over the room. Instinctively, Winston withdrew from the tribunal bench.

"Winston," the eagle at the center was speaking, a note of sympathy and tenderness, maybe even a shade of embarrassment in her voice, "something . . . unusual . . . has occurred."

"I'll say," Winston was still aware of his advantage and making use of it.

"How shall I put it?" She was obviously struggling for words. "We have asked to see you under . . . *false* . . . pretenses. I don't know what to say except that we sincerely apologize for any inconvenience we may have caused you. To be honest, there seems to have been, well, a misunderstanding."

"Misunderstanding!!" Winston raised his voice with what remained of his righteous indignation. This was not the outcome he was expecting, and suddenly, he was feeling quite . . . helpless.

"Honestly, Winston, we didn't send you this note, nor do we know why you received it. Look at the stamp on this envelope. As you may have noticed, when we want to communicate, we never use the U.S. Mail. It's much too unreliable. I'm afraid . . . you're going to have to figure this one out . . . yourself."

TWENTY-THREE

A MOONLESS, STAR-SPRINKLED night blanketed the California coast. The freeway a pale strip of light, barely a car in sight. Left and right, the tungsten glow of distant towns, settlements and even single, lonely homesteads was twinkling mutely in the darkness. Travelers (like Winston), hungry, thirsty, tired, unshaven and unbathed, are reminded when in the wee hours they see lights in other people's houses how far they are from home, how vast the discrepancy between those who are sheltered and those like himself who are not. His confrontation with those forces of Chaos had ended in . . . yes . . . chaos! Blindfolded anew, they had chauffeured him back to Hollywood, this time another driver, unseen and silent the entire way. A Beagle Boy maybe? Not important. By now he was equally depleted in body and soul. His stomach hungered for something, something more than food to fill an emptiness that was not just physical. On the other hand, given the opportunity, he probably would have willingly hit the streets of Los Angeles for some new adventure—despite nearly total exhaustion. Anything but this void that meant his escapades, his role as a person of interest, were now over. No new *dramatis personae* to smother him in an ether-soaked cloth or hunt him down or put him on stage or dispatch him to an orgy. In retrospect, it had all been a hell of a lot of fun! Already the memories were tarnishing at the edges like when you awake from some vivid dream. He tapped at his jacket pocket. Whew. The Rapidograph was still there. How would he ever manage to tell this tale . . . *all* of it? He had never been much of a raconteur. A real problem when you recall that history has always depended on someone's ability to communicate the facts, to pass on the memories. Maybe that's what made historical continuity so vexing for the dwarf.

The highway he was speeding along on was a familiar stretch of road. It was a path that always led home, and his car was humming steadily, reliably. Like all denizens of that Eden called Santa Barbara, he normally experienced a quiet exhilaration as he passed the landmarks that heralded his approach to his cozy hometown. Not this time. Apart from the fact that he had still not found an answer to his initial problem, he was also burdened with a bad conscience! And probably justifiably so. Imagine. He had succeeded in crash-landing into *Headquarters*, right smack into the center of some huge global or maybe universal conspiracy which still made no sense to him. And dammit, although he had had the opportunity—and there was no denying that!—it had not occurred to him *once* to inquire about Larez Pentius or the fate of his father. He most certainly could have questioned those eagles about their connection to all that murder and mayhem. After all, for a short while he *did* have the upper hand. That is: if there *was* any connection. And why had one eagle called him Winston and not Mr. Hewlett as the others had? There was something familiar about that voice. Now it was too late, and his questions would probably remain forever unanswered. The fact is: his journey into the belly of the whale had been in vain. And he would get no second chance for sure.

He was back where he had started and still had no clue why any of this had happened in the first place. In this empty, hopeless moment, this existential void, Gladiola Freytag came to mind. Of course! He slapped the steering wheel emphatically. Gladiola! Why didn't I think of that before!? It all makes sense! *She* was the one who had put the idea of an Empire of Chaos into his head. And that note! Yes! *She* was the one who sent it! Drop it! Drop it!! And dammit I did!!! How dumb can I get! Now the picture was coming into focus. Naturally! . . . she was JEALOUS! That's it! What else could it be?! She concocted all those stories and insinuations to sabotage my marriage, to drive me out of my mind. And why? So she could pick up the pieces! I always suspected she had fallen in love with me—even when she denied it. Boy, am I an idiot!

Now he was fuming, angry at HER, *Gladiola*, for the grief and suffering she had caused him. All that confusion! All that chaos!! His foot weighed heavily on the gas pedal. He was racing towards Santa Barbara. And what's this? An *erection* was wedged now tautly against his pants leg. An angry erection, straining against containment.

The image of Gladiola's new paramour came to mind, and that made him even angrier. Winston's car sliced through the night aggressively. Now he knew what had to be done. It was time to pay Gladiola a visit. Time for the big showdown. Yes, let's get this show on the road!

How soothing anger can be. Every cell in his body was falling into line like a well-drilled army; and in command was his erection, spearhead of a mighty force, a red-blooded general well-schooled in the art of war. "Just a Friend," a voice whispered into his ear, but he ignored that voice. He knew what it wanted. He knew its goal was to sabotage his clarity. He and his erection were a winning team, knight and lance, jousting down the freeway towards an inevitable confrontation. This war had been celebrated in sundry mythological traditions. He was St. George, and she the dragon, the seductress, the *chaos* monster.

Her cool urbanity came to mind, so young and yet so cunning. That deceptive, melancholy look in her eyes, that I-have-suffered-so-much mimicry. And he had fallen for it! He recalled her knitting basket: a receptacle of half-finished projects. Everything had to be on her terms. Once she had told him she never knitted for others, that knitting was too personal. And that was how she made love! Only herself in mind. A poisonous spider wrapping him in a web of dependency. That pretty, blond coolness, those large searching eyes, pretending helplessness. She dispensed affection in pennyworths, afraid that if she gave more, more might be demanded of her. And still, she wanted me to risk everything! Including my marriage!

Time for the final confrontation. He could see those big eyes of hers pleading ignorance. Should he tear off her clothes, throw her down on the bed in that tidy little room where everything has its place? Work her up to a froth till her daintiness smelled of earth and pungent honesty? Gently, gently, she might beg him, but no sirree, this time he would work her up to a frenzy . . . and then leave her for good! Ha! Let her new friend have the rest!

He was forging up the freeway on automatic pilot, headlights, razors of light, cleaving the night asunder. "Just a Friend," a voice whispered, but he shook his head when he heard that buzz and shooed that voice away.

Exits were flashing by in staccato blinks, *tempo accelerando*, his mind fixed on a single objective: Gladiola Freytag, more name now than face. "Just a Friend" fluttered past his ear, and he swatted at it, Ventura, then Carpenteria fading in the rearview mirror, his foot goosing the gas-pedal. Half-blind he careened through that tree-lined stretch of road at Montecito, past the Milpas Street bridge, and finally he exited at Laguna Street, turning sharply. He and his erection were fevering for revenge. He careered up Laguna Street barely heeding the four way stop signs at each crossing. And indeed, he should have, because at the corner of Laguna and Micheltorrena, another car had reached the intersection concurrently with his. There was a screech of brakes, the harsh blare of horns, and a brief, loud crack. Then all was still. Lights blinked on in the surrounding houses. Silhouettes were appearing at windows. A short-circuited horn was wailing thinly. Winston had seen red, then green, then blue and then for a moment nothing. For some minutes or seconds (so it is when you lose the ability to measure time), his hands were gripping the steering wheel fast as if he were bracing himself for a coming event already past. Then the shock began to thaw. He climbed out of his car, weak-kneed but seemingly uninjured. He surveyed the two battered cars, one his own. A bashed fender and dented door. That seemed to be the extent of the damage to his car. Then he approached the other vehicle.

"Hey, are you all right?" he was tapping at the side window.

No response.

"You, hey, are you okay?" more urgency in his voice. Someone was slumped over the steering wheel. "Hey! Open up! I think the door is jammed!" He yanked and pulled at the handle and finally managed to wrench it open. People were trickling out of their houses, perched at a safe distance in the darkness and watching, just watching. Shadows. The horn was bleeping nasally. Winston hunched over the unconscious driver and raised that body to an upright position, balancing the head against the head rest. It may not be what you're supposed to do in an emergency, but it was all he could think of. Hmm, that face. He perused the round head and bald pate, the dark-rimmed glasses ajar, the myopic eyes. I know him. He did indeed. It was Doctor Anthony Becker. Who will ever truly understand coincidences?

Meanwhile, Doctor Becker began to stir, and the crowd, boldening, was edging in on the action, necks craning. "Get some water!" said Winston to that anonymous conglomeration of contortionists. In the distance, the whine of sirens broke the silence. And soon, Sheriffs' cars, ambulances, tow trucks were converging purposefully animated. Bright lights were blinking red and yellow, bouncing off houses, reflecting on windows and mute faces. Scratchy mechanical voices jabbered incomprehensible things over wireless radios. Engines were chugging, chains clinking, cranes whirring. People were calling out orders. A voice echoed briefly: "Hey, ain't that Tony?" A businesslike policeman, clipboard in hand, was interviewing Winston who could be seen painting broad, hectic gestures in the air that reflected his helplessness.

Doctor Becker was hunched on a gurney, feet planted on the asphalt, hands tucked between his knees as if in prayer. He was conversing with a white-coated paramedic who was extending a paper cup filled with coffee towards him. The Doctor barely noticed that his car was being towed away. Two officers were stretching a tape measure in *pas de deux* fashion between chalk marks that had been hurriedly sketched on the pavement and photographed. Flashing cameras briefly illuminated this fragment of night. Another officer was scribbling notes, holding his clipboard in the glow of a streetlight.

Winston stepped over to the Doctor just as he was being helped into the ambulance. Winston wasn't very steady on his feet either, and he was feeling terrible about all this. "Listen, Doctor . . ." his voice contrite.

"Don't worry, Mr. Hewlett," Anthony Becker smiled weakly, "I'm fine. Really, I am. Please don't blame yourself."

Winston's head bobbed sheepishly. He wanted very much to show concern, but seeing the Doctor so helpless, that familiar antipathy for the man began stirring too. There was just something about that guy. He looked so . . . *ridiculous*, so pitifully *ridiculous*.

"But please," Doctor Becker was squinting through his glasses, askew on his face, one lens cracked, his eyes so small. The Doctor took a deep breath. He too was suppressing a feeling: yes, there was something about Winston he just didn't like. Was there a trace of a smirk on Winston's face? "Mr. Hewlett, perhaps we could make an appointment to . . . meet? I mean, when all this is over. It might be important . . . for both of us. I . . . well . . . think I can learn something from you." The words were spoken with courage and honesty.

"Of course." Winston was making an effort to sound solicitous, but he interpreted the Doctor's request more like a threat, a danger to his integrity. "I'll be happy to. Umm, feel free to call me. All right?"

"Thank you, Mr. Hewlett, you won't regret it." The door to the ambulance closed, and the Doctor disappeared into the night.

The show was over. The tow trucks, police cars and ambulances disbanded in sundry directions, the rubberneckers drifted back to their houses, and the corner of Laguna and Micheltorrena appeared surprisingly unscarred after the excitement. Winston shuffled numbly over to his moderately damaged car and climbed in. For a while, he just hugged the steering wheel. Mindless. Though occasionally he hovered at the brink of tears. After all, he was still not over his shock. Minutes passed, blank minutes. Only then did the thoughts begin to return, in a trickle first. It's her fault, he was thinking. It's all her fault. And gradually he managed to resuscitate his slumbering anger. What a relief to *feel* something, especially after a shock. It took a while before it occurred to him to turn on the ignition, and then he continued on to Gladiola's, this time assiduously attentive to the traffic rules. Fortunately, he was sober. That had spared him the need for detailed explanations to the powers that be as well as other consequences.

And there it was again. His erection. Snaking down his trousers. Winston quite liked the sensation. It invigorated him to know that at least one part of himself had resisted the niceties of civilization. He was delighting in the imagination of savagery. "Just a Friend" buzzed at his ear and he slapped at it like at a horsefly.

He found a parking spot directly in front of Gladiola's house (My lucky day!), jack-in-the-boxed out of the car and stomped up the porch steps. He remembered to duck, but too late. BONG! Another collision with that spider plant that hung to the left of the door. This was becoming a bad joke, but real life never plays for an audience's reaction. Colors briefly flashed before his eyes, bright like Disney frescos. For a moment he felt nauseous, then impatient, then helpless. The plant continued swinging as if mocking him. He was seconds from hurling it to the ground, a final judgement, but cursed instead and rubbed the sore spot on his head.

But back to his anger. He was savoring it like a new suit of clothes, custom-tailored; feeling attractive, powerful, maybe threatening (a sensation enhanced by his erection). Then "Just a Friend" addressed him by name. Shut up, Winston said, while depressing the buzzer longer than necessary. No response. She's probably sleeping. He pressed again, this time more vehemently. A light went on in the stairwell. He recognized those familiar, deliberate footsteps and saw Gladiola's petite form descending the steps. She was wearing blue jeans and a checkered shirt. Her hair was tied back in a ponytail, girlishly attractive. Winston desired her immediately. Grrr. Woof.

"Winston!?" a note of surprise in her voice *and* in her eyes, but also a hint of mischief in her expression, her nose wrinkling.

"Surprised to see me, I hope?" this spoken with as much bravado as he could muster. Hmm. Should he take her right there in the stairwell? He felt so . . . so . . . triumphant! And his erection was convinced that she was a sure thing. Hey . . . maybe I'm cured!?

"Well I . . ." She was clearly hunting for words, and then she noticed how wrinkled and dirty his clothes were as if he'd slept under a tree on wet grass which was not far from the truth. Moreover, he needed a shave. And then there was that wild look in his eyes.

"Let's go." The words came out as a command. There was nothing more he needed to say.

She followed him up the stairs.

They entered her living room, that familiar venue for many rendezvous and intimacies. Winston was already plotting out a sequence of events. First a nice hot bath and a shave—if she had a razor—and then a bite to eat. And then off to bed. Or should he take her immediately before indulging in civilities? He had never spent an entire night with her. How would it be to wake up next to her, experience the excitement of strange sheets, and maybe a round of early morning lovemaking? Grr. Gladiola sat down on the edge of the daybed; she was studying him, as if looking for some key. He was leaning against the window frame, arms folded. Had she noticed that ferocious bulge in his pants?

She did not speak. Instead, she reached into her knitting basket for a swatch of wool and began clicking out stitches.

There was silence, a tense silence neither was penetrating. Then the door to the kitchen swung open. *Agent* Porky, in blue jeans and a checkered shirt, which is to say, in partner look, entered the room. "Oh, you have company." His voice was lazy and familiar. He raised a hand towards Winston in a friendly wave. "Hi!" Then he sat down next to Gladiola, close, like neighboring countries sharing a common border.

That proximity did not go unnoticed. Winston also saw that both were barefoot. Barefoot and together late at night— and dressed like twins. Okay, he could put two and two to-gether.

"Oh dear," Gladiola said, "I don't think I've ever introduced you. Winston, Porky. Porky, Winston."

"Hi Winston." *Agent* Porky smiled, one bare foot covering Gladiola's and making caressing motions.

Winston nodded. "Just a Friend" was sucking the heat out of his face, desire was metamorphosing into a headache, and his shredded anger was struggling against annihilation. He could barely recall why he had come here. Some jumble of words about jealousy and sabotaging his marriage were tumbling around in his mind, but they made no sense. Anyway, he was unable to find the words to formulate them, nor was there any need to. His erection deflated silently and probably unnoticed.

"You look a sight. Would you like some tea? Or how about a hot bath?" There was a sincere note of concern in Gladiola's voice.

Winston contemplated a response—but what was there to say? Then the door to the kitchen flew open again. In came Nathan Weiss, wearing the bottom half of a bear costume, his hirsute chest bare. You might have mistaken him for a satyr. "Gangway! Gangway! Here comes the popcorn! Get it while it's hot!" He was balancing a large bowl on his head—quite skillfully in fact. Then he saw Winston. "Oh, hi! Fancy seeing you again. Hope I brought you some good news."

"You're the one who gave me that letter, aren't you?" Finally, Winston found a reason to speak. "Are you a friend of Fingers?"

"Of who? Fingers? Oh, you mean that guy with the weird hands. Yeah sure. My old buddy."

"Um . . . maybe you can tell me what he's got . . . well . . . under his kilt."

"Under his kilt? Gee . . . hmm, uhh . . . I know! A motorcycle!"

Winston's expression quickly turned unfriendly.

"No?" said Nathan.

"Winston," Gladiola interrupted, not missing a stitch, "The three of us have formed a cabaret group."

A long pause, Winston trying to find his way back to earth. "I know, I saw you."

"Oh, that's right." Silence. "Oh, and I passed the audition. I'm in the orchestra!" Another long silence.

"Congratulations." His voice flat, but at least a socially acceptable response. His hands had become alien appendages. He didn't know what to do with them except to slip them into his trouser pockets.

"She's great, Winston, she's really great," Nathan's cheerful attempt to deflect the next uncomfortable silence. "I've never seen a young lady who can toot a flute like her."

"What do you think?" Gladiola was holding up her knitting, she too trying very hard to make conversation. "I'm making a sweater for Porky."

Sadness dripped onto Winston's extremities like hot candle wax. What does *he* have that *I* don't? Why did she never make *me* a sweater? Would he have wanted one?

"Hey, dja hear the one about the guy with the trained octopus?" said Nathan. "Well, ya see, there's this guy with a trained octopus. It could play all kinds of musical instruments: tubas, trombones, violins, pianos, you name it. Well, one night the guy drops off a set of bagpipes in the octopus's hotel room expecting that by the next day, the octopus, genius that it is, will be able to play the bagpipes. Next morning, he goes into the octopus's room and says, 'Well? Did you learn to play it yet?' The octopus looks at him. He's got a tired expression on his face. 'Play it?' he says, 'I've been trying all night to lay it!' "

No one laughed except Nathan. More silence, furtive eye contact the only visible communication. Gladiola was fixing her attention on her knitting. *Agent* Porky had lowered his eyelids as if preparing for a siesta and Nathan was picking at hairs on the trousers of his bear costume. "Uh, Winston," Nathan finally broke the silence, "Do you always go around wearing your name over your heart?"

That was the cue. Winston fumbled at the QUID PRO QUO name tag and angrily tore it off his jacket pocket, crumpling it in his palm and flinging it onto the floor. "Dammit!" He looked up, somehow curious about their reactions.

"Sorry! Sorry!" said Nathan, "I didn't know it was such a sensitive issue . . ."

And now once again the door to the kitchen swung open. "Nathan, hey, you forgot the melted butter!" It was Virginia. Winston recognized that voice before she entered the room. His heart froze. She saw him, and he saw her. They locked eyes for a long long time, with intense familiarity and sharing the most diverse emotions. "Hi, Winston," Virginia finally spoke, "Want some popcorn with melted butter?"

"Virginia!?" is all he could say.

"Yes, Winston."

"I mean, what are *you* doing here?"

"Visiting my daughter and her friends. Now it's my turn. What are *you* doing here?"

"Your daughter?"

Gladiola got up, wrapped her arms around Virginia's waist and tucked her head into Virginia's shoulder, half-hidden in her mother's voluminous muumuu.

"My daughter, Winston. And I'm very very sorry I never had the courage to confide this one secret to you . . . it hurt too much."

"Do you mean to say you and Gladiola . . ."

"That's right. I was sixteen. And if it hadn't been for you, Winston, I might never have found her. Thank you." Her explanation was more detailed of course, but no need to repeat what you already know.

"Oh my God. Oh my God." Winston was hiding his face behind his hands. "I've never been so embarrassed . . ."

"Oh, don't take it so hard, Winston," said Nathan, "We still love you, all of us. Anyway, relationships with your step-daughter are illegal in the State of California. Aren't they?"

"Besides," *Agent* Porky said, "It's not as if you've lost a paramour. Think of it this way: you've gained a whole new family!"

"I need something to drink." Winston collapsed into a nearby chair.

"Coming right up." Nathan disappeared and reappeared with a POP-IT and a can of beer. "At your service."

"I kept a very intimate secret from you, and you kept one from me," Virginia's smile was warm. "Don't you think we're even?"

"I think I want to go home, Virginia," That was all Winston could say now, "I've had a long day."

But the time had not yet come for that wish to be granted. First, you might say as a nightcap, Gladiola, Porky and Nathan insisted on performing their new cabaret number for Winston and Virginia, a country-western piece. Nathan slipped into the rest of his bear costume, Porky put on his cowboy boots and a Stetson hat, perfectly matched to his levis and checkered shirt with pearl buttons. Gladiola reached for her flute. Then Porky and Nathan, cowboy and bear, began two-stepping around the room (always a blessing to have tolerant downstairs neighbors—especially if you're a musician). When the dance was over, Porky pushed Nathan the bear onto the floor and planted a boot on the bear's furry back. Then he began singing *a capella* accompanied by Gladiola's treble and Nathan's bass:

> My shoes are gettin' dusty
> from dancin' on this floor.

I'm goin' back where I come from,
ain't waltzin' you no more.
You never would admit it,
though I know that it is true,
you tol' me I was leadin',
but I'm always follerin' you.

CHORUS

I don' need your sweet talk anymore.
I don' wanna be a movie star.
I jus' wanna strum some honky-tonky tunes
a-playin' on my beat-up ole gittar.
Yer not much of a dancer.
You thought I couldn' tell,
but I don' hold no hard feelin's,
'cause I think it's just as well.
So if you wanna come an' join me,
Jus' say the word, my friend.
As long as yer not leadin',
it don' have ter be the end.

CHORUS

Nathan the bear jumps up, embraces Agent Porky, and dancing through the room, they sing the chorus one more time as a duet.

❀ ❀ ❀

Now it was really getting late, and everyone but especially Winston was very sleepy. The time to head home had come. Virginia and Winston were the first to leave. Mother and daughter exchanged kisses, and likewise there was a kiss for *Agent* Porky and for Nathan. Gladiola gave Winston a kiss too, pulling his head down to eye level and planting it on his cheek as he stood sheepishly at the door not knowing how to react. Nathan and Porky just waved to him.

And so, the Hewletts headed home to sort out their lives in private. They were holding hands as they descended the steps. On the porch, Virginia took care to steer Winston out of the path of the spider plant. Then she whispered to him gently, looking him in the eyes, "Winston, let's go home and make a baby, okay? Our baby, yours and mine." Weary Winston smiled broadly. And that's exactly what they did that night.

Finally, Nathan said his goodbyes too, leaving *Agent* Porky and *Agent* Gladiola to their privacy. He was ambling down the street to his car, a melancholy clown. It had been a strange, joyful evening, and that made him all the more aware of his own sadness now. Inside he was feeling hollow, and then he thought of the future and grew afraid. He was humming a soft, sentimental melody to soothe his soul.

When he got home, miracle of miracles, there was a parking spot in front of his building. He stepped slowly through the garden towards his front door. The air was fragrant. All at once, he sensed something strange, another presence, as if he were about to get mugged. As if someone were hiding in the dark. So what, he thought. What do I have that anyone would want? He reached into his pocket for his housekeys, expecting the worst. And then he started. My eyes are playing tricks. I'm overtired. He looked again. Am I dreaming? His heart was beating hard but not out of fear. Tears were welling up in his eyes.

She was standing there, draped in a black cape in the moonless night, her face, white as moonlight, her dark hair and dark eyes radiating with form and substance. Her mouth was suspended in a silent smile.

"Melanie?" His voice was hesitant and interrogative. "Melanie? Is that you?"

"Yes, Nathan." She was whispering softly, sweetly. "I'm back, Nathan. and I'm here to stay."

"Forever? No strings attached?"

"Yes, forever and no strings attached."

"But why now? I'm the same idiot as ever. I'm afraid I haven't improved a bit. And I don't think I ever can or will."

"I know, Nathan. And that's why I'm back." She reached out towards him and took his hand in hers. Both were warm. "You've never stopped loving me, and I've never stopped loving you. It's as simple as that."

"You mean there are stories with happy endings?" They drew close together.

"Oh yes," she said, "Lots of them, but usually they're invisible. Love is nothing you can see with your eyes." And then she wrapped her black cape around him, and they embraced. A passerby might have mistaken the sound of that caress for the rustling of the wind. Nathan and Melanie had disappeared, obscured from all roving eyes, into the privacy of their lovers' night.

Epilogue

THEY ARE STANDING on what seems to be a stage. All are in costume: Winston as a donkey, hooved feet, tail swishing, his donkey head tucked under an arm. Virginia is wearing a black muumuu embroidered with stunning gold brocade. A small child, a redhaired girl in a golden muumuu, is clasping her hand. Gladiola, Nathan, Melanie, Porky, Tony, Fingers, Wyatt, Marsy, Hermie, Bob, Iris, Doreen and many others whose faces we may or may not recognize (including Warren and Florida Freytag carrying their instruments and Virginia's parents brandishing Bibles) and even diverse goons and cretins, are dressed as scarecrows, their abundant straw stuffings scattering as they move about. They are surrounded by various Disney characters: Mickey Mouses, one with his mouse head under his arm and sporting a grey, handlebar moustache, Donald Ducks, Goofys, Snow Whites, Pinocchios, Sleeping Beauties and of course two, unshaven smiling Beagle Boys. A bevy of eagles in golden robes are poised behind the rest of the cast, and at the wings, Leland Hewlett on one side and Larez Pentius on the other are swinging tangles of clanging POP-ITs. It is curtain-call. The cast is waving, cheering, taking bows, giving the high sign. Now Porky steps forward, better said, they push him to the forefront. There is silence. A spotlight illuminates him, and he recites . . .

If we scarecrows have remembered,
do not think we have offended.
Like all who've just begun to speak,
we too must struggle and are meek.
Much time passes before you learn
to understand why planets turn
and how many things you may dream
can never be the way they seem.
Birds of paradise circle round
as you scramble on the ground,
and if they sometimes interfere,
they whisper softly, "Do not fear."
Please forgive this silly Porky.
Sometimes he is very dorky.
But now alas we've reached the end.
We ask only this: be our friend.

Porky steps back and merges into the rest of the cast. More waving, cheering, bows and high signs, laughter and hilarity. Then, as if out of nowhere, a figure in a long flowing white gown with a rippling train slowly approaches Winston. She is aglow in transcendent beauty, her long red hair purling. Winston senses the presence even before turning towards her. He is clearly searching for some key to recognition . . . "Mom?!" At that moment, a banner, till now unseen, unfurls rapidly from its anchoring on the proscenium arch. It is cobalt blue, and seven equally spaced golden apples are swinging from its bottom seam. At the center of the banner the following is imprinted in illuminated gold:

WESHALLRETURN

P.J. Blumenthal is an American writer living in Munich, Germany. He is the author of a nonfiction book on feral man, *Kaspar Hausers Geschwister (Kaspar Hauser's Siblings)*, as well as a German-language blog, "Der Sprachbloggeur." Three volumes of his poetry have appeared in the USA so far: *A Lusty Romance*, *Poems for Readers* and *Slow Train to Cincinnati*.